Black Cat

MARTYN BEDFORD

VIKING

for my daughter, Josie

VIKING

Published by the Penguin Group
Penguin Books Ltd, 27 Wrights Lane, London w8 5tz, England
Penguin Putnam Inc., 375 Hudson Street, New York, New York 10014, USA
Penguin Books Australia Ltd, Ringwood, Victoria, Australia
Penguin Books Canada Ltd, 10 Alcorn Avenue, Toronto, Ontario, Canada m4v 3b2
Penguin Books India (P) Ltd, 11, Community Centre,
Panchsheel Park, New Delhi – 110 017, India
Penguin Books (NZ) Ltd, Cnr Rosedale and Airborne Roads,
Albany, Auckland, New Zealand
Penguin Books (South Africa) (Pty) Ltd, 5 Watkins Street,
Denver Ext 4, Johannesburg 2094, South Africa

Penguin Books Ltd, Registered Offices: Harmondsworth, Middlesex, England

First published 2000
1

The extract from Sylvia Plath's poem 'Pursuit' (*Collected Poems*, edited by Ted Hughes) on p. vii
appears by kind permission of Faber and Faber.

Set in 12/14.75pt Monotype Dante
Typeset by Rowland Phototypesetting Ltd,
Bury St Edmunds, Suffolk
Printed in Great Britain by Clays Ltd, St Ives plc

A CIP catalogue record for this book is available from the British Library

ISBN 0-670-87965-7

There is a panther stalks me down:
One day I'll have my death of him.

– Sylvia Plath, 'Pursuit'

PART ONE

Balance

I

The farmer dreams of dogs. He is dreaming of something else, then the dogs encroach, savaging his dream, until there is nothing but dogs. In this dream the dogs are barking. A barking so lifelike he isn't sure if he's awake or asleep now, or between the two.

He wakes. He lies, listening.

The window is ajar and he can hear them, the dogs, clamouring below in the compound. His dogs. He gets out of bed and goes to the window. Opening the curtain, he looks out. There is no moon and he can make out little in the yard other than the black shapes of the outbuildings. He cannot see the two dogs, but he can hear their commotion: the tug of chains, paws scuffing at cement, the hollering. A fox has set them off, he thinks. Or another dog, its own cries from across the moor provoking a response. But as he stands, naked, and listens, he knows his dogs' voices contain an outrage too great for such familiar intrusions. Burglars? Poachers? Badger baiters? His wife asks what's wrong, and he understands that she senses it too: the quality of the barking. The farmer tells her he is going down.

He lifts his dressing gown off a hook on the bedroom door and makes his way downstairs, switching on lights. There are boots in the utility. He steps into them, takes a torch and lets himself out, triggering the security lamp. Light whitewashes the yard, its glare rendering the surrounding night blacker still. The dogs are unabated. Their noise is appalling; in this instant, he realizes what it is about their barking that has fetched him outside. Fear. This is no territorial warning, no challenge, no alarm call. The dogs are afraid. Not petrified with fear, but demented with it.

The farmer crosses the yard, playing his torch into their enclosure. He sees that, if it wasn't for their tethers, they would be gone.

Away from whatever it is they have heard, seen or scented that has brought them to this state. He watches them. Then he looks out over the land, as far as the torchlight allows; beyond its pale thread, the ground turns from silver to grey to black. Even the division between earth and sky is hard to distinguish. He kills the beam. He attends to a silence that isn't true quiet but a backdrop of stillness perforated by sheep bleatings and – once, twice – the call of an owl. He detects nothing uncommon. Senses nothing. There is nothing there for him. Inside the compound, he approaches the dogs and shows them they are loved. They become calmer. It's impossible to know whether it is his presence which pacifies them, or the absence – the departure – of the source of their fear.

It must be two o'clock. The farmer is cold. The dogs are not settled, but they are settled enough for him to leave them. He secures the enclosure and returns to the house. A shrug is all he has to offer his wife. Something spooked them, he says. At first light, he will venture out among the lambs and ewes scattered about the hillside to seek clues to the disturbance. He rejoins her, the chill from his body leaching into the sleep-warm sheets.

2

Her first impressions, Week One, were of noise and heat and busyness, and a palpable discomfort that included, but was not contained by, the guilt of cooked flesh. Frying bacon, sausages, black pudding for a living. Using lard. Getting it on her fingers and in her nostrils, like the last emanation of the thing that had died. Radio muzak, the mirth of men – almost exclusively men – whose sense of humour wasn't hers. Being indoors was part of it, this intermingling of strangenesses. And the faces were not ones she'd grown accustomed to, their sweaty chalk features looming at her. A cast of gargoyles.

What was she doing in this . . . this *cookery*?

Place du Roy. The decor was effervescently red, tangerine and yellow, made more lurid still by the sluice of summer light from a large picture window. The window faced south, over the town square – once a marketplace, apparently, now a pay-and-display glimmering with chrome and glass. Beyond the square, above the rooftops of shops and houses and a solitary church spire, the chocolate dark land rose skywards like the form of a gigantic slumbering dog. And here she was, confined, cooped up in Roy's place. Royston Rice, boss, proprietor. Landlord too, what with her having the flat above – rent and bills to be stopped from her pay so there'd be no awkwardness over arrears. Yeah, sure, she understood. So, a bedsit, decorated at the opposite end of the spectrum to the café itself, luminous greens and blues lending it the semblance of a marine theme-park, or a bathroom. There was a single bed, an actual bathroom and facilities (two cooker rings, a grill, microwave, fridge, sink). As if she'd want to cook up there as well as down below.

The menu, the *me 'n' you*, Roy told her, majored in dead livestock, eggs and carbohydrates. *Beans being an exception, the only good vegetable is a fried vegetable.* Place du Roy was a concept café, he said, its concept being to exist at variance with the lace-doily potted-plant tearooms and brasseries servicing the tourists and resident well-offs. This was a caff. It catered for folk who liked to eat in a caff. All this, part of her induction. He showed her the kitchen, explained the table-numbering, introduced her to Nigel, cook, and Faye, waitress. Work began at six a.m., the caff opened at six thirty. Her function: food prep, cooking, waitressing, washing up, wiping down. Four days a week, including Saturdays. Like, she'd have something else on at weekends?

'You won't make your fortune here, Chloe.'

This was one of Roy's funnies; her name – Chloe Fortune – tickled him pink. He wanted to know, among other things, how come she wore nothing but black: T-shirt, jeans, shoes . . . knickers, the implication. She told him black was all she had clean. He was also curious about the hair, the dreads. Plaits, he called them. How come a white lass had hair like Bob Marley's? She shrugged and said it was just a fashion thing.

Environmental Health come snooping, you tell 'em it's a wig.

Day One, her back ached from the previous evening, helping Roy remove the junk that had been stored in the flat for more years than he could remember. Hauling a bedstead and mattress up the stairs. Also, her gear. *Is that all?* His remark, on seeing her backpack, bedroll and sleeping bag. It took him half an hour to get the toilet to flush. And he was sure he smelled gas when he tested the cooker, until she pointed out it was electric. Did she want a telly, only he had an old portable going spare? Black-and-white.

'Forty quid.'

'No thanks, Mr Rice.'

'Roy. I just thought you might get bored, up here all by yourself.'

How bored would you have to be to resort to television? She'd slept with the windows wide open, that first night, to replace dust with air.

The din, at work, was what disorientated her most, though you could get used to anything, given time and a lack of alternative arrangements. But *this*. When the coffee-maker was in operation, it was like a geyser erupting. For ten, fifteen seconds people mimed at one another, or put their words on hold.

She would have to create a silence for herself, and occupy it.

But it was a job, with wages, and an abode, even if it was in a town she didn't know, despite camping out in its environs for a good while. And who else would employ her, who hadn't already declined thanks-all-the-same to do so? On the tenancy agreement, under Previous Address, she'd written: Flash Cleans Baths Without Scratching Village, aka Flashville. Roy had been cool with that. And with the convictions.

'Good on you, I say. Fucking bypass would've killed this place.'

The job was crucial, she'd said. He'd laughed in anticipation of his own pun: 'You can't be a fine upstanding member of the community with fines outstanding.'

That's what she was now, a member of the – of *this* – community.

Week One, Day Four, two events coincided.

First, two men arrived, not to eat but to fix something. One of them said: 'Gaffer around?'

Dark, good-looking, conceited. There'd be a wife or girlfriend somewhere; kids even. His eyes were on hers, then on his mate's, and there was an exchange of smiles between the men that was concerned with, but excluded, her. Fixerman One wondered if *she* had anything wanted fixing while they were at it?

Making sure to remain deadpan, she replied: 'I have a broken heart.'

Their expressions, at this point, being a sight to behold. Roy appeared, telling the men to come through to the back.

Second, a guy sat at Table Eight; maybe a couple of years older than her, blond hair and cornflower eyes that reminded her of Mom, and of the distance dividing them. Was mother intuitively thinking of daughter at this exact moment? It was possible. She recognized him, from Flashville, though he'd never actually interviewed her.

Roy was back by now, calling across to the new arrival: 'If it isn't that great contradiction in terms – a gentleman of the press.'

'Hiya, Roy.'

'*Monitoring* today, or a day off?' Then, to her, he added: 'Gavin Drinkell. Mind what you say to him or you'll end up in the local paper.'

She took the guy's order. On her way to the kitchen, his voice followed her: 'Hang on, can you make that coffee instead of tea?'

Roy roared. 'Journalist In Hot Drinks U-Turn, eh?'

She considered Gavin Drinkell to be the sort of guy she might end up in bed with if he turned out to be, on the inside, the way he looked, on the outside; which was unlikely, taking into account the weight of past experience. When she returned, this Gavin was saying something about a sheep.

'When was this, then?' Roy said.

'Yesterday. The farmer said you could pick up what was left with one hand.' He sniffed. 'It's this week's lead, 'less anything else happens.'

'Go on, let me guess the headline.'

'I don't write the headlines.'

Fingers to brow, Roy said: 'I see two words beginning with B . . .'

'I didn't coin the phrase.'

'Yeah, but you're happy enough to trot it out whenever anyone farts up there.' He nodded at the window, the moor. 'Load of old guff.'

Gavin spread his hands. 'I just present the facts.'

Actually, his bed prospects were looking iffy. It wasn't just the complacency, it was Richie. The lack of him. She had to take another order out to the kitchen, so she didn't get to discover the B-words, or anything else about a dead sheep that could be picked up with one hand. She tried to picture this. She flexed her fingers, imagining her grip closing on – what? – a spine, like the knotty handle of a suitcase that, when you lifted it, was lighter than you'd anticipated.

Richie.

To remove something, Mom told her, you must also remove the space it filled.

Roy went out back again; she tailed him, lugging a sack of rubbish to the bins. The fixermen were in the yard. Seeing them engaged in manly conference with Roy put her in mind of village elders huddled around the hub of their wisdom. It was warm outside and the air smelled of sewage. The fixermen's snag was Roy's snag: the only way to find the breach, they reckoned, being to have the lot up. Fixerman One drew an imaginary line with his hand across the concrete. Roy asked about cost, time, mess, all that drilling; he swore at their answer. They said if he didn't have it seen to a.s.a.p. the kitchen would be knee-deep in shit, piss and rainwater within a week.

'What's the problem?' she said.

Roy looked at her. The two men looked at her.

She smiled. 'Okay, try to pretend I'm a bloke.'

Fixerman One said: 'You're tall enough for a bloke.'

She looked at Roy.

'You plan on serving food to the customers via the drainage system,' he said. 'This is why you need to know what the problem is?'

'All right, I'll speculate: there's a sewage pipe runs under the yard, the pipe has a leak, you don't know the exact location of the leak, so you have to dig up the whole length of pipe to find it. Yeah?'

Roy addressed the two men. 'She used to live in a tunnel.'

'You want me to locate the leak?' she said.

'Four days, she's worked here. Still can't tell Table Six from Table Twelve.'

From the repertoire of moods available to her at that moment, she pulled out an appropriate selection: patience, seriousness, self-confidence, implicit resistance to piss-taking. The important thing was to focus on the task in hand.

'You can spectate, or you can go inside and leave me to it.'

The men stayed. She took position, composing herself, closing them out. She reached into her back pocket and brought out a small cloth pouch. From inside the pouch, she unwound a wooden plumb bob on a length of cord and let it hang from the thumb and first finger of her right hand. Eyes closed, waiting for it to settle.

Fixerman One said: 'Fuck me, it's Mystic Meg.'

3

'Black Beast' Strikes Again
by Gavin Drinkell, Chief Reporter

The discovery of a mutilated sheep's carcass has sparked new fears that the so-called 'Black Beast' of the moors has struck again. The body of a full-grown Swaledale ewe was found close to the famous Toadstool Stones on land owned by hill farmer Leonard Cunliffe. 'You could pick up what was left with one hand,' said Mr Cunliffe, 51. He denied that a dog could have been responsible for the kill.

'Dogs don't kill clean,' he said. 'And they don't eat the meat in this way – with dogs it's killer instinct, not for food. I've never seen anything like this,' added Mr Cunliffe, who has farmed sheep on the moors all his life. 'My dogs were disturbed in the night, so they must have heard or smelled something unusual. I didn't believe in the beast before, but now I'm not so sure.' Asked if he could think of any other explanation for the ewe's death, he said: 'Well, it wasn't suicide, was it?'

The incident is the first for four months, following a spate of attacks at the eastern end of the moors in February and March which left five lambs and two ewes dead. In the past year, a series of unexplained killings of sheep, deer, calves and goats – along with reported sightings of a mysterious 'Black Beast' – have led to claims that a dangerous wild animal is at large in the local countryside.

Amateur beast-watcher Ethan Gray, 33, who lives on the moorside, visited the scene within hours of the latest killing and says it is 'almost certainly' the work of the beast. 'Nothing indigenous to Britain would have been big or powerful enough to do this,' Mr Gray told *The Monitor*.

The Ministry of Agriculture has always dismissed the existence of a beast, blaming rogue dogs and poachers, and refusing to bow to calls from local farmers and councillors for an inquiry. An official declined to comment on this week's attack until a report has been received from the police.

A police spokesman confirmed that the carcass was 'exceptionally mutilated', but said much of the damage was probably due to scavenging by foxes, badgers and carrion crow. He would not speculate on how the ewe died until a post-mortem had been conducted by a veterinary expert.

4

She was five years old the first time a pendulum moved for her. She could still picture the pattern of its momentum – perpendicular quiescence, to discreet tremor, to hesitant gyrations that broadened and accelerated until the bob described confident clockwise loops. The tug tug tug of the cord between thumb and finger.

'I'm not making it! I'm not making it!'

And Mom's eyes telling her it was all right, it was good. It was okay. There was no need to be scared or upset or surprised. Everything was exactly as it should be.

'Is it magic?'

'No, it's magical, but it's not magic.'

'What is it?'

'What do you *feel*, hon?'

'Like when I want the pee-pee, but in my fingers.'

'So, there's your answer.'

She remembered asking if she was clever – a clever girl, being able to make the string swing – and her mother saying well, yes and no, because the pendulum wasn't really to do with being clever. But yes-and-no is a difficult concept when you're five, so the girl-Chloe had taken that as a yes. She was clever, and she could do magic.

She knew better now.

If people asked how she'd learned to dowse, she gave an easy answer – easy for her, for them – an approximation of the truth: her mom had taught her. The breakdown of what was taught, what was self-taught, what was innate and what came with years of practice was too complicated even for her to decode. And sure as shit too complicated for the idly curious or misinformed. The non-dowser. With the reporter guy, seeking a soundbite to

enlighten thousands of *Monitor* readers, flipness had been irresistible.

Gavin: 'How did you learn to dowse?'

Chloe: 'Because no one ever told me I couldn't.'

Like Charley, a caff regular – real name Dave, but jug-ears and a
passing resemblance to the future king. He drove trucks of bottled
water for a firm with a depot on the edge of town. Always used
Table Six, if free, sitting down to a fry-up, a mug of tea (three
sugars), a pack of Camels and the racing pages. Prince of the Turf,
Roy called him.

'His ears got that way from sticking Ladbrokes pens behind
them.'

Charley had heard about the business with the sewage, her
finding the leak and that. She set his breakfast down and hit the
kitchen before he could ask her – he'd do this, he was working
round to it – for a demo. Even Roy had been pressing for a party
piece, despite having already witnessed the real thing. He was still
full of it, retelling what he'd seen to anyone who'd listen, as if he
needed a story of the event for it to make sense.

Anyway, when she cleared Six, Charley took his chance to waylay
her with the form guide and a plume of cigarette discharge. 'Go
on, love, dowse us a winner.' He winked. 'Ten per cent for you, if
it comes in.'

'Sorry, Charley, I don't do future.'

Swinging into action . . . Chloe Fortune. The caption, in the paper.
Page Three. She was a page-three girl, a pin-up, on account of Roy
attaching the article to a corkboard behind the counter. The piece,
a Gavin Drinkell exclusive, described how Ms Fortune, 22, a waitress
at the Place du Roy, 'gobsmacked' her boss and two workmen by
using the ancient technique of pendulum dowsing to find a hole in
an underground pipe. As for the photo, how did a smile get to be
so inane? And the way it was used – *cropped* to fit the page design,
according to Gavin. Trimmed. The bottom of the picture sliced off

in such a way that the bob was missing, leaving the swinging, grinning Ms Fortune apparently holding nothing more substantial than a length of string.

Gavin interviewed her twice. Once for the news story, milking his luck at being on the premises when it happened; the second time a couple of days later, for a follow-up feature on dowsing and the dowser-cum-waitress who was once an eco warrior. He wanted to know, was she cool with 'eco warrior'? Actually, no.

'What, then?'

'Environmental activist. Or doesn't your paper have space for multisyllabic concepts?'

He loved the nicknames: Peg – yeah, yeah, his name was Legg; Giraffe, for her long, slender neck; Blinky, having clocked the most subterranean hours. Cilla, Candle, Sponge Cake, Apocalypse in a Minute (Lips for short), Chuff, Spig, Elk Head, Juggler, Green Giant . . . Plum, of course. She omitted Spoons, this being Richie's handle.

'What would they call me?' Gavin said.

'They'd call you a journalist.'

This second interview took place in a pub in a hamlet in a cleft of wild upland somewhere between the town and its nearest city. His idea, his car, his expenses. Being strapped for dosh, she was prepared to trade a few free beers – a night *out* – for the risk of Gavin misconstruing the evening as a date. Besides, she wasn't sure she'd binned his prospects just yet. He made room among the pints for his notebook and pen, a miniature tape recorder and, jesus, a mobile phone.

'If I can't make up my mind about something, I toss a coin.' He showed her the coin. An Edwardian penny that cost him a quid at a flea market and sat in his wallet like a talisman. 'Heads for yes, tails for no. Which, basically, is why I'm so interested in dowsing.' He smiled. 'In the multisyllabic concept of dowsing.'

'That isn't dowsing.'

'Same basic principle.'

'Nap.' She shook her head. 'Tossing a coin . . . it's random,

whether it comes up heads or tails. You aren't the one who influ-
ences the result.'

'But *life*'s random.'

Not that she agreed with this, but it was enough for now that
Gavin had a view – which he'd pondered – on what life might or
might not be. 'We're not talking about life, we're talking about
dowsing.' Using phrases filched from her mom, she told him: 'The
pendulum is me. When the pendulum moves, it's me who causes
it to move.'

The explanation of this and other dowsing-speak felled him like
the tripwires of a foreign language. And all the while she measured
him for possessiveness, insecurity, jealousy, dependence; any hint,
any symptom, any inkling of a propensity to these traits – any of
them – and that would be it. She shared her checklist the next day
with Faye, Faye's own no-no list comprising: drug dealing, football,
motorbikes and requests for anal intercourse. The inescapable paradox was that in seeking reassurance of Gavin's *dissimilarity* to Richie,
she never once during the entire interview ceased resenting him
for not *being* Richie.

What was that all about?

What it was, she sussed, was something as oblique as the reflection in Gavin's face of light from the beaten-copper surface of their
table, and her association of this with Richie's features lit by campfire
– made unusual, beautiful, by being illuminated from below in the
shifting of shadows and warm amber. What it was, also, was a
letter from him which had come via Giraffe – the only one to know,
to be allowed to know, where she lived – and which sat in the back
pocket of her jeans, unread, unopened, but which remained there
all the same and had not been thrown away.

In summer dusk, Gavin sped them home on the slim, frayed lanes
of the moorside. The slopes all about them were shaggy, blue-grey,
and made her think of mammoths herded for warmth ahead of the
long night. Up ahead, its tail-lights intermittently disappearing and
reappearing, another car traced the road for them in its red and

silver slipstream. She was sleepy, yawning, stomach swollen with beer and salted cashews. Gavin had slotted a tape into the stereo, revealing at once the full and appalling divergence of their taste in music. With him preoccupied, making believe he was a rally driver for all she knew, she gazed through the translucency of her face in the side window, as if she might catch sight of herself skimming above the darkening blur of land like a will-o'-the-wisp or a girl in a Chagall.

'Where are the Toadstool Stones?' she said.

Gavin reduced the decibels. 'West of here. North-west.' He pointed at the windscreen, conveying a vague sense of distance. 'Why?'

'I suppose I mean *what* are they?'

'Stones . . . shaped like giant toadstools.' The interior of the car was too dark for her to make out his face, but she could hear the smile in his voice. 'Two of them, on a kind of ridge. They've got cup-and-ring marks – carvings – on them; Bronze Age or Neolithic or something. We went there once on a school geology trip.'

'Yeah?' She recalled the photograph, on the front page of the paper with her on three, of a farmer in brown dungarees standing alongside a sheep that looked like it had exploded. She planted her feet on the dashboard, knees tucked under her chin. 'So, d'you think this Black Beast exists?'

'No.'

'What about the people who reckon they've seen it?'

'People see what they want.' He shifted down a gear, swung hard into a bend. 'You believe the beast is out there, you start looking for it. Subconsciously. If you ask me, the beast is a figment of the imagination.'

'And the dead sheep?'

'Sheep worrying's nothing new.'

'*Worrying*?'

'By dogs. That's the correct term for it.'

She laughed. 'Worrying. I love that.'

Next day at the caff, at the end of the shift, she was clearing up and wiping down when the phone rang and Roy said it was for her. She felt herself redden. For *her*?

Richie?

Which was impossible. And yet, taking the handset, she anticipated his voice. It was Gavin. He wanted to know, he was wondering, he was ringing on the off chance, if she was free this evening . . . As politely but firmly as possible, she declined.

5

ROD FAVERDALE (*sheep farmer*):

They done him again the week after the kill at Toadstools. I know exactly when it was 'cos I'd had Len Cunliffe on the blower the previous night on NFU business and saying: 'Oh, by the way, *your lad* is camped out up here again.'

My lad, my arse. I told Len: 'One, he's not my fucking lad, he's my tenant; two, if he bothers you that much you should start charging him rent and all.'

Five nights on the trot he'd been there, apparently, holed up on the edge of a plantation above Len's place with his X-ray specs. Vigils. Like the thing int going to smell him a mile off and steer clear.

Like I say, Ethan came back to find his place done over. He turned up on my doorstep begging a pot of paint. I could tell summat was up so I asked him straight out, and he said they'd sprayed graffiti, smashed his windows, knocked the jack out. And they'd wiped shit all over the walls. *Excrement*. Outside or inside? I said, and he said outside. Which was something, I suppose. And at least that bitch of his hadn't come to any harm.

I told him: 'Kids, from town, most likely. School holidays, they get bored and have to fuck other folk around for a bit of fun.'

Anyhow, he'd cleaned up what he could and wanted a borrow of some paint to slap over the graffiti. And a phone, to ring a glazier. I got the wife to show him where the phone was while I sorted the paint. The only outdoor stuff I had was blue but it didn't seem to bother him one way or the other what colour it was.

6

Two weeks at Place du Roy and however often she showered she reeked of washing-up gloves, bacon, stale tobacco and, overwhelmingly, of onion. Even on days when she hadn't chopped onions, even on her days off, she detected onion among the unusual fumes of her own skin. A perk of the job, according to Mr Rice, proprietor.

Parfum d'oignon, by Laboratoire Royston.

But she was doing it, the work. Being all the things she was paid to be, living in the place she had to live while she sorted her head's various messes. And waitressing – *front of house*, as Roy styled it – wasn't as bad as it might've been: busyness, banter, sashaying among the tables to the tempo of whatever track happened to be on the radio. Faye calling the orders, Nigel working his pans like a juggler, Roy whistling as he made the teas and coffees . . . these were the adopted beats of her existence.

She sent Mom a postcard, telling of her new – which was to say, transitional – life. A card, rather than a letter or call, so she could confine herself to the facts of the matter. No room for the complexity of explanations she hadn't fully sussed for herself yet. She left space at least for this: *P.S. The rhythms of my life, as it is now, are of my making, my choosing, but they're not mine. They're not my rhythms. But this life has novelty, so I guess I'll embrace the novelty while it lasts! P.P.S. I so stink of onion!*

Four times, Gavin phoned her at the caff, wanting a yes instead of a no.

Punter on Three. Roy, summoning her. Something in his eyes and in the emphasis on 'punter' snagged her interest. Disdain. Like the customer wore a pink tutu, or had a bottle of meths jutting out of his pocket. But it was just a guy on his own in an old T-shirt, patched-up jeans and hiking boots. The only obvious oddness was a tidemark around his face, where the skin altered abruptly from tan to white, and the speckling of his forehead, ears and neck with cut hair, as if his head was a magnet and someone had sneezed iron filings at him. She wanted to dab at him with a sheet of damp kitchen roll.

'What'll it be?'

'I don't have my glasses.'

She leaned forward, whispering. 'To be honest, the food isn't much to look at.'

'No, no, the menu.' No smile. 'They're reading glasses.'

Close up he smelled of dog and something synthetic. Paint. A wrist, a thumb, knuckles, fingernails, were encrusted with dried blue paint. An artist, maybe, or – more likely, given the clientele – a decorator, though he didn't much resemble the stereotype of either. She wanted him to be an artist. An artist who only ever worked with blue.

'It's the usual stuff, yeah? Bacon, eggs. We're large on chips here.'

'Bacon sandwich, I think.'

'Brown or white?'

'I In?'

'The bread.'

'Er, brown. And a cup of tea.'

She wrote all this on the pad.

'Oh, and a bowl of water.'

'A bowl.'

'For my dog.' He indicated the window. There was a golden retriever outside, looped by its lead to a drainpipe, making breath patterns on the glass.

'What's her name?'

'Erica.'

'Would Erica like a bacon sandwich as well?'

Tab Three just frowned.

'I'll take that as a no.'

He seemed distracted, impatient; his eyes were fidgety, as though he couldn't fix on anything for worrying that wherever he looked next might be more worthwhile. Other punters were, with varying subtlety, observing him. Conscious of him. She tore out the page and placed the customer copy under a ketchup dispenser in the design of a fat plastic tomato. She told him his table number and said he had to memorize it, they both did, because the very fabric of the caff's system of service was sustained by this fact and others like it.

It was a defence mechanism, this. The jokery. A barrier between him, them, or whoever and herself, her more serious self. Also, a way of discovering the transforming effect of a smile on the guy's features. Only, he didn't smile, or even appear to register what she'd said.

'She's got the Hermit,' Roy said.

'Who?' She was filling a dish with cold water, for the dog.

'Local celeb.' This was Faye, on bread duty, putting marg on a stack of sliced with automatic efficiency. 'Lives all by himself up on the moor.'

'Yeah?'

Roy pointed to his head, did the loop-the-loop sign with his finger.

'How d'you mean, on the moor?'

'A hut,' Faye said. 'Built it himself. A shack, bang in the middle of nowhere.'

'You been out to his place?'

Faye looked up at her, incredulous. 'Oh, I mean, *yeah.*'

'I thought it was a caravan,' Roy said.

Faye binned the empty tub and fetched a fresh one. Big yawn, tucking a strand of hair behind her ear, she said he'd walked out on his family. The Hermit. An image of a . . . cabin, despite what Roy had just said about a caravan; a log cabin, the guy inside, peering out of a window, suspicious, training a shotgun on an approaching visitor. On her. She was the visitor, the intruder. How old was he? Thirty?

Faye was still talking: 'Months ago, this was. Gave up his job, sold his house, the lot.'

'What did he do, before?'

Faye shrugged. 'He was on the telly a while back, when it was all going off up there,' Roy said. 'One of them fly-in-the-wotsit documentaries. It was a *caravan*.'

Or maybe he didn't sell the house, Faye said, 'cos where were the wife and kids living? Faye had read about this in the paper. Ian. Ewan. She couldn't remember his name. Whatever, he'd jacked it all in just so's he could (here, she made her voice go spooky): 'Find . . . the . . . Black . . . Beast.'

The retriever nosed her hand as she set the dish down on the pavement. *You are one skinny pooch.* The dog was less interested in lapping at the water than at a septic red welt at the base of her thumb. She let her do that. High above the moor, aircraft trails criss-crossed the sky like scattered stalks of the I-Ching. She wanted to ask Tab Three about the name. Cool, but whoever heard of a dog called Erica?

The guy was gawping at her, at her and the dog, leaning across the table so that his face was almost pressed against the window.

In Flashville, there'd been talk – scraps of rumour around the fire – of the beast of the moors. A sheep kill took place less than a K from camp and they half expected to be blamed – demonized in the tabloids as poachers or pagan ritualists. She didn't recall ever hearing about a hermit.

Bacon sandwich. She'd been disappointed when he ordered that.

Nap, he wasn't watching her, he was studying his reflection: a tilt of the head, touching his face, his scalp. What the guy was doing, was inspecting his new haircut. Not with vanity, so much as surprise. From his expression, you would've thought he'd just woken up to find he'd been given an all-over grade two in his sleep. Then his eyes caught on hers through the glass, and she was the first to look away.

*

After he'd gone, as she cleared his table, she saw the letters in a precise pile beside his plate. She started to go through them: police, district council, Ministry of Agriculture, Country Landowners' Association, National Farmers' Union, regional TV and radio, *The Monitor*, two MPs, an MEP, *Wildlife* magazine, a university research department, the Institute of Zoology . . . each envelope addressed in neat manual type.

'You left these.'

She was out of breath from hoofing it around the pay-and-display in search of them. The Hermit sat behind the wheel of a red 4WD Toyota pick-up, Erica alongside in the passenger seat. Windows open, engine off. When she'd approached, the guy was speaking into what she took for a mobile and she heard him say: '. . . I saw through a hole in the page . . .'

It wasn't a phone, it was a miniature tape recorder. He snapped the machine off as soon as he saw her and placed it on the dash. Poetry. The guy wrote – composed, *dictated* – poetry. *I saw through a hole in the page*. Saw, as in 'to saw' something? Or past tense of 'to see'? He looked at the letters. Puzzled, annoyed, relieved, grateful or what, she couldn't tell. Embarrassed, maybe. Just plain irritated at being interrupted. He accepted the sheaf of envelopes without a word.

'I'd have posted them for you,' she said. 'Only, none of them have got stamps.'

'The post office is on my list.'

He handed her a slip of paper containing a column of staple groceries. Smiling, she gave the list back. He pulled a pair of glasses from the glove compartment, glanced at the note, then rooted out another for her to inspect. *Tesco, Take A Hike, haircut, hardware, post office, petrol/oil*. Spectacled, the guy resembled Elvis Costello.

'No Place du Roy,' she said. 'Or is that on a separate list?'

'What?'

She gestured across the car park.

'That was a, that was a . . .' He removed his glasses and blinked – once, twice; the strain, she supposed, of using them to stare over at the caff when they were meant for close-up. 'That was just a whim.' He nodded, to himself. 'Spur of the moment.'

'I should be getting back, yeah?' Roy must've discovered her absence by now. She thought the guy, the Hermit, would thank her for the letters, but he didn't. There was no sign of him saying anything at all. After a pause, she said: 'I know your dog's name, but you didn't tell me yours.'

'Ethan.'

'Chloe.' Finger to sternum. 'No dots over the *e*.'

7

MR DANIEL HAULT MP (*Shadow Minister for Agriculture*):
While my right honourable friend is right to state that no species
of big cat is indigenous to this country, many of these animals live
here, or have lived here, in captivity in zoos, wildlife parks, circuses
or as exotic pets. It is not inconceivable that, over the years, one or
more of these creatures may have escaped, or been freed, and
remain at large. With specific regard to the keeping of exotic pets,
the Minister – despite her youth – may be aware that this was
something of a fashion in the sixties and seventies, when I'm told
it was no more expensive to buy a puma than a pedigree dog.
Amid concern about the conditions in which such pets were being
confined, the Dangerous Wild Animals Act of 1976 made it illegal
to own or to keep certain species without a licence, such licences
being issued dependent upon compliance with strict criteria in
respect of safety, welfare, feeding and so on. The cost of upgrading
facilities, combined with the prospect of having one's pet confis-
cated and most likely destroyed if one didn't, must have sorely
tempted some owners to let their animals loose. I am advised that
it is also not inconceivable that the escape or deliberate release of
a number of these creatures created the potential for small breeding
colonies to become established in the British countryside. In short,
we may have been living cheek by jowl with wild beasts for some
twenty-five years. If the sceptics find this scenario implausible –
and, by the evident amusement on both sides of the House, there
are those who do – may I remind them of other non-indigenous
species now known to be feral in Britain: porcupine, wallaby, mink,
muntjac deer and – yes, yes – the ring-necked parakeet.

8

You bottled it. Me, Flashville, everything. Couldn't hack it. I don't reckon you ever believed in what we were doing, did you? Not really. Not in your heart. It was a phase you were going thru: 'This year I think I'll be a roads protester.' And I was just part of the deal. Another lifestyle choice. Shag a crustie and stop the bypass. Well fuck you, Plum. Or is it Chloe again, now? Whoever you are, fuck you.

Spoons

The letter. Read, eventually; read again, then shredded into as many pieces as there were words, like its disintegration would somehow erase what he'd written from her memory, her version of events, her self-estimation.

Spoons: on account of his tendency, in the football matches, to spoon the ball high in the air whenever he kicked it. She couldn't help smiling at the recollection of his nickname echoing in the woods so that, wherever she was, she'd be able to locate him from the cries of the other players: *Go on, Spoons!* Spoons – Richie – was into the construction and occupation of tunnels and tree-houses. He didn't have much time for the folk who thought it was enough just to bed down in a bender for the duration and shout *bastards!* at the filth and the bailiff gangs. Benders were the scene of protest, sure, but not to be confused with protest itself; they were somewhere to crash, beyond that their value was no more than symbolic.

'Protest must be physical?' she said. 'As an abstract concept, it's meaningless?'

'No, I'm saying *real* protest goes on in the trees and tunnels, the places where it's hardest for them – physically, practically – to evict us. They can bulldoze a bender in ten seconds.' She recalled the urgency in his face, his voice. 'The ideal protest camp is the one where we're as immovable in body as we are in spirit.'

This discussion, having taken place underground. Even now – despite his letter, despite everything – she was in love with the disembodied timbre of his speech, there, each word encapsulated in the soil-clad dark like an individually wrapped chocolate.

In the days after she read the letter, she played the part of her usual self: quirky, perky. No glimpse of the interior from what lay on the exterior.

Even so, Roy said: 'Boyfriend trouble?'

'What?'

'You look like you've had your account closed at the Happy Bank.'

'Me? I'm all right.'

She was chalking lunch specials on the board – her job, since he'd discovered her flair for pictorial representations of food. Today, toad-in-the-hole and faggots. Her unfinished year at art college had come to this.

'When lasses are in a strop, it's either boyfriend trouble or time of the month.'

'Roy, you should get out and meet more women.'

She'd considered her mood and named it 'deflation'. Mom always used colour – assigning one to her disposition, imagining a wall in that colour and, stroke by stroke, repainting it pure white. As for her, she preferred a word, visualizing the letters and scrambling them into a senseless, impotent anagram. Sometimes it worked.

Not this time.

Richie had punctured her. He didn't begin to comprehend why she'd left. Why she'd left *him*. And she'd tried so hard to make him appreciate the crux of it. Because, in her experience, if a guy didn't get the crux straight – the irreversible finality of the decision, the reasons *why* – there would be complications. Repercussions. Guys tended to be repercussive. Gavin Drinkell, for an e.g. When he wasn't calling or waylaying her at work, or knocking at the bedsit, he sent cards whose message, subtextually, wasn't romance but arrogance; a refusal to value her no above his yes. Yesterday, Gavin had done the Interflora thing: red roses delivered to the caff while she was on shift.

Another word: purposeless. She'd replaced protest with nothing.

She showered. The caff's vapours had accumulated in her skin, she imagined, smearing her in grease like a cross-channel swimmer. She let the scented soap and the hot gush of water scour her. Back in the room she put on a CD and sprawled on the bed, wet, naked, and sank into the sound. Afternoon sun drew a stripe across the ceiling. The window at the front was open and she could hear youth-talk float up from the car park.

What to wear? She fancied a maternity dress, for the airy voluminousness. But she didn't own a dress of any sort. She towelled, put on an XL T-shirt and filmy half-length skirt – no bra, no knickers – and, with damp hair, set off to meet Faye.

'I thought you were a Goth at first,' Faye said. ''Cep you don't do the make-up.'

She tilted the bottle, the cold lager fizzing in her throat. 'Yeah, Goth was how it started, when I was at college. Now, it's kind of a signature. I *like* black.'

'With my complexion I'd just look anaemic.'

Faye looked anaemic anyway. Dark under the eyes, as if a painter had thumbed two arcs of grey there. Eighteen. Doing media studies at the tech, working part time at Place du Roy plus three evenings at the S.U. bar. They were in a beer garden, which smelled, for no obvious reason, of fresh figs. Faye said it was good not to be serving, clearing empties, washing glasses; smoking her own cigs instead of passively inhaling.

Faye wanted to know about the camp, so she told her some of it.

'I couldn't live like that.'

This was shaping up to be one of those conversations where the other woman, girl, kept relating whatever you said to herself. What was the age gap? Four years. Seemed wider. But there was booze, and this – the pub, Faye's company – was better than solitude in the decompression chamber of her bedsit, or playing gender chess with Gavin, or any guy come to that. The coasters, she noticed, advertised a new beer called Beastly Brew; its logo, a silhouetted cat – a panther – on the prowl.

'You all right now?' Faye said.

'Almost.' She indicated the bottle. 'Dr Holsten's pills are starting to kick in.'

'This Richard guy's a shit, if you ask me.'

'Richie.'

She'd been discovered – deflated, purposeless – in the backyard, on the pretext of binning a rubbish sack, but actually seeking time and privacy in which to be upset. Faye, sneaking a smoke, had caught her red-eyed. So they'd talked, and the idea of a couple of beers after work had seemed altogether cool, even on their wages.

'I was doing okay,' she said, drinking. 'Getting my shit together, yeah? Then, his letter . . . bang. And all of a sudden I'm sitting here thinking: yeah, what the fuck is this all about? I feel, I dunno, like I've stopped listening to myself.'

'So, what, you're gonna go back?'

She laughed. 'That's exactly the thing I'm *not* going to do.'

'What, then?' Faye looked hurt, sulky. 'I don't know what you mean.'

'I'm bored. I'm not interested in my job, or where I'm living . . .' She trailed off, seeing if the sentence – the thought – might complete itself, but it didn't. A shrug, a slow shake of the head. 'I should just fuck off somewhere. Do something. You know? Create the . . . *open myself up* to the possibilities of change.'

Faye, drawing on a cigarette, didn't reply. The smoke thinned in the still air.

'I thought I was doing that, here. But, actually,' she said, smiling, 'the sole purpose of my life, at the moment, is to reimburse the system for the cost of prosecuting me.'

'When I was about eleven,' Faye said, 'I wanted to be a missionary.'

'That's not much of a position.'

Faye went off to buy a round. The beer garden was busy, noisy with children in the play area. A wasp settled on the lip of one of the empty bottles and crawled inside, she could see it outlined on the tinted glass. As a girl this would've had her out of the seat, squealing for someone to get rid of it! get rid of it! Upending the bottle, she flushed the insect out with the dregs and watched it fumble on the grass for a moment before flying, swaying, away. A party of walkers approached an adjacent table, pints to hand, one carrying a stick in the style of a shepherd's crook. They looked sun-rouged and foot-weary and contented enough to have been out on the moors all day.

Faye set the drinks down. 'Sorry, I got stuck at the bar behind that lot.'

She took a long slug, eyes closed. It tasted even better than the first. This was all right. So long as she eased the talk away from how she would endure the months ahead, or what she would do, where she would go, when the time came to move on; which, in any case, came under the category of 'future'. And she didn't do future.

She grinned at Faye. 'I don't know about you, but I've got my mouth shaped for getting slaughtered.'

'You're in luck, then.' Faye used her lager as a pointer. 'I just saw some people in there, off my course. There's a party going off later – somewhere, I dunno where – and they said they'd give us a lift, if we're up for it.'

In the car, all boozing: lads up front, lasses in the back; she sat in the middle, gazing at nothing in particular beyond the windscreen as they made for some village somewhere along the valley. Occasional snatches of a river running parallel to the road lay on the land like scraps of aluminium foil. Half eight on a summer evening and still light.

Raising her bottle and lowering it again, she saw two figures up ahead on the verge: a guy and a dog, even though this was a hectic dual carriageway and no place to be out walking or trying to cross. She recognized the dog first. A hundred metres off, fifty, thirty. She saw that there was something wrong. An oddness. As the car zapped by, she swivelled to watch them, but the guy didn't register her; he didn't seem to be focusing at all, and she feared he might be about to step out into the furious spool of cars. And, with a glimpse as subliminal as a flashcard, she absorbed what it was about him that was odd. He was wet: hair, clothes, feet. Not rained-on wet, but saturated, as if he'd been dumped in a swimming pool. And his shoulders – this image lingering long afterwards, defining the moment – were swathed in green weed, like a football scarf.

'The Hermit,' she said, continuing to stare out of the rear windscreen at the rapid diminishment of the guy and the dog.

But the others weren't listening, they were talking among themselves. Then she realized that they were talking, had been talking for some time, to her; only she'd not taken in a word of it.

9

She called, collect, from a payphone in town. The postcard? Yeah, that had reached her okay. Mom would've written back, only there was no return address. Which was no big deal, seeing as a letter – one of Mom's stream-of-consciousness monologues – wasn't what she needed. What she needed was dialogue. The intimacy, the immediacy, of talking things through – as far as it was possible with the cumulative interference of two pieces of moulded plastic, satellite timelag and the lifelong grooves of daughter–mother assumptions of one another, and of themselves in relation to one another.

'I worry I'm going to end up with my dad.'

'Is that legal over there?'

'You know what I mean.'

'I lived with him for fifteen years, and now I get to hear – I get to *pay* to hear – all about guys just like him.'

'I don't have anyone else to talk to.'

'You could try talking to yourself.'

'Mom.'

'I know, hon. I know. Hey, it's okay.'

Mom wondered if she'd quit because of Spoons – meaning, exclusively because of him – and she told her no. No, not exclusively. It was more complicated than that. Not even so simple as loss of faith in the cause, or disillusionment (they'd won, they'd stopped – 'shelved', 'deferred indefinitely' – the fucking bypass!), or plain exhaustion with living rough. She didn't know what it was.

'Where's the camp now?'

'Down south, mostly. Most of the people, I mean. Airport extension.' She shook her head, pointlessly, unseen. 'Even if he wasn't there, I still couldn't go back to them. To that.' Internationally telecommunicated silence. She exhaled. 'You know me, Mom, I give up on things. I get restless.'

'Impatient, is what you get.'

It was inscribed into family lore that she was inclined to become disconnected – from people, situations – and that this discon-nectedness lay in failure to read the runes of whatever was going on around her. Haste. An impatience to interpret things as they are now, or might turn out to be, according to her own partial blueprint.

The classic, often retold, anecdotal example:

Fourteen years old, out on site with her mom for the first time; the job being to plot the precise positions of underground electricity cables before digging work could begin. Mom let her have first dowse. She applied herself, she concentrated, she took care . . . she located three ducts radiating from a central transformer, tagging them on the ground and on the plans. Mom double-checked, finding the same ducts in the same places. She also detected something the girl hadn't: a series of cross-cables connecting the main ducts. If a worker had excavated into one of these he would've blacked out a few hundred homes and businesses in the neighbourhood. Daughter asked mother how come she'd missed the cross-cables, only she put it: *Why didn't the pendulum work?*

'Okay, two things: first, I'm glad you don't automatically blame yourself when things foul up. Some women do this, and it's unhelp-ful.' Her mom let that register. 'Second, this is one time when you *should* blame yourself, because you goofed.'

'How'd I goof? I dowsed the same places you did.'

'It's not just to do with where you dowse, it's the questions you ask in your head when you're dowsing. If you don't give the pendulum the opportunity to tell you about cross-cables, you don't get cross-cables.'

Dowsing was like writing a computer program, Mom said. A program was as good, or bad, as the programmer – the hardest part being to devise the sub-programs that searched for errors while the main program was running. Every conceivable glitch had to be anticipated and eliminated for the program to be idiot-proof.

'Whenever you're dowsing, make "gigo" your watchword.'

'What's *gigo*?'

'It's a saying computer people have: Garbage in, garbage out.'

Anyway, anyway, anyway, what she didn't want from this phone call was to be dragged back to teenage speech and thought and behaviour patterns. She'd moved on – from Richie, from Flashville – and wanted to move the conversation on as well. What she wanted was Mom's advice. Because things had happened which might prove to be synchronicitous, in the scheme of things, and she had to plumb their potential.

'Do I get to know the details, here?' Mom said.

'Not really.'

'Okay, are we talking a "who" or a "what"?'

'Both, I think. All right, a guy, mostly – but not the way you're thinking.'

A guy in combination with a dog, a black beast and a line of poetry; then seeing him like that at the roadside . . . but it wasn't necessary to spill the specifics for Mom to give her general guidance on self-dowsing. Not the ritual of dowsing herself before dowsing something else: *This is what I want to dowse . . . can I? . . . may I? . . . am I ready?* No, this time she literally had to dowse her *self.* The pendulum as a tool of self-psychoanalysis, to be used with extreme caution, if at all. And not without maternal consultation, her mom having forgotten more about dowsing than she would ever, etc. By self-dowsing she hoped to reveal to herself what to do about the Hermit. Ethan. Because she wasn't certain, but maybe he was the reason she was here in this place, at this time, in this mood of directionless energy.

The transatlantic counsel: 'Be absolutely sure to dowse your unconscious mind, not the conscious. Right?'

Problem being, if the pendulum moved only in response to the dowser – which it did, any dowser knew that – then how could the dowser cause it to move in response to something she didn't even know she was thinking? The trick, Mom said, was to tell yourself the pendulum worked of its own accord.

'But it *doesn't*.'

'*Believe* that it does.'

Only then could she hope to use the pendulum to personify – make known – her unconscious reply to a specific question. Dowsing the conscious mind was easy, also redundant, because if you paid attention to yourself you already knew the answer. And there was always the risk of telling yourself what you wanted to hear. The unconscious was where it was at. The ultimate test of a dowser.

'What you're doing, hon, is training yourself to see the invisible.'

The day after talking to Mom, she was on shift when Gavin Drinkell, of the blue eyes and blond hair, came in for tea and toast. Things between them were cool again – at least, for her – and he seemed to be handling it. After the Interflora scene she'd pitched up at the newspaper offices to confront him, spelling it out once and for all; since then, the calls, the cards, the pestering had stopped. No more roses. He still came into the caff from time to time, but there wasn't much she could do about that.

She fetched his order.

'Have you ever interviewed the Hermit?'

Gavin was feigning nonchalance, and her question skewed him, took him off on some tangent outside of the strict waitress–punter relationship she had been the one to insist upon if he didn't want his food in his lap.

'Ethan Gray? Yeah, a few times.' He looked suspicious. Also, he looked like he would talk to her about anything at all just to keep her there a little longer. 'Why?'

She tidied the menus, the condiments. 'So you know him, then?'

'I wouldn't say I *know* him. He's not someone you get to know, as such.'

'Only, he was in here last week. No, it was the week before.'

'Me and a photographer went out on the moors with him a while back,' Gavin said. 'Stalking, he calls it. Thinks he's some kind of a Red Indian – sorry, *indigenous North American* – tracker. Six hours up and down hills in the pissing rain.'

'Yeah?' The image recurred to her of Ethan, drenched, draped in green gunk.

He laid a fist firmly on the table. 'This is the world most of us inhabit.' With his other hand, he flapped at the air as if swatting a fly. 'And this is the world inhabited by Ethan Gray.'

She smiled.

'What?' Gavin glared at her. 'What's funny?'

'Nothing.'

She held the pendulum in her fist till the temperatures of skin and plumb bob equalized.

When self-dowsing, have no concept of yourself, your mind, your body, or of the chaos going on inside – Laura van der Haeghe, consultant hypogealist, aka Mom.

She understood, without having to be told, that the essence of 'being' didn't reside in these awarenesses *of* herself, but in the simple fact of awareness. Not until she had stilled the white noise of her conscious self could she pay out the pendulum, trusting its responses to be true. True to her.

She was dowsing her own future; at least, her own immediate future. Except that she didn't do this. So she had to dowse the present and see where it led her.

IO

SUSAN REANEY (*housing officer*):

It was someone's leaving do and we were both the worse for wear – everyone was – and it just sort of happened. I was quite embarrassed, to be honest. The next day. But, somehow, we started seeing each other outside work after that. In a lot of ways he was quite shy. Awkward. I don't think he'd had much experience with women – there was someone while he was at university, but as far as I know that was about it until he met me. It wasn't that he lacked self-confidence, or that he wasn't good-looking – because he was, in an unconventional sort of way – it was just that, I don't know, Ethan wasn't as interested in women as most blokes are. He wasn't odd (at least, I didn't think so at the time, at first), he was just different. Semi-detached, Mr Rougvie called him.

I can't say he ever made me feel particularly loved, or special, but I seemed to fulfil some sort of need for him. As I suppose he must have done for me. But the whole situation was a bit unreal. Sometimes we'd meet up three or four days in a row – lunchtimes, evenings, staying over – then a week would go by when we wouldn't have seen each other at all if we didn't happen to work in the same place. As for holidays, we had one weekend away together in all those months. To be honest, it was one of those periods in your life when you think of yourself as being between relationships, even though – technically – you're in one.

Everyone in the office knew about us being an item, but no one said anything. Not then. Neither of us was much in the clique of things anyway, so I don't imagine they were that bothered what we got up to. Now, of course, they're full of it.

II

She carried a torch, dabbing the ground with the disc of light to be sure of her footing. This was cool. Rising out of the town, the road left houses behind; left itself behind too, dematerializing into a track of puddled, rutted earth and chips of stone. Sharpness impressed itself in the soles of her feet, in trainers whose tread was reduced by wear to a pattern of grey lines, like photocopies. The fields made a winter ocean all about her. Made her small. The daylight, what there was of it, spread thinly behind her; ahead, the sky piled up with blocks of black. How swiftly would you have to travel to beat the dawn, heading west into perpetual night? This was walking. Step step step. The sound of her feet beneath her. In town, you couldn't always hear yourself walk. She spoke her name aloud. Hearing it. Seeing it, condensed as a breathprint on the chilled air.

'Out early.'

The voice, disembodied by the dark, hit her with so much adrenalin she thought she'd been electrocuted. Her throat made a noise.

'The path bends away up there,' the man said.

He was becoming visible, black, then silver, then white against black; standing in a gateway, by a cattle grid. He was short and wide, carrying something on his shoulder that looked twice his weight. She had no idea what it was. Behind him a large stone farmhouse amazed her, as if it had just been magicked into being. She saw the track, veering to the left as he'd indicated, a diagonal line across the rising pasture. Mist lay undiffused in the hollows but, already, the gathering day was restoring colour – greens and violets – to the slow-motion uncoupling of the landscape's component parts.

'Half a mile up, half a mile back again once he's told you to bugger off.'

A caravan. Not a hut, or shack, or log cabin, but a caravan – two-berth, by the looks – pitched in a natural U of banked grazing and trees. A pair of pines beyond the caravan created the optical illusion of a sheet hung to dry between two poles. His red pick-up, TOYOTA spelled in white across its arse, dandruffed with bird gloop and fragments of tree, was parked beneath a stand of mature sycamores. She managed without the torch now, pausing – hands hipped, sweat cooling on her skin. The caravan was enclosed by a picket fence that could have been nicked from a flint-knapped cottage and replanted here. With the cabin, she'd imagined woodsmoke from a chimney pipe, cooking smells from an open door. But this place looked derelict. The roof was peeling, the curtains were drawn, the tyres were flat, there was chipboard where one of the windows should have been. The caravan was pale peach, apart from a horizontal band of recent blue paint. In a slant of early sunlight it was just possible to discern a sequence of letters, an impression of them, like secret writing beneath the blue:

CUNT WANKER NUTER

She wasn't wearing, never did wear, a watch, but reckoned it to be about six thirty. Too early for an unannounced call, for anything other than sleep, but she'd been woken by a resolve to do this. So she was doing it. The belatedly impulsive enactment of a days-old, dwelt-upon decision. Breeze blocks were stacked to form steps up to the door. She knocked, withdrawing to the bottom step to lessen the in-your-faceness.

Dog noise, muffled, frantic; the caravan palpitated with all the scampering back and forth, Erica sounding like she was howling into a hollowed log. Then, the creak of a floor beneath human feet, the snip of a bolt being retracted. The upper section of the door swung out, framing Ethan from the waist up. His chest was hairless, the torso's white Y making the tanned arms, face and neck appear fake.

'Hiya,' she said.

'Er, oh, yeah. Is it?' His hair was up in tufts, his right cheek creased, as though it had been badly ironed. 'What?'

Not 'What?' as in what the hell was she doing here, but as in *Could you repeat the question?* He seemed semi-concussed. Erica was up at the ledge of the split doorway, spending small growls and yips left over from her territorial indignation.

'It's early, I know.'

He cupped his face. It was odd to be looking up at him like this. She noticed a narrow scar, like a tick, in the chin stubble.

'I was spark out,' he said, talking into his hands, then lowering them.

'Yeah, sorry.'

'I don't have any, you know . . . um . . . I'm not clothed.'

She smiled. 'Actually, that isn't why I came.'

'Right.'

'Will I wait out here while you . . . *clothe?*'

They sat at the table, with coffees. Erica was outside, peeing. Ethan had slung on a rugby shirt and baggy jogging bottoms and had tidied his hair. He smelled of sleep and stale body heat. Now and then, their knees bumped beneath the table.

'How did you find me?'

'Tourist Information. They drew a map for me.'

'Terrific.'

'D'you know, in the shop, they sell Black Beast souvenirs? T-shirts, postcards, car-window stickers, mugs, bookmarks – the lot. They even have a plastic panther with eyes that glow in the dark. Two ninety-nine, battery not included.'

No reaction. It was hard to tell if he knew that already, or was uninterested, or hadn't even heard her. She was gabbing. It was whatever a.m., the guy was drugged by inconclusive sleep, and she was gabbing at him like this was the pub or something.

She inhaled the fumes of her drink. 'Is there chicory in this?'

'I had soup out of that mug last night.'

Again the silence, and she found herself – how? why? – saying she loved the fact that he lived here, like this. His embarrassment embarrassed her. So, okay, fine. Just sit and look around and absorb the scene and shut the fuck up. There was a big wall-map, measled with multicoloured pins. She tried to sit side-saddle, so their legs wouldn't collide, but there wasn't room. With the storage bins, the folders and notebooks, and papers bound by elastic bands, this wasn't a home, it was a stationery cupboard. A manual typewriter and transistor radio filled half the table. She took in the unwashed washing-up, the thin psychedelic curtains, the balding food-stained mud-stained carpet, the rash of black-green mildew on the ceiling. The caravan reeked of damp.

'It's all right in summer,' he said, following her gaze, giving her the spiel, like she was a prospective buyer. 'The water pipes freeze up in winter, and condensation's a problem year round. And mice get into the food cupboards, so it's all in tins now.'

She pointed at the boarded window. 'What happened?'

'I lost my keys. Had to break in for the spares.' His Adam's apple bobbed as he swallowed coffee. 'I've not long had them all done. The windows. The glazing.'

'Vandals?'

Ethan frowned.

'You can still make out the graffiti,' she said. 'Sounds like a firm of solicitors, doesn't it? Cunt Wanker Nuter, Commissioners for Oaths.'

He smiled, fleetingly, then receded into something that might've been confusion or, at least, a lapse of concentration. He excused himself. The caravan lurched with his weight as he left. For all she knew, he wouldn't come back shortly, or at all. What she was sitting on, she realized, was – had been, until a few minutes ago – his bed. A sleeping bag and cushion were stashed at one end. Also, the microcassette recorder he'd used to dictate poetry that time. *I saw through a hole in the page.* She made her way to the door and sat on the steps to watch Erica foraging in the enclosure, sniffing the rough grass. Beyond the picket, the turf was cropped short; although

there were no sheep in view, she could hear their plaintive communication across the hillside. Ethan was in the trees, squatting,
trousers round his ankles. His buttocks, in the leafy half-light, were
the colour of mushrooms.

As he re-emerged, she asked: 'How come she's called Erica?'

'Hn, oh . . . I found her abandoned in the heather.' He let himself
back into the pitch. 'I was out walking, this was a couple of years
ago now – not round here – and I came across three puppies in a
plastic sack. She was the only one to survive.'

'I don't get it.'

'Erica is the name for the heath genus of plants. Family *Ericaceae*.'

'You didn't think, maybe, you could've just called her . . .
Heather?'

Ethan said, when asked, that he'd lived out here for two hundred
and eighteen days. The caravan was his, the site belonged to the
farmer. Mr F. She cited the encounter at dawn by the cattle grid
and he said yeah, that would've been him. Faverdale. Most of the
farm was intake, land reclaimed from the moor – by hand, by his
grandfather – and sown for grazing. They were on their second
coffee, on the stoop, being his term for the breeze-block steps. An
acclimatization had occurred between them. The guy was up to
pace with her now; mentally into his stride with the day – as she'd
been when she arrived, and he hadn't. Caffeine and conversation
and the fact of being, of having to be, awake. He seemed suddenly
younger, less unfriendly, for the loss of sluggishness.

'Have you ever seen her,' she said, 'in all those two hundred and
odd days?'

'Her?'

'Cats are basically female, don't you think?'

Ethan looked as if he might be giving this theory some consider-
ation. At last, he shook his head and said that, no, he hadn't seen
the cat.

'So, are you trying to kill her, or catch her, or take her picture?
Or what? Prove she exists, yeah?' She waited for confirmation, but

he simply gazed out across the fell. The grass, in the play of light, might've been glazed with dew or fresh rain. She took a slug of coffee. 'Only, if you plan on harming her in any way, then count me out.'

He stared at her. 'Count you out of what?'

When she'd done explaining, he said: 'The pendulum told you to find the cat?'

'A pendulum is an inanimate object. It has no more intelligence than this mug.'

Ethan glanced at the mug, as if the concept would be elucidated there. The guy wasn't looking his best, but whose fault was that? Her own face felt puffy, waxy, from the early rise, now that the flush of the hike out from town had worn off. Self-dowsing, when she hadn't even offered an insight into dowsing in general, was a puzzle for him.

She took out the pouch and withdrew the pendulum. 'A shoelace weighted with the wooden pull from a bathroom light cord. That's all it is.'

'I thought dowsers used rods. Or or or sticks.'

'Yeah, some do. Me, I use a pendulum.'

He was staring at her hands. 'Do you harm yourself?'

'These?' She laughed. The livid welts, the burns, the faded cicatrices, the new wet wounds. One of them was weeping pus. 'You mean these?'

'I knew someone, a girl, when I was at university,' he said. 'Used to cut herself with a razor, or burn her arms with cigarettes.'

'Industrial injuries, in my case.' She splayed her fingers. 'Hot fat, boiling water, hotplates, grills, oven shelves, knives, cheese graters . . . yesterday, I stabbed myself when I was washing up.' She showed him. 'So, yeah, you could say I harm myself.'

'I never understood why she did it.'

She watched him, watching her hands. 'Maybe she didn't understand it herself.'

'I tried it, to see how it felt.' He mimed a cutting action on his forearm. 'With a Stanley knife. I wanted to get inside her head.'

'How far are we from the nearest phone?' He looked perplexed. '*Joke*, Ethan. Here I am, stranded in the middle of nowhere with . . . forget it, it wasn't that funny.'

He smiled now. 'No, well, I was . . . this was a long time ago. Fourteen years.'

Since his reference to the blemishes on her skin, she'd been tracing them with a fingertip in a rosary sequence of slow, unconscious caresses; she became aware, now, of what she was doing and stopped. Dropped her hands into her lap. She asked if he'd been in love with the girl and he nodded and she said she was sorry.

She handed him the pendulum. *Go on*. He dangled the weight, uncertainly.

'That's the bob, as in plumb bob. As in Plum, my nickname in camp.'

'Couldn't they have just called you Bob?'

'You can make smart-arse remarks or you can learn about dowsing.'

She introduced the experiment: the use of a pendulum to tell men and women apart. The male response being a straight line, she said, the female being a circle. She instructed him to hold his free hand, palm upwards, beneath the bob. He extended his hand. There was no response at first, then – slowly, subtly – the bob moved. A tremor, tiny fibrillations, a swing, the swing growing more pronounced till a straight back-and-forth motion was indisputable. She saw him switch attention from the bob to her.

'Take your hand away,' she said, 'and I'll put mine there.'

The pendulum kept to a straight line for a few seconds before the alteration: the swing became erratic, as if disrupted by a draught, and, by degrees, a new rhythm, a new pattern, kicked in: small languid rotations, expanding into distinct circles.

Ethan shook his head. 'I'm obviously not manipulating it.'

'Nap.'

'Is it something to do with body heat, rising up from our palms?'

'An interesting theory, Professor.'

'But that doesn't explain the male–female variation. Or are you telling me men and women give off different . . . heat auras?'

'The swing varied because I told you it would.' He released the pendulum into her palm and she made a fist, the cord extruding like the tail of a captive mouse. 'If I'd said straight line for a girl and circle for a guy, that's what would've happened.'

'But I wasn't *making* the pendulum move.'

'Not consciously.'

'Even if it was auto-suggestion . . . the swings were so pronounced. I would've had to be doing that deliberately, with my fingers as well as my mind.'

She shook her head. 'If you think of the length of the cord, the tiniest fraction of a movement at the top – unconscious, involuntary, nervous, whatever – will be very obvious by the time it reaches the bob. Basic physics.'

He considered this. 'So it is me?'

'It's what I'm saying.'

She slipped the pendulum back in its pouch, the pouch back in her pocket. The bob pressed into her with its familiar hard constancy. He wasn't having this, yet, she could tell. Something nagged at him, at his assimilation of what he'd witnessed. A vague dissatisfaction. *Is that all there is to it?* He was probably replaying the demo in his head right now. She drew an analogy between the pendulum and a weather vane.

'The weather vane isn't the wind, and it doesn't create the wind. But it makes the wind *visible*. Its direction, anyway.'

Ethan almost nodded. 'The wind, in this case, being the unconscious mind?'

'In one.'

'What if I'd been blindfolded? No idea whether the hand beneath the pendulum was male or female, or no hand at all, what then?'

'That's when you find out if you're a dowser or just someone who can dowse.'

★

He said he'd seen her picture in *The Monitor*. The photo was as far as he'd got, so she had to fill him in on the story. She was a dowser. She was the daughter of a dowser. Many dowsers, her mom was one of them, had been known – had been employed – to find missing persons, and she believed it was conceivable for her to dowse for the cat using similar techniques. Maybe. The look on Ethan's face made her feel as though this was a recruitment interview and she had to satisfy him with regard to her credentials. Experience. Aptitude. Qualifications. Her commitment.

His expression said: *Tell me, Miss Fortune, why do you want this position?*

She salvaged something for him from the jumbled factors that fetched her here, now, this morning. Or, at least, what had fetched her away from what she was doing before. What it was, right, she was fed up with existing in opposition to something – of defining herself, and being defined, by that which she fought against. Resistance. There was an implicit negativity in that. Like, nationalists – Scottish, Welsh, Irish, whatever – impelled by a hatred of the English rather than by a concept of their own, independent identity. Well, she'd been anti-roads, anti-nuclear, anti-capitalist, anti-establishment, anti-everything for so long. Years. All her adolescent and adult life. Now, she wanted to be *pro* something.

'Pro what?' Ethan said.

'Pro active.' There was more to it than that, but as a *rationale* – as part of the rationale – it was okay. Only, ascribing reasons to a decision founded in intuition was about as ridiculous as you could get. 'Basically, I dowsed myself and scored a "yes".' She gave him another shrug. 'I dowse, yeah? That's what I do. That's what I am.'

'And you think you can find the cat?'

'Ethan, I haven't got a fucking clue.'

PART TWO

Equilibrium

12

The countryside warden sets off just before dawn, in the cool haze of semi-darkness; he prefers this time of day to be working, when the land is placid and he is unlikely to be disturbed. He takes a garden sack, for the litter that townsfolk leave. A stiff uphill walk from the lay-by where he left his car brings him to a reservoir and then, skirting the perimeter fence, out on to a broad shooting track. The sack is already a quarter full. Some sheep have strayed here, picking their way between several small ponds to feed on whatever they can find in the cotton-grass and bilberry. He spots a damselfly, a common blue, skimming among a stand of rushes that tilt in the breeze. Although the sun has risen now, it is blowy up here and he is glad to have cause to keep moving.

Up ahead, an old railway van comes into view; for years it served as a shooting hut, but is now abandoned. In season, it was his task to prevent walkers from straying between the beaters and the guns; when the morning drives were done everyone would adjourn inside for sandwiches, Scotch eggs and whisky. Fond memories. The council no longer issues licences for shoots up here, and if you were ignorant of the wagon's history you might find its incongruity amusing. These days, teenagers break in to have sex, drink, take drugs, spray graffiti, light fires. He has found the evidence on previous rounds and heads there again this morning to see if there is anything for him to attend to. Picnickers visit this hillside too, for the views; hikers follow the track to the higher, bleaker reaches of the interior; others are drawn by the remnants of a stone circle, partially hidden in the heather. This early, the warden is alone. He puffs up the incline, warmed, stooping with small grunts of exertion to recover scraps of rubbish. From his perspective, the nascent sun rests on the horizon, exactly bisected by the black filament of a pole, formerly used to display a red flag during the shoots.

There is a hummocky shape right in the middle of the track. At first he thinks it is a boulder and cannot understand how it could have got there; but, as he approaches, he makes out the characteristics of a sheep. It puzzles him why the animal doesn't rise to its feet and move away. It should have picked up his scent by now, or the noise of his boots. Then he sees that the sheep is dead. This does not greatly surprise him – carcasses, in varying stages of decomposition, are not uncommon if you spend time in the country. He will need to notify the farmer so that the sheep can be removed and examined for disease. A solitary crow flaps away from its carrion. The warden bends over the remains, searching for an identifying brand on the fleece. What he sees causes him to recoil. The animal, on its side, has had its throat ripped out with such force that the head is held in limp connection to the body only by the junction of skull and spine. The belly is shredded from ribs to groin, strewing guts and blood on the ground, as if the flesh has been raked repeatedly with a scalpel. He notices, now, that steam is rising in faint wisps from the entrails. His mouth is dry, and he has a sudden aftertaste of his breakfast. When he kneels down to press a palm against the ewe's undamaged flank he finds that the skin is still warm. The warden stands unsteadily, looking all around him, before hurrying back down the track, the litter sack forgotten beside the dead animal.

13

Roy pitched up at the door to her bedsit – early, her day off – looking inconvenienced, handing her a message he'd bunged on the reverse of a junk-mail flyer. *Some feller . . . Nathan, it sounded like . . . says you're to meet him in twenty minutes.* She read the note: the name of a farm, and a grid reference. Nothing else.

'Where's this, then?' she said.

'I'm a secretary,' Roy said. 'And now I'm a geography teacher.'

'A farm?' She pushed her dreads from her forehead and let them fall back into place. 'How am I supposed to get there in twenty minutes?'

'Fucking transport consultant, as well.'

She douched, slung on some clothes and went out to buy a map before setting off on foot for the place on the note, which was five K from town, mostly uphill. The Toyota was parked in a passing place along from the farmstead, both verges lined with vehicles. No Ethan. She found him sitting on a drystone wall, using binoculars to scan the hillside's acute decline towards a sprawl of woodland. She climbed up beside him.

'Here, have a look.'

She accepted the bins. The field could've been a country showground: beagle pack, police, police dogs, foxhounds, the hunt on horseback in full regalia, men with shotguns, bystanders milling around, a TV crew, a photographer, a guy who might've been Gavin Drinkell. Voices, baying, barking and the intermittent blare of a hunting horn reached out to them in the morning chill. Like the din you'd hear in your head if you were loopy. She saw that the cattle had been corralled into an adjacent meadow.

'What are they doing?'

'What's it look like? They're going to hunt the thing. On the assumption, no doubt, that it's deaf, blind, has no sense of smell and is minus a limb.' He gave a single sharp laugh. 'As for any prints it might've left in the field . . .'

Ethan filled her in on the report on the local radio station's eight a.m. news: a 'big black animal' worrying the herd. When the farmer went down to investigate he found a calf with deep scratches to the hind quarters, cowering by its mother. Ethan, just now, had been told to fuck off. No extra info about the sighting, no permission to examine the injured calf. She got the impression that Ethan was used to being told to fuck off.

He pointed. 'There they go.'

Raising the bins again, she watched the posse of men, dogs and horses funnel through a gateway at the bottom of the field, into the trees. Only the dogs hurried; the rest advanced with military deliberation, fanning out along the delta of woodland trails. The sound of their progress continued for some while after she'd lost sight of them.

For the first time, he looked at her. 'What took you so long?'

'I don't have a car.'

'Am I going to have to give you a lift everywhere?'

'What "everywhere"?' There'd been no arrangement to work together, no deal, just a vague *let me think about it*. In the – how many? three? – three days since she'd visited the caravan, Ethan had made no contact. 'You're saying you want to do this?'

He dropped down from the wall. 'Come on, there's a dead sheep to inspect.'

They followed a shooting track, rising from the farm into rough heath. To one side a chain of grouse butts were sunk into earth mounds like anti-aircraft gun emplacements. Meadow pipits darted about, their song ricocheting across the moor. With the climb, the temperature fell and the breeze strengthened, ballooning her denim jacket; her eyes were streaming and the veins on the backs of her hands had turned mauve.

'I wouldn't want to be up here in winter,' she said.

'You get used to it.'

In winter, he said, it wasn't the cold but the brevity of daylight that hampered his work. A plane passed high above them, invisible, its tell-tale drone drifting among the fells so that the sound might've been issuing from the land itself. She asked after Erica, and Ethan said he'd left her behind so she wouldn't disturb the site. Cresting the hill, she caught a splash of colour up ahead: four plastic cones – orange, like those used on motorways – connected by striped tape to form a rectangle. Inside the rectangle was a carcass, and a figure stooped over it, kneeling, as if at prayer, or as if attempting a resuscitation. The man looked up. He wore wellingtons, a sleeveless quilted jacket and surgical gloves. The ewe was no more than a skeleton draped with shreds of flesh and fleece and guts. Brown blood stained the fleece and the ground, the turf, all about. The ribcage – bare, bleach-white – put her in mind of the framework of a half-built boat.

'She won't be winning any rosettes this year.' His accent was so public school it might've been exaggerated for comic effect. He smiled, at her. 'A disquieting sight for you to take with you, I'm afraid, for the remainder of your walk.'

'Which happened first?' Ethan said. 'This, or the attack on the calf?'

The man stood stiffly. His short hair was peach-coloured, threaded with strands of reflection like glass-fibre matting. He was wringing his hands as though drying them beneath a hot-air blower. 'RSI,' he said. 'You have no idea.'

'You're Inglis.'

'And you are?'

Ethan gave his name. The man he'd called Inglis fabricated another smile. *Ah, yes, the infamous Mr Gray.* He said he'd assumed the forename to be pronounced with a short *e*, as in 'egg', rather than long, as in 'teeth'. Ethan didn't reply to this.

'I spend far too much of my time behind a desk,' Inglis said. She was unsure if this related in some way to his last remark, or to the pain in his hands, or to the scenery – his pleasure at being out here on the moors. 'Well, zoologist and crypto-zoologist in conference. Our media friends down below are missing a photo-opportunity.'

'I have an Open University degree in zoology,' Ethan said.

'Then you will be sufficiently intelligent to understand that my use of the prefix was in reference to the status of the, um, beast, not that of the investigator.'

'Which makes you a crypto-zoologist too, for the next four months.'

'You possess a sense of irony, Mr Gray.' That smile. He batted a fly away from his face. 'For some unfathomable reason, I find that surprising.'

She was aware of a high-pitched whine; the noise had been in the background all along, she sensed, but had intensified. It took a second to identify the source: wind, vibrating a metal flagpole, making it hum like a tuning fork. Neither Inglis nor Ethan showed any sign of having noticed. She looked at the dead ewe. She didn't want to, but couldn't help, looking at the dead ewe. A short distance away, a small plastic sheet had been pegged out on the muddy edge of the track.

She went over. 'What's this?'

A paw print, Inglis explained, joining her. Protected from the elements in case the weather worsened before he had the chance to make a cast.

'What's the definition like?' Ethan said.

'Wonderful isn't the first word that springs to mind.'

'Can I see?'

The other man snapped off the gloves, slipping them inside a polythene bag and putting the bag away. He flexed his fingers, making a trawl of the horizon as though the answer to Ethan's request was contained in the view. Then he bent down, eased out two of the pegs and, with care, peeled back the cover. Ethan squatted beside him.

'As you can see,' Inglis said, 'the print is skewed in diagonal elongation – due, one suspects, to a skid of the animal's paw as it closed in at speed on the prey.' He pointed. 'The resultant blurring, here, prevents us from determining whether the rear pad is bisected into the twin lobes that would differentiate feline from canine. The claw marks are inconclusive, of course, given the circumstances.'

A neat set of nicks splayed in the soft mud at the front of the print. She asked what Inglis meant and, as he replied, she detected a subtle alteration in tone from the way he'd been speaking to Ethan. Also, when he'd addressed Ethan his eyes had been on the print, now they were on hers.

'A cat's claws, being retractable, would not ordinarily show up in the way that a dog's would. But with a cat the weight, say, of a leopard or puma, running over wet ground, claw marks would not be uncommon.' He coughed. 'So.'

'What about the size?'

This was Ethan. She found herself nodding; the print did appear to be unusually large. Inglis shook his head. He was saying something about scale being potentially deceptive, about how he'd conducted experiments with his own dog, a pedigree red setter, which produced a surprising variation in tread size depending on speed, type of surface and deterioration.

'In deep snow, an hour of thaw enlarged his tracks into the footsteps of a yeti.'

'Who was that?' she said.

They were watching him, Inglis, make his way down the slope. Ethan searched in his pack, removing a fat notebook exaggerated by loose sheets wedged between its pages. From these, he sorted a news cutting. This week's *Monitor*, he said. She held the article tight to prevent it being stripped away in the wind. It described Dr Barker Inglis, CBE, as a wildlife consultant to the Agriculture Development Advisory Service. Newly appointed by the government to investigate the Black Beast phenomenon, his remit: 'to establish whether there is evidence to support a hypothesis of predation by a species of cat or cats not indigenous to Britain'. A four-month secondment. He would conduct post-mortems, study forensic and photographic evidence and take submissions from experts, eyewitnesses and interested parties. Quote: *I come here with my mind as open as the moors themselves.* There was a colour mugshot, so grainy that his skull looked like it had been stained with orange dye in the design of a hairstyle.

'Have you added him to your mailing list?'

Ethan wasn't paying attention. He'd returned to the carcass and was organizing camera gear, a spiral-bound pad, the microcassette. Before leaving, Inglis had gestured at the remains. *All yours.* Now, Ethan was setting to work: reeling off photos from all angles, moving in for close-ups, then – gloveless – examining the animal for himself.

'Full-grown Swaledale ewe; skeleton intact; meat missing from belly, upper legs, back, throat, shoulders, rump.' He leaned right in. 'Small abrasions, possibly bites or nips, to lower limbs; ribs clean, evidence of rasping; also evidence of rasping to face. Nose absent, ears and eyes absent . . . tongue absent.'

He clicked off the tape. Producing his glasses from a pocket, he made notes on the pad, then put the pad, the microcassette and the glasses away. He wiped his palms on his sweater, withdrawing a little from the carcass. From the flies.

'You've blood.' She touched her own face. 'Here.'

Ethan wet his thumb and rubbed at the bridge of his nose. 'This was the place.' He was pointing at the kill site, the ground, the ewe, she wasn't sure. Agitated. There was an excitement about him that was almost a taste. 'Right . . . right fucking here.' A look at his watch. 'Two and a half, three hours ago this sheep was killed. Torn apart.'

'Uh-huh.'

She saw that he wasn't aroused so much as engrossed. By whatever had gone on here, by whatever had done it, by their proximity to it. She could share that, she felt it herself – the being privy to . . . this. This was just her, projecting, but the guy seemed frustrated too, feeding off the pieces, the forensics, of something he'd have *witnessed* – given anything to witness – if only he'd been here a couple of hours earlier.

'You must know your breeds to identify a Swaledale from that mess,' she said.

Ethan smiled, apparently pulled out of himself by her comment.

'Why's that funny?' Then, following his gaze, she caught on: a score or more Swaledale ewes dotted about the moorside. She laughed. 'Yeah, all right.'

They sat eating chocolate, side by side against an old freight wagon – wheelless, rimed with rust and graffiti. How did *that* get here? The chocolate was hers, it had softened in her pocket. Ethan wrote up his notes. Below, wind strafed the pewter surface of a small reservoir; lower still, lay a valley created, he said, by a glacier that had strewn the land hereabouts with so much moraine from further up the dale you could mistake this for limestone, not gritstone, country. Somewhere down there was the hunt. The cat. This was cat country. To all horizons, the moors were displayed as if in a vast aerial photograph, motionless, surreal, etched with the shadows of their own irregularity.

'Why am I here?' she said.

'I wanted you to see what I do. The science. I wanted you to understand that this isn't just some hobby.' Ethan leaned forward, then back again. 'Fieldwork. I get out there. I'm not like those cosmologists who explore, who construct a theory of the universe, by sitting in front of a computer all day. Doing maths. There's no . . . there isn't a theoretical equation for the cat.'

'Do you have an image of her?'

'An image?'

'Yeah, you know, do you ever imagine her?'

He frowned. 'I dream about her, sometimes. One time, I woke in the night and saw Erica in her basket – just a shape in the dark – and I thought it was the cat.' He paused, and she sensed him retreat. 'I thought the dreams might coincide with kills or sightings, so I kept a record of them. Dates, times. But they didn't tie in.'

'I think dreaming is cool.' She watched the liquid drift of cloud-shadows across the lilac and green and smoke-black upland away to the north. There, on one of those wooded slopes – with the map, with time, she could work out which one – was a place that had been Flashville. She ate the last segment of chocolate. 'You live out here for so long, looking for her, how are you not going to have cat dreams?'

Ethan was writing again. *The science*. She pictured the cat tagged, somehow, with a microchip so he could monitor her movements on a luminous screen; a ship's sonar operator sounding the ocean for the echo of an enemy submarine.

14

PROF. HENRY HARLEY, PH.D. (*professor of zoology*):

Lynx: With a crown-to-rump length of 80 to 130 cm, the average lynx is too small to match most of the eyewitness descriptions, which put the 'beast' at nearer 160 cm. A significantly longer tail is also usually reported. The lynx feeds on hares, rodents and young deer; it is extremely unlikely that it could kill a full-grown ewe.

Wildcat: (Bobcat, N. Am.) Because of its presence in the wild in these isles, the wildcat is often cited. Its size – barely larger than a domestic cat, albeit more robust – mitigates against this. Its British range is not known to extend outside Scotland.

Puma: (Cougar or Mountain Lion, N. Am.) Similar in appearance to a lioness. Crown-to-rump length from 120 to 150 cm, with a tail of up to 90 cm. Prey includes deer and small mammals, occasionally domestic stock (e.g. sheep, goats, horses, cattle). Its method of killing, by a bite to the throat, matches some of the post-mortem findings, but the geographical spread of kills is untypically small. Despite its colouring, the puma – when seen at dawn or dusk, or in woodland – might be mistaken for black.

Leopard: Also known as the panther, or black panther in the case of the melanistic leopard. Up to 160 cm, crown to rump, with a 90 cm tail. Lives in or near cover (e.g. forest, bush, scrub, rocky hillsides); chiefly nocturnal in areas where it is hunted or in proximity to humans. It preys on a range of mammals, also birds and fish; it kills with a single bite to the throat or skull. The black panther fits most 'beast' criteria, and has been specifically named by some witnesses. Its typical territory, 6 to 40 sq. km, is also in keeping. It is known to develop a taste for certain prey (e.g. sheep, humans).

Feral Cat: A descendant of the domestic cat, it has been wild in Britain for centuries. Its diet consists of small mammals, birds and game (e.g. rabbits, pheasants). One theory is that there is more than one 'beast', and that they are feral cats, or a hybrid of the Scottish wildcat and the feral, evolved to a size and strength capable of hunting larger prey. Most zoologists and naturalists are of the opinion that, with so much smaller prey available in the food chain, there is no logic to such an hypothesis.

Rogue Dogs: Great Danes and lurchers (a cross between a greyhound or whippet and another breed such as a collie or terrier) are used by poachers. They are fearsome animals, trained to hunt silently, usually for deer; it is not unheard of for them to be let loose among farm stock. It is conceivable that one or more of these dogs was released, or escaped, or became lost on a poaching expedition, and is now at large. If so, it would be certain to hunt for food rather than depend on scavenging. In post-mortems, numerous sheep have been found to have nip marks to the legs; it is common for dogs to bite at the hind legs and feet of a fleeing animal. A Great Dane or lurcher would certainly have the power and ferocity to kill a sheep. Dogs, however, tend not to attack and eat their prey in the clinical, comprehensive manner of a cat. Moreover, many eyewitnesses cite physical features that are characteristically feline, not canine.

Conclusion: Many of the incidents can be blamed with confidence on dogs. However, in several cases the evidence is far from conclusive, and in some it clearly incriminates something other than a dog. There is, as yet, no forensic basis for establishing beyond doubt the type of predator or predators involved. It is my opinion, therefore, that this latter category of cases must be deemed 'unexplained', pending further evidence.

15

'What did you do before this?'

'Local government,' Ethan said. He elaborated, sounding as if he was reading an autocue, or maybe as if he just didn't want to talk about it: 'I worked in the housing department, private rented sector, processing the registration and inspection of houses in multiple occupation.'

'Which is kind of ironic, seeing as you've wound up living alone. In a caravan.'

They were in the Toyota, in traffic, easing into town after the jolt down from the farm below the kill site. Flanking the road were terraces of homes and shops grimy with age, but solid-looking, attractive. She said this. Ethan told her the town's older buildings had been constructed in Victorian times with stone hauled from the moorside on quarry tracks that still scarred the slopes, if you knew where to look.

'So, where was this job?'

He told her the name of the city and she said that was where her dad lived. He was a photographer — freelance, magazines mostly. She hated the place: too big, too crowded, too expensive. There was a shallowness to the lives people lived there. A falseness. That was her impression, anyway. Ethan's face was blank. He stared straight ahead, out the windscreen. Besides, she associated the city with him. Her father.

'Did you live by yourself, before?' she said.

'Just me and Reeks. Erica.'

'Only, I heard you were married. Kids and that.'

He shook his head.

'They said you left them — your family — to come here.' She

wiped the air with her hand. 'I talk too much. Just tell me to mind my own fucking business.'

'I wasn't married.'

'I mean, the person who told me this also said you lived in a wooden hut.' She laughed. 'People say things. The garbage they'd trot out about us lot – in the papers, and that. If you spoke to them, they twisted it; if you didn't, they made it up.' She'd told him something of Flashville, then, when they were on the tops, in the lee of the disused train carriage. 'I think the truth is too dull for them,' she said. 'You know?'

Ethan didn't say anything.

'It was all *lifestyle* crap. We'd gab on about transport, or the environment, or planning or something, and they'd want to know about shagging and drugs and were we claiming benefit? The Tunnels of Love. I mean, fuck sake.'

'I'll drop you here.'

He'd pulled into a loading bay. Ahead, at the lights, was a turn that she knew would take him out towards the moorside road, towards Faverdale's place. He reached across her to spring the passenger door.

'Yeah, great. Thanks.'

The only noise was street din through the half-open door, the engine, the dunk-dunk-dunk of the indicator. And the atmospheric hum of a silence resting between and about them and mostly in her head. Where she was thinking that if she sat here long enough – not talking, not being talked to – this could develop into a scene from one of those French films where, for minutes at a time, no one speaks and you have no idea who's who or what the fuck's going on. What it was, was her: giving it large with the chatter, the Q & A stuff, quizzing him. He was pissed off. She'd pissed him off.

'Right,' she said at last. 'See you, then.'

He aimed a hand at the road. 'This is my turn-off.'

'Yeah, I'll be fine from here.'

*

In the tunnel there was no day and night, only Torch Time and Blackout. Torch Time was short, precious; she conserved Torch Time. Blackout felt eternal; the black of Blackout was true, total blackness. It filled her eyes and ears with black, black breath filled her lungs, black removed all trace of her body so that she didn't know where she ended and black began. She had to touch herself to be sure she was still there. There was no adjustment of vision in Blackout, no slow formation of shapes and shadows, no subtle gradations. No natural light whatsoever, only blackness. Even in Torch Time, the black didn't disappear, she just slit holes in it, or pressed it back to the peripheries, where it waited to engulf her again the instant Torch Time ceased.

In the tunnel you wore a hard-hat with a light moulded into it, or with a regular torch strapped on the side. To look at something, or someone, you had to move your whole head – not just your eyes – in that direction.

Puppet Neck Syndrome, Richie called it.

To her, it was an alternative definition of tunnel vision. She understood how, in neat synchronization, the brain moved the head and the head moved the light, so that the beam assumed the quality of a thought-wave made visible.

'Spoons.'

'What?'

'If I switched off my torch you wouldn't have a clue what I'm thinking.'

'You don't need to switch off your torch to achieve that.'

You had to crawl in on all fours, pushing the supplies along ahead of you. At the end of the tunnel, in the Home Dome, there was room for two people to sit up, or sleep, foetally, head to toe. Playing cards by torchlight, reading, eating, or just talking for hours on end in the dark to save the batteries. Taking turns to tell the storylines of novels they'd read or movies they'd seen.

'This reminds me of me and my sister,' she told Richie. 'We used to talk in the dark like this after we'd gone to bed.'

'Why the whispering?'

'In case Mom hears.'

He laughed. 'No, why the whispering *now*?'

'You have to whisper when you talk in the dark. Anyway, you're whispering as well and you don't even know my mom.'

Her more or less last words to him, before breaking camp, had been: *I can't go on with this.* With this, with you, the terms seemed interchangeable. With whatever. She couldn't go on. It occurred to her that her choices in life might be predetermined by a favouritism towards certain ways of expressing herself.

. . . Day One, art college, the tutor invited the students to introduce themselves, starting with her. Hi, her name was Chloe. The tutor, glancing at the register, said oh, now, there were two Chloes in the group, so which one was she?

'The other one.'

It wasn't many months before she drifted away, through with the course earlier than it was scheduled to be through with her. She just left. Because because because, from that introductory remark, there'd been an expectation of wit and unorthodoxy for her to satisfy. Because she was unable to go on with it. And because she was nineteen and it was a well-known fact she never persevered at anything requiring effort as well as imagination, which covered just about everything, if you stopped to think about it.

So she told Richie there were two Chloes: the one he wanted her to be, and the other one. She was the other one. It was as simple and as complicated as that.

On the day after the ride home from the sheep kill – with her having given up on Ethan on the assumption that he'd given up on her, even before there was anything for either of them to give up on, because whichever Chloe she was being now wasn't the one he wanted or needed or had any time for, which suited her just fine, just fucking fine . . . on the day after all of this, he came. In the doorway of the caff, dog sitting at heel, as though an invisible forcefield stopped them from crossing the threshold. She told him, sharper than she'd intended, to tie Erica up and pick a table and she'd sort him in a sec. Actually, he just wanted a word. In private.

She hesitated. 'All right if I take five, Roy?'

The boss was mopping the floor. He glanced from her to the Hermit and back again, then nodded. Outside, Erica sniffed her, excited, bum fractionally off the ground because the order to sit hadn't been revoked. Lapping at her hand, whimpering to be petted. She petted.

'You okay?' Ethan said.

'Yeah.' Nod nod nod. Stubble covered the lower half of his face in inconsistent patches. Erratic shaving, or erratic growth? When he spoke, tiny new moons formed at either side of his mouth. 'Yeah,' she said, 'I'm doing all right.'

'*Sit.*'

'It's okay, she's not bothering me.'

She tried to see if anyone – Roy, Faye, punters – was snooping on them from inside the caff, but the frontage was a mirror of car park, town and moor, with the pair of them, three including the dog, foregrounded in partial silhouette. Ethan was saying something about seeing her, talking to her. About what? About something. She wasn't really listening, being annoyed with him, and he wasn't giving her much to go on in the way of subject matter, being more concerned to get the logistics straight. The day, the place. He asked if today would be okay, or tomorrow, but she said she didn't have a day off till Friday so if he wanted to see her it would have to be then.

'In the day,' she said. 'I'm off out in the evening.'

'I can come into town.' The bridge of his nose was notched with red; she had an image of him at his desk in the caravan, hunched over paperwork for hours on end. He looked at her feet and said: 'Lunch. I mean, lunchtime.'

'Yeah, twelve, one, whenever. Come to the flat, if you want.'

'Good.' He nodded. She'd neglected Erica for too long; the dog had given up on being stroked and was lying on the pavement between them, dribbling. Ethan raised her up again on the choke and was turning to go, when he stopped and laid a hand on his scalp, as if he'd forgotten his hat. 'I don't . . . um, where is it you live?'

She pointed above the caff. 'There's a green door round the back, by the bins.'

16

SUSAN REANEY (*housing officer*):

This might sound odd, but Ethan reminded me of Aunt Carol. Mum's sister. She had a thing about Princess Diana – cutting out pictures of her from papers and magazines and putting them in albums. Half the wall units in her lounge were filled with books about Di, tapes of TV programmes about her, royal wedding souvenirs, the lot. When she died, you'd have thought Aunt Carol had lost her own daughter. She had to be treated for depression for months. Even now, she bursts out crying for no apparent reason, except everyone knows the reason but no one says anything. Her spare bedroom has been turned into a Diana shrine – candles, flowers, everything. Uncle Nigel says: *There are three people in this marriage*. It's quite funny the first time you hear it.

Obviously it wasn't Diana with Ethan, but his 'project' was taking over his life even when I knew him. Every other weekend he'd go off with his tent and all his gear. Alone. To be honest, I wouldn't have gone with him and he wouldn't have wanted me to, so it was never an issue. Apart from the fact that when you're seeing someone, you expect to actually *see* them occasionally. Even when he was home, there was the O.U. course work. Plus all the filing, and the wildlife documentaries he used to record and watch over and over. And, like Aunt Carol, there were times when he wouldn't discuss it and others when he talked about nothing else. The weird thing is, I don't think he really wanted to find the Black Beast. At first, maybe he did – well, obviously – but his project became such a part of his life that he'd have been totally lost without it. And if he found the cat, he would have to give up looking for it.

17

Using ingredients from downstairs, she fixed an omelette, fresh(ish) white rolls and an undressed tomato and onion salad. Ethan was dogless. He left his boots by the door. Through the floor came the sounds of the caff. She half expected him to mention this, or the weather, or the CD she'd put on, or something. He didn't. After the hellos, after she'd established what he wanted to drink – water – and had given this to him, he sat quietly on the only chair while she saw to the food. She couldn't decide whether it was a comfortable silence. Erica was well, he said, in reply to the one question she could think to ask. They ate off their laps: him on the chair, her on the bed.

'Sometimes, you can feel the vibrations of people talking downstairs through the soles of your feet,' she said. 'It's like you're treading on their voices.'

'Do you have any ketchup?'

She fetched a plastic tomato. He was weeding onion rings from the salad and arranging them around the rim of the sideplate.

'There's onions in the omelette as well,' she said.

'I don't mind them cooked.'

He sat there like a hobo, in off the street for a charitable feed. Unlike himself as she remembered him that first time, in the Place – hair, newly shorn – or dripping gloop at the roadside, or naked and semi-sleepy at the caravan door, or any of the times. He wasn't even familiar from the other morning, outside the caff, more or less inviting himself here. Roy, on her return, had made a hitch-hike sign at the window: 'What did *he* want?'

In Flashville, you'd saunter in and out of each other's benders for a smoke, a drink, a chat. Friends, strangers. These visits were casual, usually motiveless; no cause for communal comment or gossip or suspicion. Community, in town, was otherwise. She was disappointed to find herself adapting to its structures – analysing the Hermit's keenness to see her, so soon after his seeming keenness not to see her at all; analysing her own misgivings about that. Or maybe *here* was what it was. The oddness of him, being in the bedsit. This was her home now, for all its perversity, and she'd grown used to the things that were in it. And Ethan wasn't one of them.

'This is very nice,' he said. He sounded insincere. Not insincere, but rehearsed – like a small boy at a party under instruction to be polite, to say please and thank you.

She pointed at the floor with her fork. 'You're eating stolen property.'

He thought about that. 'Technically, the food hasn't left the premises yet.'

'That's true.'

'It would make an interesting legal test case,' he said.

Surreal was fine. She could handle surreal. There was a symmetry about him, in the way he sat and in the articulation of his limbs. His hands signed his speech, as hers did, but neatly and precisely, in harmony with the rhythm of what was being said. The meter. He was metrical. Watching him eat was like watching someone play xylophone.

'There was another kill,' he said. 'Yesterday. Did you know?'

She shook her head. Ethan told her the farmer blamed it on *gyppos*, letting their lurchers off the lead for a bit of sport and a free meal. But there'd also been a sighting, by a rambler. The account was vague, but a closeness in time and location to the taking of the sheep, of which the rambler was ignorant, lent it weight. Ethan named the area where the kill and the sighting had occurred, like this ought to be significant to her.

Sussing the need to explain, he said: 'These are the first reported incidents in that part of the moor. Outside of the previously established domain . . . the putative territory of the cat.' He stared at his plate. 'It opens up dozens of square kilometres of land that I haven't even begun to to to chart.'

'Stalking?' she said.

He glanced up. 'How d'you know about stalking?'

'Your reputation precedes you.' She smiled. 'Also, I saw you – a while back, when you must've been out on one of your hikes. Your stalks.'

'You saw me?'

'I was in a car and I saw you and Erica by the side of the road. The main valley road, yeah? The A-thingy.' She mimed with both hands, descending from her collar bone. 'You were soaking wet and had all this gunk down you. Bright green.'

'Hn.'

'I knew a guy dyed his hair that colour,' she said. 'African, with green dreads. His name was King, so we called him Lime Regis.'

She watched Ethan enjoy that.

'Fuck me, it laughs.' She made sure to laugh too as she said this, but he looked shocked all the same. Offended. She waved a hand, as though dispersing her words like so much cigarette smoke. 'Sorry, it's just . . . you're quite serious, aren't you?'

'Am I?' He frowned. 'I don't know.'

She hesitated, then decided – fuck it – to say it anyway: 'Look, what's up? Only, you wanted to see me, and now it's like, I dunno, you'd rather not be here.'

'It's just . . .' Ethan exhaled. 'It's just, this. Lunch. *Doing* lunch. I'm not used to having someone watch me eat. Apart from Erica.'

She shuttered her eyes with her hands, then uncovered them again, grinning. He was smiling as well. In fact, he'd already finished eating, so she ate the rest of hers, collected their plates and cutlery, and heaped them in the sink. She changed the CD. And Ethan, as though infused with a sudden dose of sociability, began to open up.

'I fell in the river,' he said. 'Lost my pack, all my gear – micro-cassette, camera, lenses, film, map, notebook, binoculars, compass, wallet, keys, glasses . . . I've had to replace the lot.' He cleared his throat. 'When I say I fell in the river, what I mean is I was wading across it and lost my balance.' He nodded. 'Yes, that's what I did.'

'Why were you wading across a river?'

'I had a theoretical route worked out – a hunting route – and I needed to gauge whether the cat, whether it was viable for the cat to cross the river at that point. The cat would jump across, of course, and I think it was just narrow enough to be feasible.'

'I still don't see why –'

'No, right, no – so, I wanted to pick the route up again from the opposite bank, which meant an hour's walk to the nearest bridge and an hour back again. Or wading.'

'Don't take this the wrong way,' she said, 'but what fascinates me about weird people is the immunity to contradiction of their internal logic.'

The bedsit became oppressive in the early afternoons – the sun looping to the south and heat from the caff's lunchtime rush seeping up through her floorboards like wet breath. She went over to the window and shoved it wide open. The moor unfurled in a scroll across the horizon, a child's picture of how thunder might look.

'How d'you like living up there?' She heard him shift in his chair, but there was no answer. 'I miss that,' she said. 'Can't get my head round being cooped up indoors.'

'No.'

One quiet word: no. She let it linger, its resonance drawing in the walls of the bedsit and creating a small, intimate space. Maybe he'd even get round to saying why he was here. Already she was learning that he would go missing from a conversation – verbally, mentally – and she'd have to reel him in, or just wait for him to return of his own accord. Which was fine. Diverting. She was standing close enough to where he sat to smell onions and a sulphurous essence of egg when he belched. He apologized. In the wash of light from the window Ethan's face had a texture, familiar from the camp, of chronic exposure to the elements.

'Tea?'

'Tea, yeah.' He was making an effort now. 'Yes please.'

She filled the kettle and switched it on. Ethan said he envied her ability to move around her home without having to stoop. She saw the place, then, as he might see it: its echoey minimalism, its lack of personal touches – photos, prints, books, plants – to mark her occupancy as being more than temporary, the bed with its unkempt sleeping bag, strewn clothes, a portable radio/CD along with too few discs. This could've been a room used by a squatter or by someone dossing down overnight after a party.

'You know you told me how many days you've been in the caravan,' she said. 'Well, I worked it out: First of Jan. Yeah? You moved in there on New Year's Day.'

'That's right.'

She put teabags into mugs. 'New Year's resolution, was it? Give up smoking, start an exercise programme, move into a caravan.'

'Not really, no.'

'I guess there's something, I dunno, auspicious about starting a new life on the first day of a new year.'

'It was when my notice was up at work.'

'Oh, right. Fair enough.' The kettle boiled. She filled the mugs and handed him one, along with a spoon and a carton of milk. 'I forgot to nick any sugar.'

Ethan didn't take sugar. Sitting cross-legged on the bed, she saw that the soles of her bare feet were grey with dirt. She teased out a tassel of thin black cord knotted among the dreads above one ear and toyed with it as they talked, as if it were a rosary.

'Sebum,' Ethan said.

'What?'

He pointed at her head. 'By not using shampoo, you allow your scalp's natural oils to lubricate the skin and hair. Sebum, from the sebaceous gland.'

'Yep.' She grinned, nodding. 'Yeah, absolutely.'

'I read it somewhere.'

'*I read it somewhere*,' she said. 'Ethan, I bet you have that cutting dated, filed and cross-referenced.'

But he was gone, confused by his drink, discovering the teabag floating in there and having to fish it out with the spoon, then confused by what to do with it, by where the bin was. She guessed his tea would be too strong now, the colour of burnt caramel and tart with tannin. As Ethan sat down again, she realized that until the binning of the teabag he'd held the same fixed and upright posture since first settling himself.

'How would you go about dowsing the cat?' he said. 'Tactically. Strategically.'

There. Down to business. If she'd searched scrupulously enough inside herself she might've detected the faintest taint of anticlimax that this was all he wanted to see her about. But she wasn't about to make that search. Dowsing the cat was what she'd offered him, and it was what he was offering her. Which was fine. Which was cool.

She shrugged. Not *I don't know*, but *How do I begin to explain?* 'I've only ever really dowsed for pipes and cables, underground water sources, stuff like that. If you were pregnant, I could tell you the sex of your unborn baby.'

'You said a good dowser could dowse for just about anything.'

He reminded her of her line about missing persons and she said, sure, that was in the repertoire. Though 'missing' could mean dead, and a dead person was easier to find than a living, moving one. Especially one that didn't want to be found. Especially if the dowser doing the looking was aiming, more or less, to learn as she went along.

'Yeah, missing persons. I've fooled around with that.'

'So.' Ethan spread his hands. 'Let's do it. Let's find a missing cat.'

'Is the cat missing, then?' she said. 'A wild animal, living in her habitat, doing what wild animals do – I guess the cat must be pretty happy about being missing.'

'This isn't a big cat's natural habitat.'

So this was part of it, for him, was it? Discovering the cat so that she might be captured, restored to her true place in the wild, or a zoo or wildlife park; somewhere she'd no longer be dangerous, and where she'd be safe. Was she okay with that? She thought so. She went to the sink. From the window came the sound of a car repeatedly failing to start. She allowed the water to run hot, then zapped detergent into the bowl.

'How about you?' she said. 'Would you say this was your natural habitat?'

He frowned. 'I'm here because this is where the cat is.'

That internal logic again, the blindingly obvious state of his affairs. She let this pass, smiling to herself, thinking of the job he did before – houses in, what? In *multiple occupation*; shifting paper from desk to desk in the chain of administration. Inhaling air-con. Accumulating a pension. And being *here* made him a nutter? A 'nuter'.

'Aren't you ever afraid?' she said.

'Afraid?'

'Of the cat.' She paused before adding: 'Of being killed by her, I guess.'

From his expression, this idea might never have occurred to him until now. 'If the cat knows you're near by it keeps away, if it doesn't then . . . there's no danger.'

Ethan seemed impatient with the interruption to his train of thought.

'I have a map in the caravan,' he said, 'annotated with the data from months of work. All I have to show, is a narrowing down. A process of elimination. A division of information into probabilities and possibilities. I have nothing but a set of hypotheses: theoretical lairs, theoretical hunting routes, theoretical patterns of mobility.'

She listened to him above the clack-clack-clack of crockery and cutlery being swabbed, rinsed and stacked anyhow in the draining rack.

'I have fuck all. For all the science, I have . . . I'm not closing in. I should be, by now. Making a logical progression. But I'm not. I'm going round in circles.'

'Here.' She flipped a teatowel towards him. 'Go round in circles with that.'

Ethan studied the towel for a moment, then stood up and joined her at the sink. The second CD had played out, but she felt they were managing fine now without the music. Giraffe would've cast it as a convergence of complementary star signs. But, for her, it was plain curiosity. And the fact that the smell of dog clung to him even when Erica wasn't around. You could tell a lot about a guy from something like that.

'And now I've got to widen the search,' he said. 'Survey a whole new area.'

'Uh-huh.'

He didn't know where things went; she showed him: cupboards, drawers. 'It's so, sometimes it's so fucking frustrating.'

'Science is no longer enough, in other words. Yeah?' She gave him a sideways look. 'So you're reluctant and you're sceptical and you'd be happier working solo, but you've decided to turn to quasi-science. *Crypto*-science.'

Ethan didn't have to say yes, or to nod – affirmation was encoded in the set of his face, his body. Quietly, he said: 'I don't know much about dowsing.'

'There isn't much to know. Theory-wise, I mean. Mostly it's just practice.'

'You mean no one can explain how it works?'

'Nap. I see you have a problem with that.'

He was smiling. 'Do you have a problem with me having a problem?'

As Ethan left – once they'd done with dowsing talk – he produced an envelope from his jacket and handed it to her. The envelope was obese. Inside the envelope was £300 in cash. Twenties and tens. *What's this for?* He said she needed decent walking boots, wet weather gear and that, if she was to accompany him in his work. Also, a mobile, a *vital line of communication*. He'd bought himself one. She told him there was no way she could afford to pay him back and he said it wasn't a loan, it was a wage.

18

Her eggs, Tabasco tinted, won a place on the menu. *Chloe's Spicy Scramblers*. Roy said her trial period was up; she said she hadn't realized she was on trial and he said she wasn't any more. He gave her a pay rise and raised her rent by the identical amount.

'The landlord giveth, the landlord taketh away.'

One or two punters had taken to serenading her with *lady in black*, to the tune of a song by a singer she'd not be seen dead knowing the name of. Town, being small, her appearance being what it was, folk began to recognize her in the street, in shops, in pubs; some nodded or said hello. In the only club, her singularity and barefoot dancing made her – and by association, Faye – a feature of the strobe-lit floor. The tall lass with the hair. The dowser. The girl who stopped the bypass.

Single-handed, you'd think, to hear them go on.

Work. She cut Table Seven's toast into soldiers for dunking in his three-minute egg. She trimmed the bacon rind for Table Eleven. She burned her wrist on a hotplate in her rush to keep up with the orders pinned to the corkboard like so many dead moths. On autopilot now. She experimented with this, seeking to induce a transcendent state as a way of making the day endurable. But her mind was too active. She achieved nothing but concentration lapses, mistakes, delays and the restrained wrath of Roy. Frying mushrooms. Picking at them, eating from the pan and scalding her fingers and mouth – being too ravenous to care, having overslept and skipped breakfast this morning. Roy's voice, and there was his head in the hatch asking her to lend a hand, preferably both.

'It's gone ballistic out here.'

She reduced the heat and called to Nigel to mind the fungi. Out there, cigarette smog and steam created a sauna, the window was opaque with condensation; punter-speak and radio pap buzzed in her ears like canned applause. The men, eight of them at two tabs shoved together, wore varieties of army surplus. Boxes and bags sat among the legs of their tables and chairs. They might've just participated in a sleep-deprivation experiment, or maybe they were anglers stoking up on breakfast after a night's fishing. Only, they didn't smell of fish. And they had guns: rifles, slung over chairbacks, or on the floor, or in cases unintended for snooker cues. The regular earlies – drivers, a gang of builders, a postman, overalled guys from a night-shift – were looking at the guns and at the men and were smoking and eating and not speaking much.

When she took the gunmen's orders she thought they'd mention their weapons, ask if she wanted a feel of one; but they didn't, they were too cool. It was enough for her to register the guns, and for them to know that. The guy who looked like Number One honcho wanted a bacon buttie. Deadpan, she told him: 'You don't have to shoot the pig, we have one already sliced up in the kitchen.'

It took him, them, a moment to understand just how hilarious this was. They laughed so much that Roy looked over like he was worried they were giving her a hard time, then saw it was all right. *She* was all right. Usually she hated guys looking out for her, but, for reasons beyond her, she liked the fact that Roy did. He was seeing to their drinks while she made sense of the combinations of fry-up.

It was Roy, as they tucked in, who explained: on the moors overnight, hunting, holed up in places where the beast had been seen or where there'd been kills, each man using night-sights for a glimpse, for one clean shot. She asked if they'd hit anything. Voice lowered, he said there was a rumour one of them had taken out a badger. *Go on, Brock, make my day.* The men would be out again tonight and the next night. Some were local, others had travelled miles – mercenaries, hired by a farmers' collective.

'If they get a result here,' Roy said, 'I expect they'll head up to Loch Ness. Or America. Go out there and bag a brace of Bigfoot.'

'Why do they have to kill her?'

'Kill who?'

'The cat.'

'What cat? There is no fucking cat.'

When they'd gone, and she was clearing their tables, she found a quid-a-head tip in a neat, cylindrical stack – like a miniature office block – and a slip of paper, under a saucer, bearing a guy's name and a mobile phone number. She kept the cash.

That night a noise woke her in the dead dark silence of the small hours. Waking, she made the noise real, trying to name it. An impact: a car door slamming with a whumph of expelled air; a bender flap yanked loose by the wind and caused to crack like a whip. The storms in the camp were the nights when it seemed, in semi-somnolent delirium, as if she might be swept away. But there was no storm tonight, and she was safe inside her lunar blue bedsit. Fully alert now. The noise came again; distant, unidentifiable. Shedding the skin of her sleeping bag, she moved goosebump naked to the window.

Stillness. Buildings, parked cars and quiet streets lay painted in moonlight. The moor and a cloud-streaked sky sketched stripes of indigo and black and silver above the rooftops, like the slats of a vast venetian blind. She waited for the sound to recur, seeking it with her eyes as well as her ears. It never came. But she knew the noise now, she had a name for it, she held an image of it in her mind:

A man in camouflage gear, kneeling in scrub with his rifle trained on the open slope of a field . . . a big cat bounding across the pasture, sleek black with grace, her body kicked sideways in mid-stride by the single percussion of an unseen bullet.

It was the hunters that made her mind up about the phone. Not a mobile. She would immerse her head in the deep-fat fryer before she *ever* acquired a mobile. But, yeah, okay, a phone in the bedsit, paid for with Ethan's as-yet-unspent cash. Because it made sense for him to be able to contact her directly, bypassing Roy. Also, for her to be able to call him – she was sure she'd noted down the number of his new mobile somewhere – without having to haul out to a payphone every time. All of this made sense. Only, until the hunters she'd been stalling about the phone, about the hiking gear, about the idea of working with, for, him at all, on account of who the fuck did he think he was, flourishing three hundred quid under her nose like she was on the game. Like she was *so* on the game he hadn't even bothered to discuss the cash or any of the arrangements before showing her his wad. She'd compiled a list for him, given his liking for lists, as he left her place that afternoon. A verbal list, checked off on her fingers:

1. If she dowsed the cat it was because she chose to. *Unwaged.*
2. However long it took she would pay this money back, in full.
3. No mobile.
4. He wasn't ever to fucking assume anything about her ever again.

Which cleared the air, if not her head. And which re-defined the basis for their collaboration. She'd call him once the phone was sorted. In the days that followed, she had considered dumping the whole deal, hiking out to the caravan to return his cash. Then, the hunters. The shooting. These men were intent on killing the cat and she desperately didn't want them to do that – not just in principle, but because if they killed her how would she ever know if she could dowse her?

So, do it. Just call him and go out there and do it.

Easy enough to buy a phone and to plug it into the dormant jack in the bedsit's scuffed skirting. Not so easy to have the line connected. With a zero credit rating, no track record of phone ownership and no desire to borrow yet more dosh from Ethan to cover a 'security deposit', she had to coax Roy into placing the order in his name. He was cool. *You pay the bills the day they arrive or you're phoneless, jobless, homeless.*

'They're trying to shoot her,' she said.

'I know.'

'I can hear them, at night.'

'Me too.' Ethan's voice, on the phone, was less artificial than she'd anticipated. He could've been anywhere, but she pictured him on the stoop, speaking to her with none of the self-consciousness of a face to face. 'I can't sleep,' he said. 'I just lie there waiting for the next shot.'

As she opened the shop door, a vortex of litter spiralled about her before settling again on the pavement. Sweet wrappers, chip paper, empty crisp packets. She went in. The interior smelled of the synthetic fabric of the clothing arranged on rails. Take A Hike, the place was called – recommended to her by Ethan; the town's only outdoor pursuits store, but better stocked than any in the city. There were no other customers. Behind the counter, a guy the size of a grizzly was prodding packs of cycling gloves with the nozzle of a price gun. He wore a maroon T-shirt bearing the shop's logo: a bootprint inside a jagged triangle in the style of a mountain peak. The guy appeared impeded by his surroundings, the cramped clutter, carrying himself with an impression of uneasy confinement. He made the ceiling seem too low.

'I have three hundred quid to spend,' she said.

He rested a hand on the mound of cycling gloves. 'These are nine ninety-nine a pair. You could buy thirty and still walk away with 30p.'

'Actually, it's only two hundred and something. I blew some of it on a phone.'

'Your hair looks fantastic, by the way.'

He was staring at her mouth now, as though trying to peer inside.

'What?'

'I thought your tongue might be pierced.'

'Nap,' she said. 'But I was thinking about having my clitoris done.'

A slight pause, a suggestion of a suppressed smile – the guy being less adept at keeping a straight face than her – and he was saying: 'They do the hood, don't they, rather than the actual clitoris?'

'Yeah, you know, you may be right.'

'Anyway' – he put the price gun down – 'I'm afraid we don't do piercing here.'

'It'll have to be walking boots, then. And some waterproofs – cagoule and that. Leggings.'

The guy laughed now, she did too. She told him her name, and he said his was Greg but folk called him ZZ (American pronunciation: Zee-Zee). ZZ said he could help her inflict serious harm to two hundred and something quid. Behind him a photo hung on the wall: a figure in mountaineering get-up against a backdrop of snow, snow-spray and perfect ice-blue sky, the double initials stitched into the fold of his fleece hat.

'Where was that?' she said, pointing.

He turned to look at himself, then back to her. 'The Eiger.'

She'd imagined climbers would be small, slight, wiry – something to do with the ratio of strength to bodyweight, with having to resist their own gravitational pull. ZZ had grey irises. She didn't suppose eye-colour to be a factor, climbing-wise. He handed her two walking socks from a box of seconds and told her she'd need to wear these if she was going to try boots on for size. One sock was orange, the other red. She was tempted, fleetingly, to put them on her hands instead of her feet, and wondered what it was about him that made her want to do that.

19

MEREDITH BECK (*moorland tour guide/paranormal investigator*):

Point, the First: In the last two years, 110 beast-related incidents have been reported in the moorland area at the centre of your inquiry. Plotting them on a 1:25,000 scale O.S. map [see Appendix 1] shows that 88 (or 80 per cent) occurred within a 250 metre radius of a site of archaeological interest (cup-and-ring-marked rocks, standing stones, stone circles, burial mounds etc.).

Point, the Second: Such sites date back to a period when mankind still lived in close enough harmony with nature to have an unconscious sense of its hidden patterns and energies. Scientifically verifiable electromagnetic readings and extreme temperature fluctuations, beyond meteorological explanation, have been recorded at a number of Neolithic and Bronze Age formations.

Point, the Third: Stone circles have long been associated with apparitions, visitations, psychic or supernatural occurrences and other paranormal phenomena. I personally experienced a time-slip at the Wellbeck Head circle on 31 October 1981, during which I witnessed the sacrificial slaughter of a bull by figures wearing animal-skin cloaks [see pp. 71–92, *Summat Weird's Going On Up There!* by M. Beck, Chimera Press, £4.99].

Point, the Fourth: One interpretation of cup-and-ring marks is that they are depictions by ancient man of UFOs (Unidentified Flying Objects).

Point, the Fifth: In the past two years, 40 UFO sightings, encounters, alien abductions and 'spook' lights have been reported in the area. Plotting these on the map [see Appendix 2] reveals that 32 (or 80 per cent) occurred within a 250 metre radius of a site of archaeological interest. The moor has been officially designated a Grade-AA UFO Window by the Ufological Society of England and Wales.

Point, the Sixth: Archaeological surveys of rock carvings on the moor have found that the most common symbol (after cup-and-ring marks) is the spiral. In symbolism, the spiral traditionally represents the dragon (i.e. a mythological beast, or X-creature).

Point, the Seventh: On an unspecified date in the 1930s, Philip Saville was walking on a moorland path when he came across a black dog sitting in the middle of the track. As he approached, snapping his fingers, the dog literally vanished [see pp. 19–24, *Summat Weird*]. The dog is believed to have been a boggard, or spectre; in Victorian times, the Town Book contains references to rewards being offered for 'boggard catching'.

Point, the Eighth: Witches are reputed to assume the form of a black cat.

Point, the Ninth: The Hounds of Hell are said to roam remote moorland by night, their presence foretelling the death of anyone who encounters them. It was such a beast that inspired *The Hound of the Baskervilles* (Sir A. C. Doyle, 1902). Stories of hellhounds occur across Europe, their origins found in the tales of pagan mythology.

Point, the Tenth: A fellow investigator, Mr Kirk Colquhoun, claims the beast is the lycanthropic incarnation of the son of a local landowner [see Appendix 3]. This theory awaits substantiation.

Conclusion: The connection between these moors and paranormal phenomena is well established, both historically and contemporaneously. It is my considered opinion that the Black Beast is but the latest manifestation of a force that is, in essence, the very spirit of the land itself. Bear this in mind, Dr Inglis: the world is not just stranger than we imagine, it is stranger than we *can* imagine.

20

Driving out of town, Ethan explained the lie of the land. She had her feet – her new boots – on the dash, a map folded open on her knees and was slurping through a straw from a carton of orange. The Toyota reeked of the chips she'd been eating when he collected her, their wrapping now wedged in the door pocket. She scratched her shin and saw that she'd left a chevron of white grazes. Ethan indicated a long escarpment delineating the horizon to their right; it had once continued unbroken, he said, beyond its present eastern-most point. Then, a million years ago, a glacier had come down this valley – a vast tongue of ice that forked off, to the south, carving through the ridge as easily as if it was made of modelling clay. He showed her the place on the map.

'The hill where we're headed was once part of the ridge, before being cut off.'

'Yeah?'

'An outlier.'

She gazed out the windscreen, then at the map, tracing the path of the ice. Sort of attentive, sort of not. Pre-dowsing mode: simultaneous detachment and application. The *quiet animation* of preparing herself. Not a paradox, she told Ethan, but a Zen thing; she regarded the mental coexistence of action and tranquillity as unremarkable. She sucked her juice dry and pressed the empty carton in with the chip paper.

'"Panther" means "all beasts", from the Greek,' she said. 'I looked it up.'

Ethan changed down at the approach to a junction. 'I knew that.'

'Yeah, I thought you would.'

'So, "panther", what about it?'

'Nothing. Just that, I guess.'

The road rose acutely before them. The hill: a dinosaur, fish tail or whale, he'd said, depending on perspective. The Crags, which gave their name to a heavily forested country park and to Crags Gap, the moorland pass cut by the glacier. She glimpsed the actual crags now – gritstone cliffs trapping the late afternoon light and looking for all the world like giant organ pipes. The engine pitch altered as he shifted into second. It'd been two weeks since their first phone call; fourteen days of waiting for the cat to act. Meanwhile, she'd bought one of those toy panthers from the Tourist Information shop and stood it on her window sill. When Ethan asked what function this would serve, she said it wouldn't serve any function at all that she could think of.

The pot-holed car park jolted them, jogging his shoulder against hers so firmly she was aware of the hardness of bone beneath flesh and fabric. A transit daubed with the local council crest was leaving. *The removal of the bodies.* She turned to watch it pass. A police motorcycle led the van out, a car completed the convoy – the cortège – its occupants dressed in white overalls. One of them, the one with vivid red hair, was Dr Barker Inglis. Ethan parked.

The narrowness of the trail compelled them into single file. Ethan leading, walking as if conscious of being scrutinized in the banality of putting one foot ahead of another. She could see he was unused to this, to her, to not being alone. His *working procedures*, the most mechanical action, assumed the quality of a performance, so that he'd grown unsure even of how to be himself. Whatever that was. In heavy-duty boots, green T-shirt, khaki trousers, and with a water canister suspended from his daypack, he could've passed for a squaddie out on a training yomp. He could've passed for one of the hunters, actually, which made her smile to herself at the irony of it. The forest smelled musty and, oppressively, of chlorophyll. The descending sun dropped bright shapes on to the ground, but it had rained earlier and it was muddy. Her boots were clogged, her clothes damp from the waterlogged foliage. Her boots were being unkind to her heels.

Ethan had the map now. 'We have to cut through here,' he said.

In the clearing, some trees still wore frayed belts of police tape. She'd expected the stench of decomposition to linger, but the air here wasn't noticeably different. And there were no immediate visible signs, except the remnants of the cordon, to mark this place as special. Only a close inspection of the soiled, spoiled ground enabled them to approximate the positions of the dead deer. Reportedly, two does, two fawns. *Like an elephants' graveyard*, the radio had said, recycling a description by the woman jogger whose dog discovered them. Although deer, unlike elephants, Ethan insisted, were not known to gather together to die. *A poachers' cache* was another theory, the carcasses abandoned when the poachers were disturbed before they could dismember them for removal. Or a hoax, intended to perpetuate the 'Black Beast myth', or evidence of a satanic ritual slaughter. In the days ahead, Dr Inglis would decline to confirm or deny any of the speculation. The deer had been so grossly scavenged, he would reveal, that even cause of death was uncertain, beyond proof – by analysis of water samples from nearby streams and of digestive tissue – that they hadn't been poisoned.

'In the wild,' Ethan told her, 'a big cat will create a hoard of meat.'

'She brought them here, then? This wasn't where they died?'

'They'd either be dragged along the ground' – he indicated a set of scuff marks – 'or carried on the cat's back like a . . . a sack of potatoes.'

'Uh-huh.'

'But you would expect it to take the carcasses – the young, at least, being more manoeuvrable – up into the branches to keep them safe from ground scavengers.'

Ethan needed to commit this to tape, and to take photographs, make sketches. He withdrew to the edge of the clearing, where their packs stood back to back. She remained among the disturbed soil and leaf litter, its damper stains still busy with flies and dislodged maggots. She took sedate, meditative steps between each of the places in turn where the deer had lain, her eyes half closed. Inducing a fluid, balletic grace, the burnished skin of her arms luminously green in the fading leaf-filtered light. When she'd paced out a connection between the four absent corpses, she approached the bole of a nearby pine, squatted, and began probing the ground-layer of needles with a stick. Humming to herself. The tubular locks of hair kept rhythm with her movements.

Ethan's voice rang out in the woods. 'What exactly are you looking for?'

'A sample.'

'The whole site will have been forensically examined . . .'

'I don't mean something physical, necessarily.' She spread her arms, as though summoning a definition from the air to clarify her meaning. 'It's kind of like an aura.'

She smiled at him, then resumed, as absorbed as if the interruption hadn't taken place, oblivious even of being observed. Ethan said later that she'd resembled a child at the seaside, turning the sand in search of shells.

She drew a slow circumference of the clearing with herself, stopping here and there to dowse. Eyes shut – facing the centre, then out – right arm at right-angles to her body, pendulum making a right angle with her hand. Doing the symmetry. Richie used to say she looked like a sleepwalker. *One of them B-movie zombies.* She was a zomnambulist. His word. Being trippy at the time, she'd found this enormously funny. A blind woman feeling her way out of a room, was how she thought of herself while she dowsed.

She loved being in woods again. Spoken words clunking like clogs, or like pine cones landing on a sawdust-earth of dead needles. When you talked among trees it was as if what you said was contained in a box. She sang to herself in the woods; she was singing now, immersed in distilling some essence of the cat. A sample. A *witness*, Mom would call it. She sang also to seal herself off from Ethan, with his questions and the click-click of the recorder, the camera; the unintelligible dictation.

What it was, with Richie: he hated being shut out of whatever place her head went to when she was dowsing.

There was a salty, chippy afterthirst in her mouth. She went to the packs and pulled out a bottle of water, slugged some, then offered it. Ethan came over. That scar again as he tipped his head back to drink. Midges scribbled on the air above him.

'Did you have to wear a suit in your job?' she said.

He handed the bottle back. 'What?'

'I can't picture you in a suit.'

'We, no, we . . .' He smiled, shook his head. 'D'you know, I can't remember.'

She asked about the scar under his chin and – reflexively, self-consciously – he touched it; he'd come off his bike when he was ten. She swallowed more water, then stowed the bottle. Ethan looked at his watch. There wasn't much daylight left, he said, so they should crack on. Like, you needed a watch to know that.

Hide-n-Seek. A game for two people, though she supposed it would work just as well with a human and a wild animal even if the animal wasn't, technically, participating or even aware that the game was in progress. She explained the rules to Ethan: Player 1 hides in the woods, Player 2 counts to a hundred, then goes after Player 1 – the object being not just to find her but to plot the route she took. The method: dowsing.

'Mom and me played this when I was little, to give me pendulum practice.'

'Did it work?'

'We found each other, if that's what you mean. Most of the time, anyway.'

'The cat could be anywhere,' he said. 'Twenty, twenty-five kilometres away.'

'Yeah, and she could be in those bushes.'

Ethan looked at the bushes. He asked if she seriously expected to find it (her) right here, right now? *Nap.* This was an experiment, she said. To do with seeking more than finding. He'd been working the cat for months, but she needed time to attune.

'I just want to get a feel for her, pick up a trail and see where it leads. Yeah?'

What she'd dowse for, she decided, was the most recent point of departure – the cat's last exit route from this place. First task, to create a mental picture of her – not the face, but the hind quarters – as she withdrew. The feline gait. A flick of the tail, the step-step of the rear feet, the alternating rise and fall of the hip joints like pistons beneath black velvet. Carrying this image with her as she dowsed the margins of the clearing. *This is what I seek, this is who I seek, here is where I seek her, now is when I seek her.* In the absence of a physical sample, it would do.

What she had to blank from her mind was the shadow of Ethan's expectation; the idea that, despite everything, he couldn't help wanting a tangible outcome.

In time, she tidied away the internal and external clutter; in time, the pendulum gave her a positive. She opened her eyes to orientate herself and, signalling him to stay silent, set off along a rabbit run through wet bracken, the brush of her legs against the ferns releasing a scent of almonds. Every so often, she dowsed for confirmation. *Was she here? Is this the way?* Searching in vain with her eyes as well as the pendulum, for clues: a paw print, a snag of fur, trampled vegetation, a piece of broken claw, a stool. At one point, where the path forked, the response stalled her. Ethan drew up behind, so close his breath filmed on her neck when he spoke.

'What is it?'

'I'm getting a "yes" for both directions.'

Mom would've said: *If the answer is unhelpful, there's a fault in the question.* So she dowsed again, with precision, asking not only if the cat had been this way, but if she'd been this way most recently. Yes/no for the right fork, yes/yes for the left. She went left, Ethan following. And, with each step deeper into the forest, the absorption deepened; the erasure of distraction – wind in the branches, the shifting pattern of light, scuffing feet, bird calls, midges, mosquitoes, a nettle sting, chafing shoulder-straps, her new boots, thoughts of him and herself and the what and why of this . . . everything, until all that remained was a pure and perfect visualization of a black panther moving ahead of her along the path. *This* path.

They trailed the imagined cat, stop-start, for seventy-two minutes. Ethan timed them. Walking and dowsing, back-tracking, diverting, zigzagging – it was the passage to the centre of a maze, without the maze – coming to a halt, finally, where the ground cover was densest. There had been no path at all for the last few hundred metres, just a slog, a wade, through chest-high bracken and brambles and low-slung branches that distressed her clothes and scripted shocking pink calligraphy on her forearms. Her legs were shrink-wrapped in damp, sweaty jeans. She would fall uncomplicatedly asleep the instant she was able to lie down somewhere soft and warm and dry.

'We're here,' she said.

'Where?'

'The place where the dowsing brought us.'

She let him do his thing now: the forensics – disappearing into the embankment of chaotic scrub, ivy and oak roots where they'd fetched up. She waited, sitting on a stump, eating chocolate. Snatches of colour or noises like an animal foraging for food, or the twitch of a tall fern, located him for her. Light and warmth leached from the day; she took a sweater from her pack and put it on. To be sure of finding their way to the Toyota they ought to set off soon. Even as she thought this, she was indifferent. It got dark, so what? Worse things could happen than being lost in woods after nightfall.

She heard Ethan, talking to himself in there.

He'd entered on all fours and exited the same way, only backwards. He stood, turning to find her; hair in a frenzy, shirt rucked up under the arms, shreds of flora all over him. He was a child. A boy. But his hands and face were a man's and were empty of anything but dirt, exhaustion and disappointment.

'Fuck all,' Ethan said.

She shrugged.

'It has all the makings of a day-bed.' He glanced back at the undergrowth. 'But there's nothing in there. Not a thing to show the cat's ever used it.'

They sat and shared water. Ethan used a thumb and index finger to tweezer a fragment of fern from his watchstrap, head tilted, as though listening to something.

'Two long, one short,' he said. 'Dash-dash-dot, in Morse.'

'What is?'

'The pigeons.' As he spoke she became aware of the trees, all about and above them, conversing with the purr of unseen wood pigeons readying themselves to roost. 'Pigeon-talk,' Ethan said, 'is an endless repetition of the letter *g*.'

'Yeah, right.'

If this was the way his mind worked, fine; just so long as he raised himself – as he seemed to be – from the downer of drawing a blank. He was talking, telling her a story about these woods: 1981, two people below the crags claimed to have spotted a pterodactyl. Dusk, like now. Ethan said it was most likely a heron, being a weird sight in flight if you've never witnessed it, or possibly a child's kite.

'At work, after they caught on to my project, they treated me as if *I'd* said I'd seen a pterodactyl.' His gaze was turned away. 'I could see it in their eyes, in the way they they they humoured me. But it's not comparable.' He looked directly at her again, face looming out of the gloom like a paper lantern. 'It's not the same thing at all.'

'Why tell them about the project?'

'I didn't.'

'So who did?'

'My . . . fiancée. Susan.'

Having divulged her name, her existence, Ethan gave the vibes of not wishing to talk about this ex-fiancée any more than he had done. She stared beyond him, at the site she'd brought them to, merging now into the grey coagulation of nightfall. Susan. He had been with – been *engaged* to – a woman called Susan.

'What's a day-bed?' she said.

He took a moment to align his train of thought with hers. 'It's like a lair or den. Except, a leopard doesn't stay put for long, so rather than a permanent "home" it has a network of places to rest up during the day, between night-time hunting expeditions. These will be scattered all over its territory – usually in dense undergrowth, like this. Or the cat will make use of caves or tunnels or natural hiding places it comes across.'

'Nomadic is the problem, actually.'

'From a dowsing point of view?'

She nodded. 'In theory, I could dowse a trail that takes us right to the cat. But, say she was here, I dunno, a week ago – she could've travelled hundreds of kilometres since then. Ten K here, five there. We could be doing join-the-dots for weeks, months, trying to plot her route. And we'd never catch up 'cos she'd always be on the move to someplace new. That's the trouble with wild animals.'

'I used to believe if I sat in one place long enough,' Ethan said, 'eventually, I'd see it.' Hands framed to mime a camera. 'Law of averages, you'd think.'

'I don't believe in the law of averages.'

Ethan ignored that. He'd used time-lapse video cameras, he said, he'd used a hide and a telephoto and, going technical on her, something about an image intensifier for night shooting . . . hundreds of hours of observation. *Nothing.* She had nothing to say about that. Soon, they'd have to stand up, sort the torches, shoulder their packs and return through the woods. The forest. She hoped to see bats.

'I enjoyed this,' she said.

After a pause, Ethan said: 'Me too.'

'I saw her, in my head. I *saw* her. That's an okay place to start, if you ask me.'

*

On the drive home she rode shotgun in the rear of the Toyota, for no other reason than the bounce of her body and the cold thrash of the air in her face and the solitude.

21

GREG 'ZZ' HOLLAND (*shop manager/climber*):
Look, he bought his gear here, that's all. Hiking equipment, clothes, boots, camping gear, stuff for the caravan. Gas. I sold the bloke bottles of gas. He must've come into the shop half a dozen times in twelve months, if that. So, no, I didn't *know* him.

What did I think of him? You mean when he came in? As if my *impression* of him counts for anything, makes him more real, more substantial?

. . . All right, I think he was unusual. No, I think he was the type of bloke most people would find unusual or odd or unnerving or just too fucking unconventional for them to feel comfortable with. Serving him was like serving someone with amnesia, because he always lost the plot of why he'd come into the shop in the first place. No, I can't think of a specific example. I think, possibly – *possibly* – his concentration span was affected by the fact that shopping was a waste of his time when he could've been out there on the moors, doing his thing. I think he intensely disliked being in town. And if you want psycho-wank, I think his social skills left scope for development. Basically, I think he fished in a different river to most of us. That's what I think.

Does this add up to madness? Listen, I climb mountains for kicks, so who am I to say what's mad and what's sane?

22

Spying on him from the stand of sycamores. Not spying, observing. She'd quit the track between Faverdale's place and the pitch, on a whim, skirting into the trees to sneak up on him. Believing it would be simultaneously interesting and entertaining to watch Ethan while he was oblivious to being watched. And there she was, concealed, on her haunches, eyes on the stoop, where he sat knifing dried mud from the soles of his boots. Erica slept in the shade, the rise and fall of her flank punctuated by nervous tics. Ethan worked intently, methodically, picking at the tread like a dentist inspecting teeth for cavities. She'd hoped he might talk to himself, but he didn't. Cupping a hand to her mouth as if it was a microcassette, she whispered: *Full-grown Caucasian male; age thirty-three; height, approximately 1.8 metres; weight, approximately 65 to 70 kilos; hair uncombed; mood unpredictable; no visible evidence of death by predation* . . . Her breath was moist on her palm. Ethan looked at his watch, then at the track along which she was due to appear any time now.

She glimpsed a memory of Richie – Spoons; of coming across him in the woods at Flashville, alone, playing the clarinet. Usually, he played for everyone – last thing, when the food and talk had eased down and the fire embers were dying and folk were sleepy but not ready to turn in. But there were occasions too when he'd slope off by himself to make his music in seclusion and privacy. She'd watched Spoons for maybe a minute before he'd become aware of her and glanced up, pleased to see her. He wasn't solitary in the way that Ethan was. Spoons included those around him, whereas Ethan excluded them, or excluded – removed, detached, distanced – himself from them. Ethan was a separatist. And yet, spying on him, she recognized that this very alienation was integral to what attracted her. Looking at the people repelled by him, she found herself repelled by them. Also also also, in her experience the defining characteristic of *Homo sapiens* (male) was amplification of his own existence, while Ethan's – so far as she could judge – was the diminution. The reduction of himself to the enactment rather than the declaration of whatever compelled him to live.

He set one boot down, started on the other. They hadn't worked together for a while. In the week after the deer, there'd been no cat-related incidents to investigate. Then, Ethan had gone off with Erica on a *stalking expedition* – three nights, four days, camping out, charting land previously calculated to be outside the cat's domain. More pins to perforate his wall-map. He'd asked her to accompany him, but her shifts didn't allow for more than one day off at a time. So – rusty, and in any case unsure of her capabilities – she'd practised map-dowsing instead. Map-dowsing, dowsing 2-D, being just about the only way she could conceive of doing the business, cat-wise.

Grid method, à la Mom: dowsing the map square by square for a positive, subdividing that square and dowsing again for an exact fix. Slow, laborious, difficult. With Faye's help, she tested herself. Map-dowsing at home, then going to the dowsed location to see if the dowsed object was there, dowsing for it again *in situ* if necessary: a magazine hidden in a rubbish bin outside the train station; a glove on a wall; Faye herself sitting on a bench in the municipal gardens. From the inanimate to the animate.

Visualization, visualization, visualization.

You dowsed the map, rather than the land it represented (how long would *that* take), conjuring an imaginary 3-D world from the flat features and picturing yourself in it, dowsing for a visualized object. Four places had to be caused to coincide: the 'here' of the map, the 'here' of the imagined world, the 'here' of the physical world, the 'here' of whatever you sought. *Real*-izing the imaginary, in Mom-speak.

Your unconscious mind makes contact with the universal, omniscient mind.

She spared a gobsmacked Faye this explanation; Ethan too,

seeking the theory behind the technique. A shrug: *It works 'cos it works*. What else was there to know?

Besides, map-dowsing a nomadic, uncooperative cat would be another matter.

At so many quid a minute, she'd phoned the US. Mom's first words, after the surprise-surprise hiyas and how-you-doings and laughs of catch-up chatter, being: 'Hon, are you dowsing again?'

'Why d'you ask?'

'You sound happy, is why.'

She explained about the cat, expecting to have this demeaned in some way, but a transatlantic pause ended with Mom saying that, if *she* worked in a café, she guessed she'd go out and dowse a possibly fictitious panther, or anything at all, just to keep her brain from turning to slop.

'So, you want to talk to me about the cat, or this guy Ethan?'

'The *cat*, Mom.'

They discussed map-dowsing for animates. She wanted this conversation to be taking place from chair to sofa, two beers on coasters, a bowl of something. Popcorn, nachos, whatever. Instead, they had satellite static and a fractional timelag that caused their sentences to overlap.

'I tried to call you a couple of times.'

'I've been away,' Mom said. 'Bolivia. Surveying locations for copper mines.'

'Didn't the Bolivians kill Che Guevara?'

'That was more than thirty years ago. The poster came down *ten* years ago.'

'Who d'you have now, Oliver North?'

The connection between dowsing and happiness, she decided, was that the caff was no longer the biggest figure in the sum of her existence. You get happy in one part of your life, it infects the rest.

'Way I figure it, hon, you have two major challenges.'

'Yeah.'

'One is displacement, two is temporality. Uh-huh?'

The crux: you could map-dowse where the cat *is*, with no

guarantee she'll wait for you to turn up; and you could map-dowse where the cat *was* – an hour, a week, a month ago. But how to map-dowse where she *will* be?

Somehow, she was going to have to do future.

'Hi.' She gestured behind her, at the trees. 'I was just using your loo.'

Ethan had finished cleaning his boots and, having withdrawn into the caravan, was outside again. He held a pyrex bowl of water in one hand, a polythene sandwich-bag in the other. Steam rose off the water. She let herself through the gate in the picket fence, let Erica greet her. It was humid away from the coolness of the sycamores, the sky so milky with haze it was possible to stare directly at the sun's perfect white disc.

'Look.' Ethan raised the polythene bag. 'I found this yesterday.'

'Is that what it looks like?'

'I have to send it off for analysis.'

'You're posting a piece of shit to someone?'

'There's a zoology professor. Henry Harley.' He nodded in the vague direction of the city beyond the moor's southern extent. 'At the university.'

'I'd like to be at the guy's breakfast table when he opens the envelope.'

'It doesn't look like fox or badger to me. Or deer. And it's way too small for horse. Wrong shape and texture, as well.'

'Oh, texture. Absolutely.'

He'd discovered the stool on the last afternoon of his stalking trip, deep among bramble roots. Half a kilometre from the tent. It was recent; not moist enough to be fresh, but not too dehydrated to be of no value. Similar in appearance to the droppings of a domestic cat, he reckoned, only larger; dog-sized, but not dog-like. He placed the bowl on the steps, broke the stool in two and dropped one piece into the hot water.

'I'd prefer tea,' she said.

'Cat's lick themselves.'

'They do. I've definitely seen cats do that.'

Ethan had been watching the shit dissolve, encouraging it with the handle of a wooden spoon. He looked at her. 'Hairs get into the cat's mouth, the cat swallows the hairs, the cat's shit has hairs in it, you separate out the shit, recover the hairs, analyse them by microscopic comparison with known hair-types, you identify the species.'

'Look, Eeth, I didn't mean to –'

'Eeth?' His expression: surprised, amused, disorientated. *'Eeth?'*

'You ever noticed that "Ethan" is an anagram of "the" and "an"? A definite article and an indefinite one, yeah?' She grinned. 'Anyway, whatever.'

He was studying the bowl again. The water had turned a weak, cloudy brown, particled with excrement in lazy, sedimentary suspension. No hairs. Ethan tipped the whole lot on to the grass. The other segment of stool, he would parcel up, he said, for Professor Harley. There was no optimism in his face or in his voice.

'I brought *The Monitor*,' she said. The gunmen had been out again – a second, final, three-night deployment. She showed him the headline, SHOOTING FIASCO!, and read the first sentence aloud: *The police and the RSPCA have blasted a team of marksmen whose moorland hunting sprees fetched a haul of three foxes, one badger, a pet pooch . . . and no Black Beast.* There was a picture of a dead black labrador called Dave.

Ethan spooned dog food into a dish and went inside with another. She heard the pump-pump-pump of the treadle, the asthmatic spit of the spigot. Erica was gulping the meat as though she would happily choke, blonde straggles of belly-hair snagged with pellets of mud that swung back and forth as she ate. When Ethan returned with the water, she asked how long it was since Erica had eaten? He couldn't recall. And how long since *he'd* eaten? He couldn't remember that either, but guessed at yesterday breakfast.

'You came here to bring me the paper and to lecture me about nutrition?'

'Nap. Well, yeah, partly – but, nap.'

'What, then?'

'I'm here to admit you into the realm of my imagination.'

She imagined Ethan in the heart of dense woodland, stripped to his boxers, shin-deep in a beck and stooping to douche himself, the cold shock of the water exacting a series of rapid inhalations. She imagined him regaining the bank to dry off and dress, walking back up the shallow slope to the tent, towelling his hair, talking to Erica like a parent including an infant in a monologue beyond its comprehension. *Right then, Reeks, shall we fix some breakfast? Eh? Yeah, I think so.* She imagined him making coffee on a Primus, heating tinned beans and sausages, rescuing one of the miniature sausages with his fingers, juggling it, blowing on it, feeding it to Erica, who snapped it down whole. Ethan, eating straight from the pan, gazing about him in a sieved light that picked out silver birches in a luminous gloss, so that they seemed to be cast from aluminium. Their leaves were the first to have turned – yellow, but not yet fallen – though it wouldn't be long before autumn redecorated these woods in its colours. She imagined the place to be so remote that Ethan had encountered no one in days. Or maybe, while he was out stalking, he'd heard a shriek of unseen children and had changed course to avoid them. There was no avoiding the sounds of rifle fire. Each night the reports had woken him, she imagined – some near by, others further off, muffled but unmistakable. He had lain awake or dozed fitfully from shot to shot. Because for so long all he'd dreamed of, all he'd worked towards, was to be the one to find the cat, to prove its existence, and now some bastard with a gun might deny him. She imagined him, increasingly tired, aching from a succession of nights on hard ground, on a thin foam mat already patterned with a partial impression of his body. She imagined his knuckles, irritable with insect bites. She imagined him scratching them until they bled.

. . . and she stopped there. Ethan was trying to conceal his hands. Then, smiling, he splayed the fingers to disclose the damage done to them, to the skin.

'If you'd imagined yourself further up that slope, you'd eventually emerge from the woods on to this this this exposed hilltop,' he said. 'A lookout point. I hiked up there every morning, before breakfast, to take a peek at the caravan.' He talked across her interruption: 'It was way, way off along the valley, but the view – the angle – meant you could just about pick it out. A blob. A dot.'

'And, what, you'd just sit there and gawp at it?'

'There's this short story, about a creature living in a burrow who becomes so paranoid about intruders that it digs a second burrow in order to spy from its entrance on the first.' Ethan nodded to himself. 'Kafka.'

'Maybe if you didn't read Kafka,' she said, 'you wouldn't be so paranoid?'

'I don't know.' He seemed momentarily lost. 'I don't know what I am.'

The sound of a tractor engine, growing louder, from beyond the trees. She thought the farmer, Mr F., was about to pay a visit, but as she watched the track the noise lessened, moved away. The vehicle must've turned into one of the lower fields. Shortly, she saw it, drawing baled feed across a pasture towards metal troughs, sheep congregating in its wake. From this perspective it appeared as though they were being towed by the tractor, rather than pursuing it.

'You're trying to tell me you dowsed my campsite?' Ethan said.

'Mom said I shouldn't do this. *Get hung up on proof, hon, where's it end?* I said to her: I don't have a problem with proof, I have a problem with a guy who has a problem with proof.'

'That . . . description.' He shook his head. 'Educated guesswork. A secluded location in the woods, next to a water supply. Logical, I would've thought.'

She drew her daypack on to her lap and opened its neck so wide, reached in so carefully with both hands, you'd have forgiven Ethan for imagining she was about to produce the cat's severed head. The plastic carrier bag must've been anticlimactic.

'Your campsite.' She made a loop in the air with her hand. 'It could've been anywhere in all these hundreds of square K.'

'I told you the name of the area,' he said.

The speculative vagueness, the looseness, had been gathered in and made tight. She became serious, purposeful. Focused. Defining the stages of the process for him:

Visualization . . . map-dowsing . . . site visit.

'I was out there this morning, after you'd packed up,' she said. 'Long bus ride, even longer walk – but it was worth it. Nice spot, actually.'

'You weren't there.'

'The track where you must've left the Toyota – how far d'you reckon that is from where you pitched the tent?'

He frowned. 'Five kilometres.'

'So, okay, I knew the general area, but even if I fluked the track, at πr^2 when r = 5, that would still mean a search area of almost 80 square K. Yeah?'

She took the map from the carrier, already folded open, and showed Ethan the place she'd asterisked. She kept quiet, looking around, not looking at him. Erica was propelling the empty food dish with her tongue. She took it from her and skimmed it away like a frisbee. *Fetch.* The dog watched it go with interest, but uninterested in recovering it. Ethan explained that, despite being a retriever, she didn't retrieve.

He handed the map back. 'This isn't proof.'

Reaching into the bag again, she removed the rest of its contents, item by item, and placed them in a line on the step: a tent peg, two spent matches, a plastic fork and an empty can of Heinz bangers 'n' beans. She smiled at him.

'You really ought to clear up after yourself. Countryside code, and that.'

PART THREE

Vision

23

The name of the place is not what has attracted him here, although the vicar will smile in retrospect at the associative irony. The Twelve Apostles. He counts thirteen. But, no, the stone circle is an archaeological curiosity – an addendum to his excursion, not its primary objective. He is here for the birdlife that the higher ground – the tops – promises, even at this time of year with the summer visitors mostly gone and the winter migrants yet to arrive. Already, during the hike up from the car park at Sun and Moon Rocks, he has noted a pair of curlew, three red grouse and a kestrel. He believes a few pairs of lapwing nest on the bare parts of the high moor, and there may be some golden plover and redshank hereabouts, although he knows these are more likely to declare their presence with a call than an appearance.

The vicar sits against one of the Apostles – a suitable backrest, and a wonderful vantage point. The ground is damp, but he is wearing waterproofs. He is peckish and, even though it is short of ten thirty, he opens the packed lunch prepared for him by the retreat centre. Fishpaste and cucumber, again. An occasional cry or movement causes him to pause and to pick up the binoculars. His notebooks are within reach: one for the birds, the other for jotting down thoughts and images which he might work into a sermon. A germ of an idea is forming already, inspired by the autumnal condition of the bracken that, every year, appears to have annexed a greater part of the moors. The lush green ferns of summer are turning the colour of grubby straw – a bedraggled, dehydrated and degenerating mass that will remain dormant, now, until spring. Odd sentences string together: notions of transience, death and rebirth, nature's relentless cycle . . . half-formed thoughts that may or may not solidify into something of symbolic utility. The vicar listens to himself rehearsing, in his mind, the isolated snatches of oration. He bites into another sandwich.

It is the crows that draw his attention to a concave sweep of old and blackened heather, where the land falls away from the circle before rising again. Crows, not rooks, the harshness of their cries distinguishing them; half a dozen, no seven, creating a raw commotion, flapping about above the scrub and dive-bombing. The object of their fury is obscured by a dip in the ground. The vicar raises the binoculars and pulls the birds into focus. They are easing away from him, at a distance of eighty to a hundred metres, driving along whatever it is that bothers them. Then he sees it, moving up the slope. A dog, possibly. He refocuses and sees right away that it is not canine but feline. Unquestionably. The shape of the head, the tail, its carriage, all identify it as a cat. A cat the size of, and perhaps bigger than, a large labrador. The creature takes a couple of fierce swipes at the crows – which are still pestering it, mobbing it – and then breaks free from their attack, pelting away up the hill so swiftly it is lost from view for a moment. He has it again. There. *There.* Running like a greyhound, forelegs pushing through the hind legs, hind feet striking the ground in advance of the head. Jet black. And quite beautiful. He has never witnessed such grace and aggression in harmony. The cat vanishes over the crest of the incline. It is gone. The vicar continues to stare at its point of departure for some time before, finally, lowering the binoculars into his lap.

24

Laid out, the map of the moors filled half the floor of her bedsit. She knelt – barefoot, eyes closed, her back to the window and the real, physical moorland beyond the town. Was she ready for this? Was this ready for her? In her left hand, the plastic cat, in her right the pendulum bob, their textures and temperatures harmonizing within the gentle enclosure of warm, slightly moist skin.

She opened her eyes.

The creases of the map where it had been folded formed a natural grid. Starting in the north-west corner, she placed the cat in one rectangle after another, posing the internal question: will she be here? Visualizing, realizing the imaginary. Hers was the effort of effortlessness, not willing a response but permitting it to happen; like falling asleep at night with a problem and waking up in the morning with a solution, as though it had materialised of its own volition. She became ignorant of the passage of time. A spectator might've assumed she'd induced a self-hypnotic trance with the swing of the bob. Back and forth, back and forth. Then . . .

Yes. A circle, the long, lazy loops of a widening circle. *Yes*.

Ethan said he trusted her logic – *What logic? I don't do logic* – that predicting the cat's movements, if achievable, promised more than pursuit based on her past whereabouts. What he struggled with was the method and principle of map-dowsing.

The concept.

He quoted to her from a book: *A map-dowser requires extrasensory perceptions akin to those of a psychic.*

'You've been *reading* about dowsing?' she said.

'Hn.'

'You might as well read about the futility of language.'

'No, it's interesting.'

'Yeah, right.'

'Which method do you prefer: triangulation, coordinates or grid?'

'Ethan, please, burn that book. Tear the pages out and burn them one by one.'

But he persisted with the questions. She told him dowsing, for her, was tactile rather than technical; it was a state of being, of seeing, and of doing. Anything about dowsing that could be written down wasn't to do with dowsing but with writing. When Ethan asked if she might be psychic, she said: 'How should I know?'

It worked because it worked. But, with Ethan, it hadn't. So far. Not just the snags of displacement and temporality Mom had warned about, but the unquantifiable distraction – the *ether* – of Ethan. Working with him, working with him in mind, being with him, thinking about him when the screen of her imagination needed to be clear of everything but cat. Three outings, *exploratory operations*, since she'd map-dowsed his campsite had produced sweet zip. Visits, typically at daybreak or sunset, to locations identified as auspicious by use of map, pointer and pendulum. Anticipating the cat. And they'd sit there – *had* sat there – in a hide, watching and waiting for nothing to happen. Gazing out into the dimness of her prediction.

Another extract from the Book of Ethan: *In all dowsing, but in map-dowsing especially, to be driven by 'results' is to be driven mad.*

Three ops, three blanks.

Which was fine. Which was cool, because there were more appalling ways for two people to spend time than hiking the fells and sharing some of the contents of their heads and then sitting absolutely still for an hour or two in silent, serene introspection, listening to one another breathe. Even though, for her, it was mostly a case of listening to – of absorbing by a process of emotional osmosis – the unspoken, expectant edge of Ethan's patience. She wasn't sure, but she suspected he was putting her off. That she was being put off by him meant she was effectively distracting herself, seeing as other people could only fuck with your mind if you let them in there. One way to find out being to go on a solo op, see how close she got to the cat by herself.

So, yeah, solo. Eethless. The laying out of the map on the bedsit floor.

Ski-jump steep, the moorside road brought her buzzing, breathy, to the car park below Sun and Moon Rocks. She'd not walked this route before, though it was there on the horizon whenever she looked out of the bedsit window. At night, black moor on black sky, the unlit road, the land itself, vanished and the beams of disembodied headlamps hovered above the town. Today, low cloud wrapped the road, the car park, the rocks in grey gauze. It had rained, and would rain again. The Moon was the colour of wet cement, bulbous, perched at the crest of a flagged path like a giant's football, as if one kick might send it down and down; the monolithic Sun sat beyond it, in partial eclipse.

She heard the men before she reached them. Then, there they were, in a vast horseshoe of quarried face behind Sun Rock, climbers in fluorescent reds and blues – starfished in mid-ascent, or abseiling down to land, thump, on the slick ground. Richie had taught her to abseil from a thirty-metre oak. Flashville meant climbing trees for the first time since girlhood; making dens: tree-houses, benders, secret tunnels. Protest had a primeval appeal that became an end in itself, if you let it. And in any case you weren't just fighting roads, houses, airports or whatever, you were embracing a way of living. The map steered her left, a representational route picked out for real in a rising ribbon of threadbare grass. She stopped to breathe and to drink and to watch the men.

'Zee-Zee!'

The cry came again. She tracked the voice with her eyes, a lad squatting on a rim of sheer crag, calling down before lobbing a coil of rope over. It hit with a smack. A second guy, waiting, collected it and gave a thumbs-up. The grizzly. Here, away from the constrictions of the shop, he moved as though he belonged – fitting himself

and his surroundings, doing what he was doing. A hard-hat, hanging
by its chin-strap from his fingers, was initialled with a double-Z.

'Hi.'

ZZ found her face, her hair. 'Zoe?'

'Chloe.'

'I know.' He smiled. 'I thought it would have a subtle effect on
the balance of our acquaintanceship if I appeared to misremember
your name.'

She tapped her temple. 'I think you've spent too much time at
high altitudes.'

ZZ's laughter was the sound of pebbles in a barrel. She had no
idea how old he was, but decided right there that he was twenty-
eight. His hair was moulded into the shape of the absent hard-hat.
She drank some more. The water tasted good. The skin of her face
felt taut with dried perspiration from the uphill hike and her T-shirt
adhered to the length of her spine. ZZ watched the lad begin his
descent, climbing, not abseiling.

'How are the boots?' he said, returning his attention to her.

'Getting better.'

'Darren! Three out of four!' His shout echoed in the amphitheatre
of rock. To her, he said: 'Four appendages: two hands, two feet. I
drum it into them that they must keep three out of four in contact
with the face at all times.'

'Karabiners and belays,' she said. 'That's the limit of my climbing-
speak.'

ZZ indicated the gaggle of pupils. 'Wednesdays and Saturdays,
nine till noon. Just turn up. First lesson's free and all the gear's
provided.'

'My ex was into climbing.'

He looked at her. 'So you're not?'

'Nap. It's him I'm not into.'

She went to say something else but ZZ was looking beyond her,
scrutinizing the relentless rise of land into which she was headed.
His grey eyes appeared damp in the rainy wash of light from the
sky. She focused where he was focused, aware now of the noise

that must've distracted him: a swooping sound, like the pulse of radar.

'Lapwing,' he said.

She spotted it herself, black and white, soaring and diving erratically above an expanse of heather. They watched the bird until it was no longer there to be watched.

'Where you off to?' ZZ said at last.

'The Twelve Apostles.'

Walking on a track between a sunken beck and a line of yellow posts. A boundary, maybe, or markers to guide hikers down in a winter whiteout. Here was no place to be in a blizzard. How long since ZZ? Half an hour? Whatever, in that time two boys on mountain bikes had been the only people to pass her. Where the ground softened to bog there was a section of boardwalk, then dirt again. Rising, still, the land lacquered black and brown and green by fine rain.

The suddenness of the stones surprised her. A shallow swell of land, and she was almost among them. Blackened tooth stumps. Gravestones, slumped and broken and weathered. Dwarves seized in perpetual ossification by some malevolent spell.

Here.

The stones defined an area of cropped grass no more than twenty paces across. Dead centre was a bald spot, worn by the feet of those who'd stood – as she now stood – because something in the nature of circles, sooner or later, attracts you to the hub.

No cat. Nor a place near by where it might be. This was a treeless dome of high moor – the bracken battered flat, the heather shallow, charred bare in patches from selective burning, and not even a gorse bush to provide cover. But, *here*. She revolved on the axis of her heels, eyes wide, dragging the horizon in her wake till its features bled with centrifugal force. Then, halting. Steadying herself, letting the world resettle into its arrangement. In the distance, the weird white orbs of a US monitoring station. Spoons, Giraffe, some of the others, lived there before the road camp, pitched outside its perimeter fence in caravans, a hand-painted sign saying: *Hoot if you support us!*

'Glorious views up here.'

A guy, fifty-something, was sitting on one of the stones, plucking burrs from his bootlaces. He tipped his face to grin at her from inside a rainhood. She hadn't heard him approach and wasn't sure whether he'd seen her, spinning.

'Yeah,' she said. 'Even on a day like this.'

They swapped ramblers' talk: the weather, how far they'd walked, where they were headed. She told him she'd come to see the stones. *Neolithic*, he said. Had she counted them? Because, although they were known as the Twelve Apostles there were in fact thirteen. They were named by early Christian elders to disguise the site's pagan origins. *Four thousand years ago, mankind made this circle. Personkind, that is.*

'Legend has it, it's impossible to count them correctly at the first attempt.' The guy reached into a pocket and offered her a card. 'Meredith Beck, at your service.'

Step Back in Time: Tours of the Prehistoric Moor. Half-day or full-day. He gave her another, Voyages into the Paranormal.

'The Wild Hunt is reputed to set off from these stones – dead souls led by the Devil, flying out across the moors in search of victims. Also' – he made jerking motions with his hand – 'fairies have been witnessed here, dancing.'

'What about UFOs?'

'Absolutely. It's well documented, the association between sacred sites and alien manifestations.' He lowered his hood. 'In 1976, members of the Royal Observer Corps, up here on manoeuvres, saw a bright object hovering right above this circle.' He sniffed. 'Nothing on film, *malheureusement*.'

She didn't say anything.

'I'm a licensed ufologist.'

'Yeah?'

He frowned. 'Are you local?'

'Nap.' She pointed north, across the valley she'd just walked out of. 'I used to live in the protest camp. You know, the bypass?'

'Ah.' He fished out another card. The Green Guide – Moorland Conservation and Nature Trails. 'I've started Black Beast tours as well, but there's been a cock-up at the printers. First batch of cards had *breast* instead of beast.'

'I've known guys who would pay to go on a tour like that.'

He readied himself to leave. 'It's no accident, us meeting here. In this place, at this time. Nothing in this world happens by accident. You do know that, don't you?'

She nodded. 'Convergence.'

'Exactly. *Exactly.* We have converged.' He looked elated. 'You know, as soon as I saw you, I thought to myself: Meredith Beck, you are in the presence of a shaman.'

She waited for him to become a toy, way below on the path which had fetched her here. Then she prepared to dowse. The location, the circumstances, were inauspicious. First ZZ, then him: chance encounters, if you believed that chance, being random, was immune to the imposition of pattern. Also, the circle itself. Whenever she'd worked ancient sites the results had been erratic, as if any force they channelled or emitted was a source of interference. Electro-magnetism, Mom reckoned. Whatever, the pendulum would go haywire – fibrillating in vertical suspension, like an earth tremor was going on beneath her feet; or gyrating fiercely, almost horizontal, so that the bob might at any moment fly from her fingers like a bolas. And if she touched one of the stones, her palm would tingle with static. *What shape d'you see when you dowse these places?* She hadn't considered this before, but her mother's question flashed the answer in her mind: a spiral. If she was to dowse for a cat (that may, or may not, be here – when? – soon, an hour from now, a day from now), she'd have to find some way to harness the flow of the spiral, or be spun off course by it altogether.

No.

This wasn't right. *Here* wasn't right, for her. Maybe it was the pull of the site itself that had drawn her to this spot. Maybe the stone circle, marked and identified on the map she'd dowsed, had misled her unconscious mind, triggering a false – falsely positive – subliminal response. The idiot response.

She would not dowse. The decision lifted off her like a weight.

What she did, instead, was sit in the drizzle with an Apostle for a backrest and eat the food she'd made. Resting up before the long trek home. As she finished the last of the sandwiches, she heard voices. In a moment, the people appeared – heads, bodies, legs, feet – rising, almost levitating into view where the path bisected the arc of a slope. Two men. A policeman in uniform, and a fat guy in an unzipped purple cagoule and a dog-collar. The vicar was pointing beyond the circle, talking about crows.

25

PROF. HENRY HARLEY PH.D. (*professor of zoology*):

In response to my previous submission, I was invited to make further observations with regard to the behavioural habits and traits of, in particular, the melanistic leopard. This, as I understand it, with a view to determining whether your inquiry might authorise an attempt to track, entrap, drug or kill such an animal; and, by so doing, confirm beyond doubt its presence in the local countryside.

The first point to note is that the leopard, melanistic or otherwise, is a solitary and exceptionally shy creature, wary of humans. It will avoid contact, even proximity, with mankind wherever possible; it depends upon its secrecy and stealth, not just as a predator but in its avoidance of danger or capture. In common with all cat species, the leopard is intelligent and inclined to be devious. If these 'personality' traits contribute to its elusiveness, its patterns of activity and movement are no more encouraging to the would-be captor. It will hunt at night, or at dawn or dusk, and sleep during the day in dense and obscure day-beds. Being nomadic, it has no lair, as such, rarely resting in the same place on consecutive days. The leopard has no fixed routine – it does not eat or drink at a particular hour, nor does it use the same routes with any predictability. It patrols only half its range regularly, the rest less often, but again with no appreciable pattern. All that can said by way of narrowing down the search is that a leopard keeps to cover wherever possible and, like most cats, dislikes wet, muddy terrain. Moreover, the prospects of 'finding' a leopard improve marginally in winter, when the receding vegetation restricts its ability to roam and/or hide.

In conclusion, it should be evident from the above just how difficult it is to pursue the leopard or to forecast, with any certainty, where it might appear next. It is arguable that one might establish locations where a leopard has been sighted, if such sightings can be relied upon, or where 'suspicious' kills have occurred or prints, stools etc. have been found. If these sites are assumed to be part of the known or putative territory, an attempt could be constructed to capture the leopard – literally, or on film – by the placement of some kind of trap, lure or camera. Even then, I would contest, the probability of success is small. A leopard can scent humans from a hundred metres, or more, and if it is in any way suspicious of a human presence it will simply keep away.

For many months, if not years, trackers, hunters, wildlife photographers, field zoologists, the police and assorted 'Black Beast' enthusiasts have been endeavouring, with varying degrees of professionalism, to 'find' the leopard. It is an irony, as well as a frustration, that those who search for the leopard are not the ones who see it. Each of the reported sightings in this case has happened by chance, to witnesses who had not planned to encounter the leopard and were, therefore, unprepared and unable to produce any valid evidence beyond their own testimony of what they saw. If I might be allowed, finally, to exchange the language of science for something closer to Eastern mysticism: you do not find the leopard, the leopard finds you.

26

They arrived to find Dr Barker Inglis making notes on a clipboard, one leg protruding from the open door of the car, trouser cuff tucked into his sock as though he had been, or was about to go, cycling. The hair was less vibrantly orange than she remembered.

'We meet again,' he said.

'Hn.'

'Hiya.'

The inquiry inspector's eyes, and smile, dislodged from Ethan to her. 'Ah, yes, we were never properly introduced, were we?'

'Nap.'

Inglis continued studying her for a moment, then, indicating the entrance to the oratory, addressed Ethan: 'Your witness awaits.' He lay the clipboard on the passenger seat, interlocked his fingers and extended his arms. 'Thin pickings, I'm afraid, for an investigator and his, ah, consort.'

'I'm here in a consultancy capacity,' she said.

'Consultant in what?'

She shed rain from her dreads with a shake of the head. 'If you think of Ethan as a kind of zoological alchemist, yeah?, well I'm his *soror mystica*.'

Once Inglis had gone, Ethan asked her to talk him through the exchange.

'One, he's government. You ask me, inquiries aren't set up to inquire, but to pronounce. Two, nothing this guy says or does will have any relevance to the existence or otherwise of the cat. Three, he's a wanker.'

Ethan liked that.

'*Consort*,' she said. 'I mean, jesus.'

'I don't even know what a *soror mystica* is.'

'Mystic sister. Basically, your traditional alchemist – male, natch – required a muse – female, natch – to assist in the spiritual fusion of his experiments.'

Ethan frowned. 'And that's how you see us?'

'What do you think?'

Via Calvaria. White script, the sign fixed to a door in a newly creosoted fence. The entrance, set back among trees, would've been easy to pass by. Unlike Inglis, they'd parked at the monastery and walked here through the grounds. The rain had turned Erica's coat the colour of toffee, curtained beneath her in wet tassels. Ethan's hood was drawn tight around his face. He made Erica sit, securing her to a NO DOGS notice planted in the verge. Her distress at being deserted pursued them inside the oratory.

'Reverence.'

'What?'

She splayed her arms at her sides. 'Can't you feel it?'

At first the way was made gloomy by waterlogged branches pungent with pine. Then, a bright place: a lawned glade of oak, sycamore, beech and yew – tall and evenly spaced, like arched columns in a cathedral. An avenue of statuary depicting the stations of the cross guided the path to a grotto adorned by three plain wooden crosses. She saw him, the vicar. Same lurid purple wetgear. Same bulk. Facing one of the statues as if it was a museum exhibit, and only a slight shift in posture to betray an awareness that he was no longer alone. The inscription read:

Jesus is stripped of his garments

Glancing at her, then back at the carving, the vicar said: 'Is that Gore-Tex?'

'I guess it would've been some kind of woven cloth.'

He laughed loudly, infectiously. 'Mine doesn't breathe, you see. I get so damp with sweat I might as well get rained on.'

She drifted, circling the statue, wandering on to the lawn – mostly moss, if you looked closely – and taking immense care not to step on any of the fallen leaves. She heard the guy ask Ethan if they'd arrived today.

'We're not on retreat,' Ethan said. She saw him gesture in the direction of the monastery. 'They said you might be here.'

'Ah.' The vicar nodded, smiling. 'Which newspaper?'

'We're not reporters.'

'I can't even *type*,' she said. 'Spelling. Don't talk to me about spelling.'

The men looked at her, then at one another. Ethan introduced himself. The guy reciprocated: Ralph Wilson. 'You know, I've heard about you,' he said. 'The Hermit.'

Ethan didn't reply.

'Tell me, what were you before this?'

'What d'you mean, what was I?'

'I've heard so many versions – everything from zoologist to geography teacher to council tax officer. You're a man of rumour, Mr Gray. The Ministry chap – Inglis, d'you know him? – he informs me you used to be a Formula One motor-racing driver.'

She had to cover her mouth.

'Ah,' the vicar said, 'I suspect a practical joke at my expense.' He smiled. 'It is supposed that we clerics, believing in God, will believe in anything.'

She stood on one leg, stork pose, extending and retracting her non-standing leg at right-angles to her hip, conscious of being observed.

Revd Wilson projected his voice. 'You have great poise, young lady.'

'Thanks.' She smiled, lowering her leg and approaching them across the grass. The shower had eased. The vicar's eyebrows, she saw, were beaded with raindrops and moisture had collected in the fleshy clefts of his jowls. 'Chloe Fortune. I dowse.'

He shook her hand. 'Weren't you at the Twelve Apostles yesterday?'

'Uh-huh.'

'I thought so.'

'I was freaked, actually.' She mimed an explosion, the detonation of a charge inside her skull. 'Otherwise I'd have come over and said hi.'

'You were dowsing up there?'

'Kind of.'

'For what?'

'The cat.'

Beneath the affability, the vicar now seemed a little disorientated, discomposed. Smiling, opening his arms as if to restrain her and Ethan, or to shepherd them away, he said: 'Let me show you the grotto.'

The stone archway was too low for them to enter without stooping. Inside was a bench, and a shelf arrayed with devotional offerings: wildflowers, crosses constructed from twigs bound with twine, or just laid one over another. The simplicity, if not the theology, appealed to her. Their feet and the drips from their clothing had marked the cement floor. When the cleric spoke, his voice resounded.

'I come here every day while I'm on retreat.'

Producing the microcassette, Ethan said: 'Is this okay . . . for my files?'

'Another statement.' Revd Wilson's tedium sounded contrived, like he'd also been freaked by the Apostles and needed to talk about it to anyone who'd listen. 'I fear there's always a risk of embellishment if one repeats a story too often.'

Ethan dictated the vicar's name, the date, the date and location of the sighting. He asked what time it had occurred, but the vicar interposed a question of his own, to her.

'Are you saying that you *divined* my encounter?'

'I dowsed the cat and the place.' She sat on the bench, drawing her knees up under her chin. 'You just happened to be there.'

'I suppose I ought to be impressed.'

She hoped her expression said: *Please yourself.* 'I've never met anyone who's seen her for real.' She widened her eyes. 'You know? Actually *seen* her.'

'Dr Inglis asked if I'd heard the stories about the Black Beast.' A rasp of Velcro as he undid his cagoule. 'The implication being that this might've prejudiced me. That I might unconsciously, even consciously, have wanted the animal I saw to be the beast.'

'That can happen,' she said.

'I am a birder.' He stressed the word. 'You become quick at noting identifying detail: size, shape, colour, markings, action. A glimpse may be all you have. It's the difference between an experienced observer and an inexperienced one.' Adjusting one of the flower arrangements, he said: 'I told Inglis: there is no more reliable eyewitness than a birder. Cats, birds – the basic principle is the same.'

'What did you observe?' Ethan said.

'He showed me a book with photographs of various animals and asked me to point out the one that most closely resembled what I saw.'

'And?'

'Melanistic leopard. Black panther, to you and me.' He closed his eyes when he laughed, the sound – a solitary bark of amusement – reissuing with a slap off the walls of the grotto. 'The good doctor wondered if it could've been a Great Dane.'

Revd Wilson gazed out. She did the same. The rain had stopped altogether and the oratory was streamered with feeble sunshine. Ethan was saying something about how the statues to one side of the path stood exactly in the elongated shadows cast by those opposite and how, if you knew the place intimately, you could calculate the time by this. She pointed out a rainbow, faint and diluted as a smudge of watercolour.

'You know, Inglis had the audacity to quote the Bible at me?' the vicar said. '"Blessed are those who have not seen and yet have believed." John, chapter 20, verse 29. Well, I told him I *have* seen. Saw it with my own eyes.'

She made a circle with her thumb and middle finger. 'Nice one.'

*

Afterwards, after the vicar had described the sighting for the tape, she came away with a mental picture of a creature created by his words. It was a picture of beauty. She said so to Ethan and he nodded and she saw that he possessed it too, this picture.

'Other eyewitnesses,' he said, 'they only ever talk of of of fear, astonishment, shock, terror, excitement, panic, disbelief, dread, menace . . . speaking of themselves, of the cat in relation to themselves.' She had the sense that Ethan wasn't sharing this with her so much as working through a private thought, a sudden internal revelation. 'To them, the cat is a thing of ugly, bestial savagery. A killer.'

'They see death,' she said. 'Not life.'

'Yes. Yes, death. That's what they see. Death.'

'How about you?'

'Me?'

'Yeah, have you ever imagined her as a creature of beauty?'

'I . . .' He stopped, right there on the path, as though it was too complicated to think and talk and walk at the same time. When at last he found what he wanted to say, his words were released on a pale breath of regret. 'I'd like to have seen what he saw.'

They resumed, in silence, emerging from the oratory to an exaggerated display of pleasure by Erica. She untied her before she choked herself or yanked the sign from the ground, presenting her face to be licked, lapping at the dog's snout in return.

'Serious halitosis.' She dried herself on the back of her hand, quietening Erica. 'Would it be enough for you, d'you think?'

'A sighting?' Ethan said.

'Or would you still want proof? Something to show someone else – this Inglis guy, or whoever.' She took off her cagoule and fastened it to her waist by the sleeves. 'I mean, *you'd* know, wouldn't you? You'd *know*.'

'No.' He looked to be measuring the truth of this. 'No, it wouldn't be enough.'

Here, the air was sharpened by a coal-tar stink of creosote from the fence and by warm, wet dog. Even though it had ceased raining,

Ethan still wore his hood. Being sure and neat and practical about it, she unpicked the knot beneath his chin, slackened the drawstring and drew the hood back. *There.* His hair was flattened, matted, but she wasn't about to ruffle it for him, given his evident confusion over the hood business. A spliff would've been good right now. She wondered what Ethan was like spliffed. He was sorting his pack, stashing the microcassette, the notepad.

'How did the vicar's description compare with your visualized image?' he said.

She smiled, turning away. Not answering.

'What?'

'Visualized image,' she said. 'A guy sees the cat and it blows you away, but if someone "sees" her' – she wrote inverted commas in the air with her fingers – 'you can't quite get there, can you? Houston, we still have an acceptance problem.'

'I accept that what he saw was more real than what you saw, yes.'

'The cat has many realities.'

Ethan shook his head. 'It has one reality. There is one real, physical cat. What you're talking about is the, is the . . . multiplicity of people's experiences of the cat.'

'Same thing.'

'It's not the same thing at all.'

'You don't consider experience to be real?'

'That isn't what I'm saying.'

Erica raised her head, ears pricked, staring into the woods which would return them to the monastery. She looked too, but could see and hear nothing unusual.

'What you're having trouble accepting is that I dowsed her.' She shrugged. 'You probably think it was just some amazing stroke of luck.'

On the phone, and driving out here, he'd been more interested in discussing her reasons for going solo on this one. Not that she gave him more than an edited version. So he was startled by the outcome of the op, sure, but there was still no way for him to know, to verify, to *prove* that (a) she'd dowsed the cat, or (b) the vicar had seen it.

'A coincidence, maybe,' Ethan said. 'An amazing coincidence.'

'Ethan.' The pitch of her voice rose, she was close to laughter. 'That's what dowsing *is*. A coincidence. A concurrence – a convergence – of incidents.'

Erica began to bark. And there, materializing on the rough track along which Inglis had departed, was another car arriving. The car mounted the verge and braked hard to a halt close to where they stood. Gavin Drinkell and a guy she recognized as *The Monitor*'s photographer got out.

Gavin's stare shuttled between her and Ethan, then settled on her. Ethan would be thinking – what would he be thinking? – he'd be thinking that the reporter, here for one story, had chanced upon another. Beast Man Puts Faith In Diviner's Intervention, or something. Some shite. As far as Ethan knew, this was the essence of the encounter. This was all there was to it. But if he was reading Gavin's face right he would find the other story. Because Gavin didn't look smug, the way he should've done, and he didn't look pleased with himself, or with the situation, or its journalistic implications. And he sure as shit didn't look pleased with her.

'This is space to be by yourself, is it?' he said. Calm, controlled. 'This is guy detox?'

She let the forward tilt of her head drape her face with hair, then raised it again.

'Him?' Gavin was pointing at Ethan, but still looking at her. '*Him?*'

27

SUSAN REANEY (*housing officer*):
Ethan never seemed especially interested in my previous boyfriends, but he didn't seem all that bothered if I mentioned them either. One lad I went out with was so jealous, I had to act like I had no 'past' at all, like he was the first boyfriend I'd ever had, even though I was twenty-six at the time. Insecurity, I suppose. Ethan wasn't insecure. Or, at least, he didn't come across that way. And so, over the months we were together, I must've made a few casual remarks about my exes. Maybe he'd ask the odd question about them or, you know, they'd just crop up in conversation the way they do . . . and he never batted an eyelid. And all of this was fine, of course. All perfectly normal and mature. Then, near the end I was looking in his drawers at work for some document or other he was away from his desk – and I saw a sheet of paper with a list of names on it. Nothing else, just six names in block capitals. And as I read them my stomach went flip, because they were the names of all my serious boyfriends since fifth form, in the exact order I went out with them.

28

Driving away from the monastery the silence between and inside and about them filled the Toyota with the cold shadows of unsaid words. Not a word on the hike back to the monastery, not a word now. She wanted to, but resented feeling obliged to, explain. Ethan was no business of Gavin's and Gavin was no business of Ethan's, and yet – one with his words, the other with his wordlessness – they were messing with her head, as if it was theirs to mess with. Ethan surprised her by being the first to speak. Hands at five to one on the wheel, eight whitened knuckles in a row.

'What was that all about?'

'It was about me,' she said. 'Not you.'

'It sounded like it was about both of us.'

'That's how it seemed to him.' Staring out the passenger window at a drystone wall, shredded into a chalky, chequered blur by the speed of their passing. Waiting for him to say something else. But he'd shut down on her again. 'If this wasn't the middle of nowhere, I'd make you stop the car and let me out.'

'It's not a car,' he said. 'It's a pick-up.'

'I'd slam the door and stride off across the fields, *magnificently*.'

Ethan swung into a passing place, pulling up so abruptly that their gear, in the back, scraped to a stop with a thud against the cabin. 'Go on, then.'

She observed him – gripped, eyes front, so serious he was funny. 'Ethan, this is not a movie. We don't do melodrama. So, I'm gonna sit here and you'll take me home, please, and somewhere along the way we will deal with this.'

Soon, but not too soon, he drove off. She half thought he'd do it with a spit of grit from the rear tyres, but he eased away smoothly, checking in his wing mirror, even offering the stammering blink of an indicator to the empty road. There was a continual alteration in the light from the arched branches of the trees overhead. Barcode bands of bright and dark scanning their legs, laps, chests, faces.

She inhaled through her nose. 'Gavin interviewed me a couple of times, and took me for drink. Once. Months ago. He asked me out again, and I told him no. And that was that. Well, apart from the pestering.' She told Ethan about the pestering.

'You finished with him?'

'There was nothing to finish. But, yeah, in his terms I suppose I did.'

Ethan was quiet for a moment. 'Did you sleep with him?'

'What the . . . no, hang on,' she said, 'I have to get the emphasis right, here . . . what the fuck, what . . . the . . . fuck, what the *fuck* has that got to do with you?'

There. She liked the way the words sounded. This was shaping up into a proper quarrel. A row. Only she couldn't keep the amusement out of her face or her voice, and she could see that all she was doing to Ethan was puzzling him.

'Gavin seemed to think you're sleeping with me.'

'I mean, jesus, I'm supposed to care what he thinks?' She tried to make Ethan look at her, but he kept his eyes on the road. 'What do you think? Do you think we're sleeping together, you and me? Or d'you want to check with Gavin?'

Ethan didn't answer.

'This is playground stuff,' she said. 'This is all just so fucking juvenile.'

'You cared.'

'Sorry?'

'Back there, you cared what he thought when he found us together.'

She shoved her fingers in among the dreads and massaged her scalp, moving skin back and forth against bone. Firmly, then less so. The smells of the pick-up – dog, dozing in the footwell; sweat, his and hers; seat leather; diesel – were suddenly and oddly familiar. Comforting. Ethan was right, she had cared; though not about

Gavin's reaction, but his. She allowed herself to be driven, getting her head round the why of it all and the precipitating clumsiness of guy-think.

'What would you've done if I'd got out?' she said, at last.

Ethan unfurled his fingers, then closed them again on the wheel.

'You'd have left me there, wouldn't you? Miles from anywhere.' She laughed and saw that he found it funny too, despite himself. 'You fucking would've!'

Ethan dropped her at the corner of the street behind the caff. She jumped down and Erica, awake now, jumped up into the passenger seat. Talking across her through the open window, she smiled and thanked him for the lift.

'Am I still in your gang?' she said.

Ethan hadn't let go of the steering wheel. A toy driver fixed for ever inside a toy car. Which was to say, a pick-up. 'You want to keep on dowsing the cat?' he said.

'Be cool with all this, yeah?'

'Yeah.' He nodded once, twice. Then he smiled too. 'Yeah, sure.'

She headed off, turning to wave as she reached the entrance to the yard. The Toyota remained at the kerb where she'd got out. Immobile shapes of man and dog were all she could distinguish. The cagoule was still slung around her waist. She drew it up behind her and wheeled into the yard like a child playing aeroplanes – past the bins, and right up to her door, even though Ethan would no longer be able to see her.

That night – late, twelvish – the phone rang and her first thought was Ethan, seeing as no one else but Roy and Faye knew the number and, besides, she wanted it to be him. But it wasn't. It was Gavin. *How did you get my . . . ?* But this wasn't dialogue, it was monologue. Drunk, swearing, working off on her all the confusion and hurt and shock and humiliation that, a few hours earlier, had been condensed into the contemptuous repetition of one word: Him . . . *Him.*

She hung up on him mid-rant, dialled Ethan's mobile, and they talked for ages without mentioning Gavin or anything that wasn't to do with the cat or dowsing.

Science needs a body – skin and bone – to make a definitive classification.

Ethan's bottom line, when she presented the Apostles as a breakthrough. By way of example, he updated her on the shit sample he'd sent for analysis – conclusion: inconclusive. But even if it had been positively i.d.'d as stool-of-leopard, how could he demonstrate, beyond doubt, that the find wasn't faked in some way?

'The cat would have to walk into the lab, in full view of a team of independent zoologists and several TV cameras, and crap into a petri dish.'

Being just about the funniest remark he'd made to her in all these weeks.

She'd sussed that Ethan wasn't there yet, with what he called the methodology, but she'd sussed too that even if he wasn't sure whether to believe in dowsing, the concept, he believed in Chloe Fortune, the dowser. Which was something. Which was a start. Because, although it wasn't necessary for someone else – least of all a guy – to believe in you for you to believe in yourself, it weighed on you when they didn't. It weighed on you and it sapped you and it dragged you into the low places, where your own buoyancy wasn't always enough to raise you back to the surface.

'You sure he believes in you?' Mom said, via satellite, collect call, seeing as she was wide awake now, post-Ethan, still in the mood to talk, and it was teatime on the West Coast. 'To believe in the dowser, but not the dowsing – where does this sit with a guy you say is so stuck on logic?'

'I think he takes me seriously. I think he knows what it's like to be ridiculed for believing in something most people don't believe in.'

'You don't think, maybe, he's so desperate to find this cat, so frustrated by the failure of his own methods, that he'll try anything? Any*one*. Huh?'

'He's with me 'cos he's desperate. Thanks, Mom.'

'He's *with* you?'

'*Working* with me.' She exhaled. 'All I'm saying is, when I'm with him and I'm dowsing, he doesn't look at me the way Spoons used to. Like, I dunno, like he's trying to say something really important but he can't make himself heard 'cos you're listening to some crappy song on the Walkman. You know? Ethan doesn't do that.'

'Hon, I seem to recall a time when Spoons didn't do that either.'

No matter what you do as a dowser, some people will refuse to believe in you. This isn't about dowsing, it's about belief – Mom, c. 1987.

Yeah, yeah.

There were also those, she knew, who would always believe in you, no matter what. And this wasn't about dowsing either. People at the extremes of belief she could handle. Extremity was easy, part of the binary code – the yes/no – of dowsing itself; only, done properly, you offered the pendulum more options than positive or negative. There were the anti-idiot responses, safeguards against false assumption: neutral; don't know; unask the question. Her dowser's take on life, so far, was that complexity – and, therefore, interest – resided in the space between yes and no.

Which placed Ethan where?

He was an unask-the-question kind of guy in most respects, but he demanded a yes on dowsing. She could tell. He wanted a yes, or he'd assume the no. Mom, of course, would say a dowser has no obligation whatsoever to prove anything to anyone except herself. And yet she wanted to convince him.

There was a complexity to Ethan, beneath all the proof stuff, that hooked her. He'd sought the cat long before she coincided with his life and he would go on seeking after she'd moved on; she liked this about him, the fact that she wasn't the focus of his need. She liked him. She liked to spend time with him. She liked to dowse. She liked the idea of the cat. Okay, so the Gavin encounter had dislocated them, or threatened to relocate them somewhere they weren't – *she* wasn't – ready to be just yet. So what? Where was the harm in staying with this for a while and seeing where it went?

29

RHIANNON SPALL (*mythologist*):
There is a preoccupation, among officialdom and the media particularly, with whether or not the 'Black Beast' exists. What is far more interesting, in my view, is its existence as a phenomenon within our intra-millennial culture. And the creature's mythological or legendary status, if that is the case, in no way reduces its sociological significance.

It is through myth that we – as individuals, as societies and as a species – make sense of experience and through which we attach meaning and purpose to the everyday mundanity of living. Myth is at the core of humankind. The truth contained in myth is outside of scientific truth and immune to its applications. Science is thus at odds with human experience in that it seeks to undermine the mysterious, the miraculous and the unexplained. Imagine a world in which there was nothing beyond what we can prove – logically, rationally, empirically – to be true.

Human beings believe in things for which there is no conclusive evidence. This is universal. Cultural anthropologists have been unable to identify a society anywhere in the world that does not have well-established and complex systems of belief in the paranormal operating within it. So natural do these seem to our thought processes, and so adaptive are they, that they may be genetic in characteristic. We have a basic, innate need and desire to tell ourselves stories. And underlying each story – each myth and legend – is a tale of human experience.

Historians who deride or ignore the study of superstition take a narrow view of human history. Many such beliefs are rooted in a time when the natural world was both feared and celebrated: at once a source of life and of death. Even today, in our more scientifically aware and technologically developed society, the mystery of the unknown persists in tantalizing us. Monsters, so to speak, are still out there. We may no longer believe in dragons, but we might construct a belief in a known creature inhabiting an atypical environment. No one disputes that the melanistic leopard exists, but does it exist here, in this place, at this time? Possibly. Plausibly. Conceivably. This is the dragon in its modern, sophisticated incarnation – roaming the overlap of scientific understanding and mythological premise. It may exist, it may not. What is certain is that the 'Black Beast' exists for those who believe in it. It exists too as an object of disbelief for those who do not, and as an object of scepticism for those who are unsure. As such, it can be said to exist for all of us. That is its magic.

30

She handed him a paper bag. Inside was a small cactus shaped like a hand, with four fat oval fingers and a thumb stump.

'What's this?' Ethan said.

'A cactus. *Opuntia microdasys*, I expect you'd call it.'

'No, I mean . . . why?'

'A present.' She shrugged. 'A token of whatever.'

'Hn.'

'This place needs something homely.' She was standing on the steps, looking up at him framed in the split doorway, as she had done on her first visit. Only this time he was dressed. Erica was inside, fussing to be outside. 'I painted the pot myself.'

A uniform egg-yolk yellow that surprised him, he said, for not being black. He might've thanked her at this point, or at least conveyed a sense of gratitude beneath his awkwardness. But what he said was that, with it being a cactus and the caravan being cold and damp, and with winter approaching, the plant would probably die.

'You've hurt yourself,' she said.

He revolved his hand to inspect it, as if she'd drawn his attention to something he hadn't noticed. The knuckles were grazed, abraded, the skin grated away to leave tacky wounds that she imagined, if she touched them, would adhere to her fingertips. A fall, he said. He'd been out on a stalk the previous day, while she was at work – surveying a gully, a dried-up watercourse overgrown with hawthorn, gorse and nettles. A putative route to and from a defunct, partially collapsed railway tunnel the cat may have used as a temporary lair or meat store. The gully sides were steep and loose with scree, and he'd had to lift Erica over a razor-wire fence at the top, then climb over after her. Only, he caught his jeans and landed heavily, and the next thing he knew he was at the bottom. His ankle was done. Sprained, not broken, but it had taken three hours to walk the three kilometres home.

'I can't put any weight on it, now,' he said. 'Can't even get a boot on.'

'Today's off, then?'

'I called last night to cancel, but there was no answer.'

'I was out.' No need to tell him where or who with, but she did so all the same and wasn't sure why. 'Clubbing, with Faye.'

'I thought you'd assumed I was Gavin.' Frowning, he said: 'We should devise a code – I'll let it ring twice, then hang up and call back straight away.'

'He came into the caff yesterday. Into the *kitchen*. Roy went ape.'

Mostly, Ethan was cool with the Gavin-thing, so long as he could categorize it as a practical, rather than a personal, hassle. But there were times when she'd mention the latest nuisance call and he'd disappear into one of his moods, *inner journeys* as she'd come to think of them. Sometimes, being with Ethan was like watching someone dive into a lake and never knowing where to look for them to break the surface.

'D'you play the guitar?' she said.

'Me? No.'

'I think you should take lessons. Or teach yourself, that would be cool.' She gestured at the stoop. 'Imagine sitting out here in the evenings, singing and smoking dope and playing the guitar. Acoustic, obviously.'

'It's the last week of November.'

'Get a fire going or something. Anyway, by the time you've learned . . . yeah?'

Ethan was still holding the cactus. He tested the spines with his thumb; and she knew from having done the same that they weren't sharp, but downy – like the bristles of a toothbrush. She thought he might be wondering about teaching himself guitar. He unbolted the lower flap of the door and let it swing out, letting Erica out too.

'Come in.'

'Can we stay outside?' she said. 'Only I need to loosen my head.'

'D'you want coffee?'

'You got any paracetamol?'

'I think so. Somewhere.'

'Hangover. Seven on the Richter.' She set her daypack by her feet. Her eyes felt bruised from lack of sleep. 'Or Solpadeine. Anything.'

Ethan smiled. 'I thought you'd be into herbal. Homoeopathic.'

'Yeah, like I'm gonna get that here.'

He fetched two tablets and a mug, hobbling, slopping water. She swigged both pills at once, pulling a face at their bitter aftertaste and at the drink's anaesthetic chill. The water from the plastic keg under the caravan was cold enough in summer, but this time of year it hurt your teeth, your gums. It tasted of metal. It tasted of the dentist.

She yawned profusely. 'Is that new?'

He looked down at his red and white hooped sweatshirt, then at her. Deadpan. 'I haven't bought any new clothes since 1994.'

'I've not seen it before.' She was aware of the effect on him, on people, of her disjointedness, and of their confusion, their coercion into the syncopated structures and cadences of her speech and thought patterns and subject matter. It was just the way her mind worked. An idea would occur to her – in this case, an image, Ethan's shirt – and whatever was being talked about she'd have to hit the tangent. 'Suits you, actually.'

'Have you had breakfast?' he said.

'Nap.'

He fixed coffee and toast. The thought of food made her nauseous, but once it was there in front of her she ate, suddenly *famished*. They shared the stoop, a plastic plate between them, heaped with halved slices of unmarged, slightly burnt bread. When she asked why he'd trimmed the crusts, he said the outside of the loaf was mouldy.

'I don't know if I'm glad you told me that.'

'I can tie her up, if she's bothering you.'

'She's fine.' She fed a scrap to Erica. 'I like her wet breath on my hand.'

The air was cool and dry and still, the sky an unbroken screen of high cloud. A ewe had ventured near to the fence, browsing, raising its head occasionally to study the dog through the pickets; the rip-rip-rip of grass being wrenched from the ground was audible. Shorn of its wool, the animal resembled a goat.

'Did you see *The Monitor?*' Ethan said.

'Uh-huh.' Another yawn. 'Roy cut it out and pinned it on the menu board.'

Gavin's speculative diary piece about their 'wacky double act', illustrated by a cartoon panther pawing like a playful kitten at a pendulum bob. Ethan reckoned one of the nationals might follow up the story. Like she cared. She'd already had her picture in the tabloids, she said, being arrested after surfacing from a subterranean stint.

'I looked like a miner. Like Al Jolson.' She made staring eyes. 'I sent a copy to Mom and she said I shouldn't let Dad see it 'cos he'd be upset by the composition.'

'Did he ever take pictures of you?'

'Nap. Well, yeah, family snaps and that, but not studio stuff. I never *posed* for him,' she said, making her voice actressy. 'He only photographed women he wanted to fuck, basically. Mom, then whoever.'

What did she know of Ethan's folks? Zip, apart from: mother deceased, father estranged. Father estranged, or Ethan estranged? It amounted to pretty much the same thing. Also, a sister (married, kids) he'd lost contact with long before this, the caravan, the cat. And an ex-fiancée he'd referred to once and never again. Walking, swaying, away from the club with Faye, their talk about Ethan had centred on this, on how little he had divulged of himself. Of his past. In all their hours together, he'd listened more than he'd spoken. And if he did speak it was usually about the present – about the cat, about anything but himself, except himself in relation to the cat and the finding of it.

What Ethan is, right, is a maze disguised as a one-way street.

Faye thought it was stunning, the crap people came out with at whatever a.m., boozed up to the skull. Her own take being something along the lines of: you fancy a feller, you invent nice things to plug the gaps in your knowledge of him. Only, who'd said anything about fancying? She looked at Ethan. He was talking.

'When I think of the protest camp, I don't picture you in a tunnel,' he said. 'I see you high up in a tree – hanging on to a branch, lobbing abuse at the police and the bailiffs.' A slow smile formed, he was nodding to himself. 'I don't think of you as a a a troglodyte, more . . . to me, you're more *simian*.'

She laughed. 'You're saying I remind you of a monkey?'

But Ethan wanted to show her something, a photograph. They were discussing photographs and, despite the monkey banter, he wanted to show her a photograph that illustrated some point or other. It was a famous photograph, heralded as *the* definitive picture of the Black Beast, he said, and still reproduced in the papers from time to time. When he retrieved it from his files, she recognized it right away, although she didn't recall having seen it before. But, yeah, it was definitely familiar.

It was perfect.

Dusk. A large black cat in silhouette, half standing half squatting on a drystone wall, as though poised to pounce on a cow in a field that sloped down in the direction of the camera. The cow's head was turned towards the cat, its body seemingly rigid with fear. The size of the cat, in comparison with the cow, was startling.

'Did you take this?' she said.

Ethan shook his head. He said when the shot first appeared, in a Sunday paper – WORLD EXCLUSIVE . . . FIRST PICTURE OF THE BLACK BEAST! – he'd suspected a hoax. But it turned out to be a genuine misinterpretation. He showed her another cutting, dated a week after the original article. Blah blah blah, then the pink-highlighted quote, from a Ministry of Agriculture official: *The reliable indicator of the cat's actual size is not the cow in the foreground but the wall upon which the cat is standing. Thus is the optical deceit of perspective eliminated*. They'd measured the wall, Ethan said, and from this the ratio of cat-to-wall in the photograph was a straightforward calculation. The 'Black Beast' was no more than 30 cm at the shoulder – roughly equivalent to a domestic pet.

'I don't see the attraction,' Faye said. 'No offence but, me, I'd be too spooked.'

'Spooked?'

'I like a feller to be . . . normal.' Faye made two parallel lines in the air with her hands. 'Straight, I suppose. I like to know where I am with him.'

'He's looked inside himself.'

'Hasn't everyone?'

'Not in my experience, no. Not properly.' She might've been sick at this point, or maybe just the first flush of saliva warning her of the sick to come. 'Nobody could spend so much time alone and not look inside. I like guys who've done that.'

She was spent. A hungover fatigue of such yawning magnitude that Ethan could go on about the interpretation of photographs for as long as he wanted but all she craved was sleep sleep sleep. Right away. To lie down and sleep immediately.

'Eeth, can I use your bed?'

His face being a sight to behold. She was wrecked, she said. So wrecked she could just slump down right here, shut-eyed, on the breeze blocks of his stoop, or head off into the trees, the sycamores, and lay herself down among the papery debris.

So, please?

Inside, she drew the curtains. They were thin, unlined, admitting a glimmering film of light like aerosol spray. She took off the denim jacket, the joggers, the trainers, making a casual pile of black on the floor. The T-shirt and knickers, she kept on. She'd sleep on, not in, the bed, she decided. Zipping the sleeping bag shut, smoothing it flat for softness beneath her on a base as firm as a floor and narrow enough to roll right off. No pillow, just a cushion covered in fabric with a raised design that would etch her cheek as it had done Ethan's, that first morning, awakened by the unexpectedness of her. Seemed an age ago. And, now, she was using his bed. The weirdness of these, or of any, circumstances residing only in their perception. She relaxed her limbs in turn, relaxed her breathing. Closed her eyes. Drifting, she wondered whether he would come to her and what she'd do or say if he did.

31

Cold.

A scratch-scratch-scratch near by, so close that an insect might've been fretting at the coarse cloth of the cushion. She heaved her head, her shoulders, up and opened her eyes. No insect. The light had faded. Her neck was stiff, her body too, from, she guessed, making herself pencil thin in this strange bed for unconscious, dormant fear of falling. Gluey lips. She registered the cold again, and a large towel draped neatly over her, like a sheet, from chin to shins. Propped on her elbows, she absorbed the gloom. Seeing Ethan, across from her, wearing his reading glasses and sitting at the table with papers arranged before him and a pen poised above a page. And now she knew what it was that had made the scratching sound.

'I couldn't use the typewriter,' he said.

Her own words came in croak. 'What time is it?'

'You've been asleep for eight and a half hours.'

'Shit.' She deposited her head cushionwards. 'I haven't, have I? *Shit.*'

He adjusted the valve of a wall-mounted lamp; there was a whisper of gas, then the odour. She watched him strike a match and, tentatively, introduce the flame to the mantle. *Phiszsh!* The bulb hung in flaps of singed gauze, a bluish jet shooting from its gape like the blowtorch of a cigarette lighter on high. Ethan swore and shut off the gas. Finding another mantle, he replaced the broken one and tried again. A creamy bloom filled half the caravan, daubing abstract domes of white on the walls and ceiling.

'These fucking things are so fragile.'

'The light is good.' She sat up, dislodging the towel. 'Better than electric.'

Why a towel? Why not a blanket? Maybe he didn't have any. She thanked him for letting her sleep. She saw that the light accentuated the tan on her legs and turned their dark hairs blonde. Trousers. On the floor, where she'd left them. Easing out from between table and bed, she went to the darker end of the caravan and drew them on. Speculating, unable not to, how long Ethan had been sitting there, how long before the towel, how long he'd looked – gawped – at her as she slept. No. You invite yourself for a lie down, a nap, on a guy's bed, in a guy's home, and then, half naked, zonk out for eight and a half hours, *eight and a half hours, jesus* . . . she was the intruder here. All he'd done, that she could be sure of, was cover her up.

'Was I snoring?'

'No.'

She had dreamed, in his bed; she couldn't recall what about, except that she'd awoken flushed with a residual, inner warmth to contrast the external cold. At the sink, she stamped the treadle till her cupped palms filled with water, sluicing her face, mouth and neck, taking her breath away.

A discussion on temporality. The unresolved problem, Ethan said, was that they still hadn't done future. *They.* She liked that. In the guttering light, his face was the colour and – to the touch, she was sure – the texture of parchment. Of linen soaked in amber. She offered him some Mom-speak:

The future is facts that haven't happened yet, which means they're imaginary.

Using a pendulum to work with time, it was essential to understand you were handling probability, rather than actuality. The coincidental probability that, given all the variables, this event will occur at this time in this location. You were seeking the most likely future from a finite number of possibilities. Not a statistical forecast based on interpretation and extrapolation of known data, but an imagined one. You didn't *compute* the future, you *visualized* it.

Quoting her mom again, she said: 'A statistician engages in probability theory, a dowser in probability practice.'

Ethan didn't buy this distinction. 'Sounds like educated guesswork to me: bit of dowsing, bit of knowledge about the cat's habits. It's predictive calculation.'

'Okay, you have to know what questions to ask the future and how to interpret the responses, but that's where the similarity ends. What you do, what I have to teach myself to do, is *create* an imaginary future in the present reality of my mind.'

'But the uncertainty is still there,' he said. 'The possibility of being wrong.'

'How can there be certainty about something that hasn't happened yet?'

'What about death?'

'Yeah, like: where, when and how.' She laughed. 'D'you know Faye, at work, she went to a palm reader and this woman told her she'd already lived exactly one fifth of her life. Which means she's going to die when she's ninety. Five quid, that cost her.'

Ethan removed his glasses and rubbed the bridge of his nose. Erica, who'd been asleep in her basket, got up and stretched and sniffed at the door. She let her out. The dog's claws on the stoop made the sound of knitting needles. Remembering the cactus, she looked for it, spotting it on the table among the piled jigsaw pieces of his books. It hadn't died on them yet, for all their talk of death.

'I'm going to make us a brew, yeah?'

'Hn. Yes, go ahead.'

She filled the kettle and put it on, sorting out mugs and teabags. 'If you knew where, when and how you were going to die, you'd spend your life trying to make sure it couldn't happen.' Pointing a spoon at him, she said: 'Date, next Friday; time, 18.30 hours; location . . . I dunno, some moor top; cause, mauled by a black panther.'

Now it was Ethan's turn to laugh. 'How about you?'

'I'm gonna die in a tunnel, or falling out of a tree,' she said. 'Or run over by a JCB. Why d'you think I quit the camp?'

They drank at the table. Easing the curtains apart, she emptied the window of condensation and saw it was almost dark outside. A long trek home, torchless, on the broken ground. But she was bang awake now and fine, full of energy; the prospect of hiking back in the black – just treading out over the fields, the moor, all night if she wanted – wasn't so bad. Barefoot. The chill of damp grass against her soles and among her toes. Ten, midnight, two a.m., whenever, she'd sooner be out there than scuffing along under the sodium lights of some brick backstreet.

'This place looks so different once the light's gone,' she said.

'I don't think so.' The subtle clunk of Ethan's mug being replaced on the table. 'If you spend long enough gazing out across those fields you never lose the points of familiarity. Even when the snows come, the structure of the land doesn't alter.'

She looked again at the darkening landscape, picturing it buried, laminated with snow, then closed the curtains and turned to look at him. He was tidying the desk, slipping paperwork into folders, sleeving photographs, removing the earpiece flex from the micro-cassette and ejecting the tape for labelling and filing. His actions set up small tremors in the surface of her drink.

'Another poem?' she said, smiling, eyes on the tape. He smiled too.

She'd asked about the poetry during one of their ops, baffling him. Even when she'd re-created that scene in the car park outside the Place (him, in the Toyota, her overhearing the line . . . *I saw through a hole in the page* . . .), Ethan hadn't been able to make immediate sense of what she was saying. Then, with understanding had come his enjoyment of her mistake, and of his being taken for a poet. But no explanation. No placing of those elliptical words in context for her.

'They must mean something,' she'd said.

And he'd replied: 'Why must words mean something?'

'Ethan, you're starting to sound like me.'

She asked again, now, in the caravan's milk-and-honey illumina-tion. Hesitant, watchful of her face, as if his decision was concealed there, Ethan retrieved a shoebox of sequenced microcassette tapes and flipped through them for the one whose neatly printed dates enclosed that day they'd first met. Screening with the earpiece, he fast-forwarded, played, rewound, until an alteration in his expression told her he'd located it, the line. He unplugged the earpiece and pressed play:

The girl in the café is the same girl I saw through a hole in the page.

He clicked off. 'The newspaper,' he said. 'There was a story on the front of *The Monitor* that week about a sheep kill at the Toadstools. I clipped the article for my files, and there you were, on page three, smiling out of the hole at me.'

'Is that it?' She was neither surprised nor flattered to be worthy of a dictated mention, seeing as she'd heard him mutter all sorts of non-cat related stuff into that gadget. 'You didn't think that, maybe, it was some kind of a sign? Only, seeing as you don't believe in signs, you just put it down to your definition of a coincidence. Yeah?'

Ethan didn't reply.

'And *then* I turn up at the caravan, offering to dowse the cat. Even at the Ethan Gray Academy of Science two coincidences must equal an omen?'

He was restoring the tape to its proper place, looking anywhere but at her; she thought he might be enjoying the tease less than she was, or that he was regretting the sharing of the secret with her of the poem that wasn't a poem. She eased off.

'That was such a crap picture,' she said. 'The missing bob. The inane grin.'

Ethan's comment was soft, almost inaudible, so that she misheard him as saying *I thought you were so dutiful*; which made no sense, until she swapped a b-sound for the d-sound and allowed herself a moment to be stunned by that.

'Tell me about Susan.'

'Susan?'

The questions: Was *she* beautiful? Do you miss her? Did you love her?

Ethan said he had loved her, then ceased loving her, had missed her, then ceased missing her, and that she had been beautiful, then ceased to be beautiful. She thought of Richie. And she realized that in asking Ethan about Susan she was really asking herself about Richie and about the perception and cessation of beauty.

She had no idea of the time or of how long they'd been talking. The lamp was making her woozy with its warmth and the faint tang of gas – nice and mellow woozy, spliff or booze woozy. Also, the lulling cosiness, the intimacy, of their voices, the roll and pitch of head-to-head speech in a small place. She had the sensation that the caravan wasn't grounded, but afloat, drifting like a life-raft, and if she drew back the curtains now there would be only the limitless undulating grey-black-blue-black of an oceanscape.

'Is there anywhere we can go skinny-dipping?' she said. Ethan looked at her, like he was trying to work out if she was joking. 'A lake or a river or something?'

'There's the tarn.' He pointed east. 'But it's an hour's walk from here.'

Her next words were a mistake. She knew as soon as she'd said them, as she was saying them, as they formed in her head. But, she said them. Because because because they were so close to what she wanted they felt right even in their wrongness. It was as if the words held a meaning separate from the fact, the act, they implied, and had to be spoken for the sheer irresistible thrill of their impact. She said: 'Or we could just take our clothes off anyway. Here.'

She recognized her mistake in his face, and inside herself. There could be no simplicity in the consequences of the simple, physical enactment of her proposition; not this, not now, not with him with all of his confused expectations.

'Look, Eeth, forget I said that.' She pinched the end of her nose till it hurt, till her eyes watered, then let go. 'Shit. I'm so sorry. I'm . . . look, I think I'm going to go now.' She nodded to herself. 'I'm going to go home, yeah? Yeah.'

She left. Ethan said nothing, nothing at all, and she apologized once again and got her gear together and left alone on foot in the dark.

32

GAVIN DRINKELL (*journalist*):

TALES OF A RAMBLING MAN, was the headline. Nice pun. I don't write the headlines, but I liked that one. I'd have preferred them to work 'stalking' or 'stalker' into it, but these have a more sinister double-meaning and the slant of the piece, in line with the brief, was 'gentle mockery'. *A profile of the loner who quit the rat-race to go on a wild cat chase.* Apart from which, Ethan Gray's definition of stalking didn't square with most people's. Six hours, I spent with him – up hill and down dale in the pissing rain – and I'm still none the wiser. To be honest, I don't think he knew what he was up to either.

I've got the cutting here . . . yeah, this is him on stalking:

'To know the cat you have to know the territory – think as the cat thinks, live as the cat lives, walk where the cat walks. At first I used to see the cat in every shadow and unexplained shape: a tree stump, a boulder, a rubbish sack caught in a bush. Then I stopped looking for the cat and started looking for myself. Stalking is tracking without tracks. It's a matter of both seeking and of becoming that which is sought. If I was the cat, how would I behave? What would I do? Where would I go? Which route would I take? When I stalk the cat, I am the cat.'

I asked him straight: what would you say to people who think you're barmy?

This stuff never made it into the final piece, but I've got it all on tape . . .

Do you think I'm barmy?

No, it's . . . thing is, it's what some people might think.

I don't have anything to say to people who think like that.

[*pause; sound of teeth being tapped with plastic biro*]

You like it out here, then, do you?

Yes, I do.

Hey, live and let live, I say.

Do you like living where you do?

Ethan, I'm just trying to understand what makes you tick.

No, you're not. That's precisely what you're not doing.

[*pause*]

Don't you miss companionship? Human contact? *People*, basically?

People like you?

Look, I'm just doing my job.

And this is my fucking job.

Wandering around aimlessly in the mud all day, getting rained on.

[*long pause*]

It it it doesn't always rain.

[*click*]

See what I mean? An undiagnosed care-in-the-community case, minus the care and minus the community – that was him.

33

With Richie, there was no cataclysm. No instant of vitriol or violence or revelation that could be isolated as the fatal point, the *cause*, of their disintegration. It wasn't even a break-up so much as a dispersal. Chronic, and unilateral. Her feelings towards him had simply – not simply, complicatedly – lost coherence; scrambled by Richie, or at least by a gathering sense of his reluctance to let her breathe her own air as well as his.

'Spoons, being with you, being with *us*, isn't enough for me – I also need to go on being all the things I was before I knew you. All the things I am.'

'You can.'

'Not with you, I can't.'

'You mean dowsing?' he said.

'I just don't understand what it is about me that makes you feel so threatened.'

'Threatened? You're the one who feels threatened.'

'Okay, you build tunnels. That's your kick and it's cool. It's cool. You build a tunnel, and I crawl right in there with you and it's your tunnel and I'm cool with that. I love that. Yeah?'

Spoon-faced. Blank with incomprehension.

'But you . . . what it is,' she said, fumbling for the words' meaning even as she formulated them, 'what it is, right, is you don't love the places I have to go to that are mine. That aren't yours.'

All this being part of the rambling, spliffy, post-spliffy hour upon hour of head-to-head bender-speak on what turned out to be her final evening at Flashville. Dowsing wasn't the whole of it, but it was a chunk. There were fragments too – an accretion of gestures, glances, words, actions, moods brought them to this.

'You know your trouble, Plum?' he said. 'You live, you *choose* to

live, in this fucking fantasy world where reality and intuition are in
communication breakdown.'

'See, you're doing it now.'

'Doing what now? Christ's sake, doing *what*?'

The decision to leave wasn't made during that last night of talk,
or declared to him then, or at all, as it happened. In the morning,
while Richie slept, she packed and left. No note, nothing. The guilt
of this remained with her. But what could she have written that
hadn't already been said? Apart from the deliciously, maliciously,
ironic: *I dowsed myself and the pendulum said: Go.*

Tumblejack Hill. Invisible to them, even though they were ascend-
ing it. They'd driven as far as possible, then proceeded on foot,
torchlit, shy of sunrise and the approximate, appointed time. Walking among trees, at first; a managed wood, its clearings stacked
with pyramids of irregular logs. A wood pigeon started up near by
with a whipcrack of wings, and pheasants' cries measured the
human intrusion. At another time of year, she thought, this place
would be perfumed with wild garlic. Now, it smelled damp and
wintry and of decomposition.

Out of the woods, and on to the open fellside. She was warmed
from the hike, though the air smarted her face and filled her lungs
with cold. Ethan kept his beam on the track, she used hers to sweep
for the sheep whose bleats betrayed their presence in the darkened
pasture. She asked about the name of the hill, assuming a connection
with the nursery rhyme; but he told her of a reclusive seventeenth-
century prospector, called John, who'd panned the streams here for
minerals, semi-precious stones and ore, washing his finds in a
tumbling barrel. Besides, wasn't it Jill rather than Jack who took
the tumble? Her smile at his technicality created a grey plume of
breath. Three hundred years ago, Ethan said, the slopes would've
been entirely wooded, but depletion for timber and for grazing had
shaved them almost bald. He stopped talking abruptly, as if irritated
by himself, or afraid that she might be. Unconsciously, they'd fallen
in step, establishing a momentum that seemed to generate its own

energy. Coarse stone chips crunched beneath their boots, made louder still by the black, enveloping hush. Like the sound in your head when you ate biscuits.

'I missed you,' he said.

She hesitated. 'I guess I must've missed this too, or I wouldn't be doing it.'

She'd phoned, the morning after, to apologize for walking out on him like that, as if the walking out was the issue. She'd rung again, a week later, to ask if he was all right. He said he was confused; being pretty much how she felt, and seeing as life was so confusing, which it was in her experience, maybe confusion was a natural and only-to-be-expected state for them, or anyone, to be in? *Maybe, to resist confusion is to go against the grain of what it is to be human, yeah?* He told her she was talking crap and she laughed and said he was dead right. But that didn't mean she was ready to see him, or for them to deconstruct all of this. The third call was made while she was still allowing Ethan time and space to accustom himself to her absence: she had dowsed the cat at Tumblejack Hill and how was he fixed for dawn the following day?

'Here.' She mimed a triangle on the map, its area defined by a Neolithic long-barrow, an O.S. trig point and a ruined Victorian tower. 'All we need now is cover.'

They were on a bench at the base of the folly, recuperating from the last section and sharing a water canister. Night was being dispersed by the first slow seepage of a lightening horizon. Rabbit excavations perforated the earth at their feet and, below the lookout, the craters of long-defunct stone pits combined with the half-light to lend the land the semblance of a shell-damaged battlefield. Much lower still, a canal and a river drew parallel metallic lines across a plain of partially flooded meadows. And beyond that, a ridge that rose out of the valley like the terraced tiers of a vast sports stadium.

'Cover, up here?' he said.

'Well, up here is where we wait, so . . . yeah.'

Ethan turned, and she looked where he was looking: the exposed interior of the plateau. A scattering of defoliated silver-birch saplings was the only obvious break in the rough grass, heather and crowberry. Sheep had strayed here, foraging, flushing out an occasional grouse. *Go-bak go-bak go-bak-bak-bak urrrr*. He used the binoculars, right to left, right to left, then froze. Handing them to her, he said: 'What d'you reckon to that?'

She lifted the bins, sharpening the trig point, then the shallow hump of the burial mound, tracking across the moortop – the dowsed triangle – for whatever hide he had spotted: a pocket of gorse, a drystone wall, a grouse butt. 'Where?'

'On a direct line from here to the long-barrow, about three-quarter distance.'

'Where? Oh, yeah, yeah got it. What is it?'

'A bothy, I'd say.'

'Uh-huh.' She lowered the bins, grinning at him. 'Cool.'

Now that they were working, now that the op framed their conversation, Ethan seemed to ease into the fact of being here. The contagious tension of the rendezvous, the drive, the climb, had lessened almost to nothing. He was back in his element. Only, she wasn't sure if his mood change contained her as well as the situation, or how she could tell. What she did know was that her lips were greasy with flavoured salve, and whenever Ethan took a slug of water he would taste cherry on the neck of the canister.

'We should hike over there and get ourselves set up,' he said.

Footsteps. A woman in a yellow vest and shorts appeared, running hard up the track which had fetched them. She halted, hands on hips, head tipped back. Gulping air. Her top was tongued with damp, and moisture pooled in the hollow at the base of her throat. A chunky black watch enclosed her wrist like one half of a futuristic pair of handcuffs. The runner registered them in turn. A grunt, a slight shift of the eyebrows was all she could manage by way of hi.

'Hiya.'

Ethan didn't say anything.

'Don't . . . make me . . . talk.' She was thin, pale, the skin drawn taut over sinew and muscle and the knotty articulation of her skeleton. She bent over, touched her toes, held the position, then raised herself again, unclipping a water bottle from her waistband and taking neat, rationed sips. Still breathless, she said: 'Going far?'

They answered simultaneously. *Nap. No.*

The woman used the bottle as a pointer. 'Here it comes.'

To the north, diagonal streaks of charcoal-grey sketched the space between sky and land; a curtain, progressing almost imperceptibly along the dale, dampening the air where they stood with its imminence. She sensed a tightening in her temples and at the backs of her eyes from the alteration in pressure. A wind got up, making flapping flags of their waterproofs as she and Ethan hurried to put them on.

'The tower is haunted, you know.'

The words tugged her attention to the folly. When she glanced at the woman again, she found herself being stared at. A look, even though they were strangers, of recognition – or wariness or complicity or alarm; whatever it was, it was written in the gaunt, sweaty features. And in the eyes that were too large for her face.

She was about to ask her – ask her what? something, she was about to speak, even if it was only to wonder aloud what she meant about the tower – but this fleeting connection between them had been broken. The runner was resetting her watch, doing the jogging-on-the-spot routine. The limbering.

'That's me, then.'

She watched her descend the steep trail past the quarry delphs, skittering, arms pecking the air as if jerked by a puppeteer, watched her reduce to a vivid yellow stripe among the gloom of a copse where the drop of land merged from olive to shadow to black. Ethan urged her to come away, but she continued to watch the runner until there was nothing left of her to see.

'What's wrong?'

'Nothing.' She closed her pack and shouldered it. 'Come on.'

'Do you know her?'

'Nap. Forget it, it's nothing. It's just me, spooking myself.'

34

PROF. HENRY HARLEY, PH.D. (*professor of zoology*):
I understand he had some schooling in zoology; certainly, his early
reports displayed a degree of objective rigour. However, I began
to observe a change in tenor and content in the final months.
Methodologically and empirically, his fieldwork became less sound,
his submissions poorly reasoned, subjective, factually flawed and,
frankly, downright eccentric. One was typed in green rather than
the usual black – due, his postscript said, to a discrepancy between
the stated and actual contents of a box of typewriter ribbon. I cite
this by way of illustrating a general deterioration; more troubling
was the, by now, marked deviation from good science. By good
science, I mean the traditional strategy of thought, observation,
formulation of theory, prediction, experiment, accumulation of
evidence and counter-evidence, amendment of theory, etc. Mr
Gray, increasingly, was deploying dubious experimental methods
allied to the selection of 'facts' which fitted his theory and rejection
of those which did not. Most disturbing of all, was his claim that,
with the aid of his 'lover' – a water diviner by the name of Cleo
Fortune – he had forecast the incident in December at Tumblejack
Hill. Verification was impossible as the papers reached me, and
were postmarked, several days *after* the said incident.

I am neither qualified nor willing – even with the benefit of
hindsight – to say whether he was predisposed towards obsessional
behaviour. But it was evident to me from his reports that a legitimate interest in proving the existence of a non-indigenous big cat
had developed into unhealthy frustration at his protracted failure
to, as it were, 'bag the beast'. By the end, I believe Mr Gray was
demonstrably irrational.

35

They sat cramped in the drystone shelter; half its four walls remained intact, forming an L that supported enough of the corrugated-iron roof to protect them. The sleet set up a fierce clatter directly overhead, peppering them with grains of rust. The bothy was damp and draughty and stank of lanolin and sheep shit. Across the rubble of the two disintegrated walls, they surveyed the moor through slanting sheets of white.

'I loved weather like this at the camp,' she said. 'It's just so, I dunno, so . . . awesome, isn't it?'

Ethan had primed the cameras, but there would be no filming until this lifted. He spoke the date, time and location into the microcassette, raising his voice above the downpour. 'Conditions: *awesome*; visibility: thirty metres.'

'And, afterwards, everyone would come out of their benders and stand around looking, and taking the air, like something fundamental had happened. Like something had changed.' She inhaled. 'I used to get such a buzz.'

'Elemental.'

'Yeah, elemental. Exactly.'

They were sitting side by side, compelled to huddle so close that any movement – the raising of a hand, the stretching of a leg – produced a synthetic whisper from the friction of their waterproofs. She was shivering.

'What are you thinking?' he said.

'I'm thinking I'm hungry. I'm thinking we should eat before this clears.'

Ethan yawned. Knowing him, he would've slept poorly, anticipating the dawn. Aiming a hand at the sleet, the inhospitable bleakness of the moortop, he told her the sighting of a cat, or any creature, was *improbable*. She wanted to say that the purpose of waiting was to wait, the purpose of being here was to be here.

What she said was: 'I should've dowsed for this.'

'What?'

'Weather. I should've dowsed for it.'

Her hands were clasped around one knee, fingers interlocked. The skin, where it wasn't whitened by pressure, had been discoloured with the cold – violet, as though stained from dyeing clothes or from picking blackcurrants.

'You should get yourself some gloves,' Ethan said.

'I have gloves. I have two pairs of gloves, I just don't have them with me.' She pulled the cuffs of her jacket down. 'Or were you suggesting that as a life option?'

'Are they thermal?'

She laughed. 'Ethan, it's whatever time it is and I'm hungry and we're sitting in a shepherd's bothy and I am not going to discuss gloves with you.'

The sleet shower appeared to be intensifying, contracting still further the hub of visibility which they occupied. She searched in her pack, bringing out two parcels of food: marmalade pancakes she'd made early that morning, rolled up and sheathed in grease-proof paper.

'All ingredients by unwitting courtesy of Place du Roy.'

Cold and oily, but delicious. Ethan opened a flask of strong-smelling coffee and filled two beakers. It was unsweetened so she fingered a scoop of marmalade into hers, aware of him watching her. Then, he did the same. The odd simplicity of this replication made her unaccountably sad. And, when he spoke, there was a sadness in him too.

'I don't understand what happened that night,' he said.

'Me neither.'

'I don't know what you want.'

'You have to stop saying things that require me to answer "me neither".'

'Chloe, d'you think . . .'

'Look, Eeth, I'm not a very tidy person to be around right now. Yeah? Since I came here, since the camp . . . basically, I came here to sort my head of guys – of one guy in particular. Richie, okay. Spoons. I'm not really untangled from all that just yet. In my head, I mean.'

'Spoons.'

'That's what we called him.'

She looked down at their feet, four boots in a line on the compacted mud of the bothy floor. Hers were not much smaller than his, and she was surprised to be noticing this for the first time.

'You wanted to go skinny-dipping with me,' he said.

'That night.' She ate, washed it down with coffee. 'That night, I was horny – horny enough to push things, push *us*, to a place where I didn't think we should go just yet. Or at all, I don't know. But I started to push, and then I stopped myself. And I'm sorry. I really am sorry.' She turned to look at him. 'Does any of this make sense?'

'What place?'

'I'm a mess at the moment. *We* would be a mess.' She sighed, facing out again into the harsh white of the sleet. 'It's . . . actually, what it is, is I think I, Ethan, I think I could really like you. And I suppose I wish we hadn't met when we did, so soon after Richie. Fuck. Look, I shouldn't be saying any of this.'

'I can't stop thinking about you.'

She found herself attending to the quality of his voice – its clipped clarity in the chill air, in the retort of the roof, the drystone, the bare black mud, and in the palpable contraction of his vocal chords. What he was saying – what was he saying? – she didn't want to think about what he was saying. What he'd said. It was only sounds. If it was only sounds it didn't have to mean anything. Her hands were tacky with marmalade. She ran a fingertip along a fold in her cagoule so that it collected a film of orange rust.

'It's starting to clear,' she said.

She stared out at the thinning sleet. Her mind should've been reeling with him, with this, but all she could think about, all she could see or feel, was the woman. The runner in the sweat-soaked

yellow vest. The woman, the freak weather, Ethan . . . this whole
dowse was going weird on her. She made herself concentrate on
him, on what he was doing and saying. He wasn't eating. He was
holding the pancake and not eating it. He was heavy alongside her
in the bothy with the weight of his own words.

'You came back,' Ethan said. 'I didn't think I'd see you again, but
you you you came back.'

'Yeah, well, there's a cat to find.' She nodded to herself. 'I think
we should be professional about this, don't you?'

The sleet had stopped. If the cat appeared now her blackness
would be resolute against the gleaming salty-white surface of the
moor. Together, they waited in silence for the manifestation of the
panther.

36

The sheep carcass was discovered in woods below the hill three days after the vigil in the bothy. The post-mortem report was leaked to the press two days after that. But Tumblejack Hill still bugged her. The pendulum response had been her most potent yet – too strong, too complex, for her to ascribe it to the kill alone. Leaving there that day, she'd contained an overwhelming sense of departing from the vicinity of an event, the completeness and non-intuitive facts of which eluded her. And she sussed, she *felt*, that the woman – the runner in the yellow vest – was right there, buried deep beneath the layers of the dowse. Only, days later, she still didn't know how or why; or whether she would ever get to find out that there'd been more to all this than a savaged ewe.

She called her mom, who said the name of the place was terrific.

'Mom, this is serious.'

'Hon, you've been telling me about Tumblejack Hill for, I guess, ten minutes, and, if we're keeping a tally, I'd say "Ethan" is beating "jogger" and "cat" five to one. You want an unaccounted variable, I offer you the phrase "look no further". Huh?'

Ethan.

To begin with, even before they met, she'd seen his lifestyle as a celebration of individualism, a rejection of society's conventions and constraints. Now, she wasn't so sure that what she'd taken for robust independence might not be mutating into joyless and debilitating and dysfunctional anomie.

'I thought I was reading things wrong because of him. Maybe it's *him* I've been misreading. D'you think?'

'It's possible,' Mom said.

'Or maybe I'm misreading myself?'

'You know my take on the idiot response, hon.'

When an idiot invokes the idiot response, she questions only the response.

Telling ZZ of her anxieties about the jogger – the spooking of herself, then and since.

'It wasn't just me. She sensed it too, you could see it in her eyes.'

'What you saw in her eyes might've been a reaction to what she saw in yours,' ZZ said. 'You spooked yourself, you spooked her too.'

'Nap. Something happened to her that day.'

They were sitting on Moon Rock after climbing tuition, cross-legged, surveying a landscape glazed in light the colour of diluted apple juice. Her first lesson, with him. He was more patient than Richie, more composed. She asked how she'd shaped up and ZZ said that in a crisis she would be an extreme liability. The tips of the middle fingers of her right hand were moist pink ovals. Her wrists ached. Her back, neck, hips, every part of her ached so much it felt good. Way below, the town arranged itself in the dale like too many dice tumbled at once along a groove. The Zeez asked if she smoked and she said no, then he explained himself and she said yes. He rolled one to share.

'If we were at my place now,' he said, 'I could show you a picture of a ghost.'

'Yeah?'

'Taken on the approach to the summit of Yr Wyddfa. Snowdon.'

ZZ described the photograph: a man stands at the edge of a ridge, beyond and slightly to one side of him a huge greyish figure floats on the mist looming out of the valley below – vaguely humanoid, faintly haloed by the colours of the spectrum.

She watched his face. 'Go on, then.'

'The man on the ridge is me. The *ghost* is me.'

'So what is it, some kind of optical illusion?'

'A Brocken Spectre.'

Named, he told her, after mountains in Germany where the phenomenon was commonplace. In the early morning or late afternoon – depending on the position of the sun, favourable weather conditions and a suitable precipice – a climber's own shadow could be projected, vastly magnified, on to lower-lying cloud.

'Must be pretty amazing.'

'It's not connected to you, like a normal shadow.' ZZ animated his words with his great hands, his arms that looked too heavy to be raised away from his body even by their own implicit strength. 'It's out there, hovering.' He smiled. 'Freaked me out, until the bloke who took the picture explained it to me.'

She unravelled the reason for the anecdote and, shaking her head, said it wasn't at all the same as her encounter with the jogger. A dowser learned to recognize when she was or was not projecting herself on to a situation. The real and the imaginary, and their points of overlap and separation, were the raw materials she worked with each time she unpouched the pendulum. They were her medium.

'Zeez, that woman is out there somewhere with the secret of what I dowsed.'

'I should get a print of the Brocken Spectre for you to give to Ethan. Pin it up in the caravan for him.'

'Anyway, I actually believe in ghosts.'

They passed the spliff back and forth in silence for a while, the smoke almost blue in the frail winter sun. *This rock I'm sitting on is 320 million years old. I am twenty-two.*

Dope-think. She smiled and drew some more of the stuff inside her. This was good, being here, doing this. There was an equanimity about the guy that made him easy company. Also, an integrity that inclined her to find reasons to dislike herself, but, curiously, not to dislike him for making her feel like that.

'So, where does "ZZ" come from?'

'From my ZZ Top beard.'

'You don't have a ZZ Top beard.'

'I used to.' He stroked his chin, whiskery with several days' inattention. 'I still grow one every December. A shorter version.

For cold-weather climbing.'

The Zeez told her he was planning an expedition next year, to the Himalayas; only, strictly speaking, it was the Himalaya, no *s*, this being as close as he'd come to sounding anything like Ethan. Although he also said he didn't reckon you'd give a fuck about correct plural forms if you were stranded on Dhaulagiri in a blizzard.

After another spliffy lull in the conversation, he released some more words on a smoke-breath. 'Do you believe the cat exists?'

That depended on how he defined 'existence'. Oh, and 'belief'. ZZ smiled at her and nodded and flicked ash, and confessed to being a simple mountaineering man who, generally, kept his philosophizing to himself.

'You know what I'm asking you,' he said, still enjoying this. 'And if you want to hand me some bollocky psycho-wank, fine. But don't expect me to join in.'

'You're asking if I believe in the existence of the cat – yes or no, yeah?'

'Yep.'

'Well, it depends how you define "yes". Oh, and "no".'

'Fuck off.'

ZZ was laughing. They both were, though what with the blow and the affability of sitting, jawing, on a rock, it was hard for her to tell what caused either of them to be amused, or even to say the things they said.

'I hope your mate appreciates the way your mind works, for both your sakes.'

She gestured at Sun Rock, at the old quarry. 'Can you see Ethan doing this?'

'Climbing? From what I know of him, he wouldn't make a climber all the time he's got a hole in his arse. He'd be fixated on the summit, the conditions, the gear, or whatever was going on inside here.' ZZ tapped his head. 'That isn't climbing.'

'What is climbing, then?'

'Climbing is climbing. It's handholds and footholds. It's about being absolutely concentrated on where you are now and how to get yourself a few centimetres higher.' There seemed to be nothing intentionally cool in how he spoke, or to suggest he even valued her evaluation of him. 'Climbing is as easy as that.'

She might've felt protective of Ethan, but ZZ's tone wasn't derogatory, it was matter-of-fact. Not arrogant matter-of-fact, just matter-of-fact. She watched him take a final drag of spliff, then flatten the tip between finger and thumb, slip the butt in his pocket and zip the pocket shut. The Zeez looked her full in the face now, being what she was waiting for him to do, and the smile was there, also waiting for him.

'What about me?' she said. 'Would I make a climber all the time I've got a hole in my arse?'

She ached even worse the day after the lesson. Moving with such robotic stiffness that the least of her hassles were the two thimbles of sticking plaster. Roy relieved her of washing-up duty because of them, and food prep, what with the hygiene implications. *In future you injure yourself here, not in your own time.* First thing, he'd sought a quiet word. He was staring at her fingers, but he didn't want to talk about them, it was just someplace to look that wasn't her eyes.

'The old boy in the flat above next door.' Roy nodded towards the launderette. 'Jeff. He says there was a bit of a row going on last night. Out the back of here.'

'Oh, yeah. Yeah there was.'

'Friend of yours, was it?'

'Kind of.' She wanted still to be in bed, and what she should do was tell Roy to tell this Jeff to get a fucking life. She emptied her lungs, then refilled them. 'It was just a guy, banging on the door and mouthing off 'cos I wouldn't let him in.'

He looked at her. 'Not that Hermit nutter?'

'No, no, not him. Just some rat-arsed guy.'

The boss smirked, and she saw the price of last night would be a period of piss-taking – and what was new or unmanageable about that? 'Drunk with love, was he?'

'Roy, I'm a very attractive woman after ten pints.'

Despite the distraction of work, her thought-processes, post-Tumblejack Hill – Ethan, the cat, the jogger, Mom, ZZ, Roy, last night – were dishevelled. What she'd said to Ethan about dwelling in a natural state of confusion wasn't crap, it was the way she was. She'd dowsed her shape, years ago, and she was the shape of the fractal.

The Zeez had wanted to be absolutely and unequivocally clear about the way of things between Ethan and her. Perched on the Moon, post-spliff, discussing the skinny-dipping scene and its aftermath and the bothy-talk which had, but hadn't quite, sorted matters. *There's still, I dunno, an . . . expectancy.* Saying this to ZZ, and him nodding, nodding, and asking for whom, and she said for Ethan. And he'd nodded some more and gazed out wisely and serenely over the town, where she was looking.

The banging on the door. Easing out of bed, slinging on a gown and going downstairs – stiff, aching, raw-fingered – to use the spyhole. Even though she'd guessed it would be Gavin, an image of Richie flashed across her anticipation, but sure enough there was Gav, face like plasticine in the fish-eye, blond hair black with rain. Making her furious, and sick in her stomach. Who the fuck was he to be doing this to her? She'd wanted to yank open the door and confront him, abuse him as he was abusing her. But she didn't. She went back upstairs. In the bedsit, his commotion was louder still, amplified by the echo-chamber of the yard and the metal bins. *Fuckenloonybitch. Iknowyoucanhearme you . . . fucken . . . slag.* Footsteps, outside. Something thudding against the wall. She went over to the window, careful to keep out of sight, peering obliquely into the street, where Gavin stood yellowed beneath a lamp-post, swaying, looking around as if for another missile, but finding only an empty beer can. The shouting started up again, face tilted towards her window, which would be dark and impenetrable and vacant to him. Fuck him. Fuck him. The noise, she could shut out of her head. What really shook her, what couldn't be so easily sealed off, was the incredibility of the timing. The negative serendipity not just of him but of what she could also see from her window.

The coincidentality of it all.

There was Gavin. And there, parked up the street – lights off, engine off – a 4WD Toyota pick-up, its red bodywork discernible at the dim reaches of another light.

Cold goosebumped her arms and legs. She shrugged off the gown and retreated beneath the warm sleeping bag, unzipped and splayed duvet-style across the mattress. She'd not noticed until now but the room reeked of pizza, red wine and dope. She lay looking over at the window. He was still standing there, motionless, peering out as she had done, withdrawn from view and from the glare of sodium, the room's dense grey-blue making a statue of his naked-ness. Making him pale and smoky.

'D'you want me to go down?' ZZ said.

'No,' she said. 'I want you to come back to bed.'

37

MR HAFEEZ ALAM FRCVS (*veterinary pathologist*):

Firstly, I am examining the exterior – particularly the neck, throat and breast areas – for signs of injury. We see, here [points with tweezers to bloodstained puncture], where a tooth – probably an upper canine – has gone in. If I skin the neck right down to the flesh [peels fleece back], we get a clearer look at the penetration. It's quite horrendous, actually. Skinning the rest of the upper body [displays lacerations in fleece] we can identify claw marks in a group of four. The distance between the outer incisions [uses calliper] is 75 mm, suggesting an animal larger than a labrador. As for the flesh [points with calliper], we note that the cuts are, again, deep. Just here, on the opposite flank, is another wound. As you can see, a gaping, ragged hole. Really, a quite horrific injury. Three ribs have been broken – here, here, and here [points] the bone is shattered. The ewe has, literally, had a hole punched in its ribcage.

The injuries are consistent with a hypothesis of this sheep being attacked from the rear – the predator leaping on to its back and striking a ferocious blow to the side of the body with one paw while grabbing hold with the other, using the claws to drag its victim down. With the ewe grounded and restrained, the predator delivers a deep, immensely powerful – instantaneously fatal – bite to the neck, severing the spinal cord. In my opinion, it is unlikely in the extreme that a dog – or any other indigenous British predator – would have attacked in this way, or with the power and ferocity to inflict damage of this type and to this extent. If this was the Serengeti, I would speculate with confidence that we were examining the consequences of a leopard kill.

PART FOUR

Oscillation

38

It has been five days now, and still the nightmares persist. She might yet report the incident, if only in the hope that by infecting someone else with the horror she will free herself of it. Many times, in her head, she has made that call, opened the door to the police officer, admitted him to her house, watched his expression alter as her statement progresses. Initially, it is straightforward: the steep track down through the trees from Tumblejack Hill is slippery and a few times she nearly loses her footing. But soon she is out among fields where the descent is less severe. Sleet begins to fall as she crosses a meadow to join the canal towpath, gaining intensity, so sharp on her skin it is like being pricked with pins. High above, the skyline silhouette of the folly – the moortop itself – are obliterated by the downpour. The policeman will be politely attentive, making notes, posing an occasional question. Taking her seriously.

As she runs, she thinks about the couple. Will she mention this? She recalls the surprise of encountering them; most mornings she meets no one, and has the bench to herself. The girl's hair is extraordinary. She wonders if it requires effort to create that style, or whether it is the result of careful neglect. When the girl smiles, her own smile is accompanied by an involuntary contraction of her facial muscles and a sour, hollow taste in her throat. No, there would be no reason for the policeman to know of the girl. And if she omits the girl she must omit the man; this is less problematic, for her impression of him is non-visual, incidental – a brooding sullenness. Moreover, unlike the girl, he figures in her nightmares, and she decidedly does not wish to tell the police or anyone else about those.

Her statement would continue with the finding of shelter, squatting in the hollowed-out bole of a diseased tree in the woods that flank the towpath. The sleet eases, then stops. She emerges, speckled with flakes of rotten bark, so stiff and cold she must limber up before setting off again. Her feet splash the insides of her legs with the surface water that has collected on the track. It is now, she will tell the policeman, that she hears a noise. Not a noise, so much as a commotion. This will sharpen the officer's interest. Two sheep burst out of the woodland scrub to her left, less than ten metres ahead. She thinks they are about to leap directly into the canal but they career towards her, almost tripping her as they hurtle by. She registers, without analysis, that this is odd. Now, she has come to realize that the sheep run towards her, rather than away, because they are less afraid of her than of what it is that pursues them.

She sees the cat. It crashes from the undergrowth, slewing to a halt on the path in front of her, so close she could reach out and stroke it. It is entirely black, and as big as a wolfhound. The policeman's rapt fascination, at this point, will be qualified by investigative scepticism, the scrutiny of her face, mannerisms, words, for evidence of delusion. Or of falsehood. Or the possibility of error and misinterpretation. She will speak of the split second of petrifying alarm. Then, before she can act, think or even scream, the beast rears up on two legs and swipes her across the face with its right forepaw. She feels no pain, she feels only the engulfing shock of water. Surfacing, she manages to believe that the canal will save her because a cat will not follow her into water. She surfaces again – stunned but conscious, treading water, choking it up. Alive. She looks for the cat. But the cat is gone. The officer will stare at the vivid jawline contusion, the fractured cheek, the black eye, the cuts. He will assess alternative explanations, perhaps. Human brutality: a husband, a lover? An accident? A self-inflicted injury? But he will not put these to her until the police surgeon has an opportunity to evaluate the injuries.

There, she has rehearsed the separation of the real images from those of her nightmares. Yet she knows, even so, that she will be disbelieved and that there will be nothing, forensically, to substantiate what she says. Too incredible, too fantastic. It will be harmful, humiliating and degrading to her – personally, professionally – for her story to be made public. Also, she is scared that she might break down in the telling: facts blurring with the fiction of her hallucinations, spilling everything in a cathartic release, relieving herself of the pressure of containing the visions that fill her head. Every hour. Every day. Every night. She sees the cat crouched over the freshly killed corpse of a sheep, its bloodied muzzle buried between the hind legs as it feeds there, pulling away raw flaps of skin, flesh and muscle. And then it is not the sheep upon which the cat is feeding but her: eating her buttocks, her thighs, her puden-dum, eating right up inside her – vulva, vagina, cervix, womb – gnawing, tearing, feasting on her. She has hold of the cat by its ears, pulling, bucking against the clamp of its jaws. When at last she tugs the head from between her legs, she sees it is not the cat that has been devouring her, but the man. The enigmatic, laconic, unsmiling man at the tower. The man is smiling now, though – with relish, half his face drooling gore.

She sits alone at home and tells no one any of this. As far as the casualty staff, the GP, her family, friends and colleagues are aware, she slipped on a muddy towpath, smashing her face on the corru-gated-steel retaining wall of the canal as she fell in. She is recovering well, thank you, from the physical and psychological trauma. Soon, she will be better. The true, false and imaginary versions will fuse into one, sealed away in a private compartment of her brain where they can cause no contamination.

39

Ethan pitched up at the Place on Christmas Eve, lunchtime, amid all the decorations, a medley of festive muzak, the cracking of crackers, staff and punters in paper hats, and the hectic cooking, serving and gobbling up of turkey roll plus trimmings. Her own hat – navy, given the unavailability of black – being fixed to her dreads with Blu-tac. In the neon-lit fumy swelter his face looked waxen, his clothing uncomfortably hirsute. He was standing at the counter, clutching a laminated menu as if for the sake of occupying his hands. She steered him to Table Eleven, well out of Royshot.

'This place is tropical,' she said. 'There's mould in the kitchen that only grows in equatorial regions.'

Ethan made no move to strip down. She asked if he wanted anything to eat or drink. He didn't. He'd brought the menu with him, which meant there were now three at the table, instead of the requisite two, and one short at the counter. The boss, she said, was the sole custodian of the gravity of this anomaly.

She placed a hand on her breastbone. 'I am talking so much crap today.'

'I need to speak to you,' Ethan said.

'Sure, sure.' She shot a look towards Roy, busy beveraging. Punter waiting on Seven, Tab Four to be cleared and re-laid. 'Hang on a sec, yeah?'

Seven was reading sport. A roll-your-own balanced in the slot of a foil ashtray, attached to the smog above his head by a perfect vertical thread of silvery-blue smoke. At her approach, the thread quivered and separated. He picked up the cig and sucked, squinting up at her. How did a face get to be so cerise?

'Xmas special, is it?'

He grinned. 'Fancy a pull of my cracker, sweetheart?'

'Double entendre. Normally, we only get single in here.'

'Doobel what?'

'Sorry, I'm just confused over whether you want a meal or a hand-job.'

The guy looked offended, appalled. Tabs Six thru Nine were loving it. Ethan, maybe near enough to eavesdrop, maybe not, but it was easy for him to suss the scene. Witnessing this aspect of her life that was lived apart from him. She could sense him, watching her work, her rhythmic movement between the tables. Soon as she was clear, she returned to him. Leaning close, she noticed the smell. The oddness. Ethan smelled *odd*, even in here with all its intermingled aromas, only she couldn't identify the smell or say for sure whether it was pleasant or unpleasant.

'Look, Eeth, we're shutting after lunch today.' She handed him a key. 'Half an hour. I'll be up as soon as I'm done.'

'Half an hour.' Ethan checked his watch, checked the key. 'Okay.'

She was wiping his table even though he'd ordered and consumed nothing. His chair screeched as he stood up. She walked with him to the caff door, telling him to make himself at home, make a brew, put a CD on, whatever. As he let himself out, a wedge of cold air was sucked in, and her ears popped like there'd been a sudden drop in altitude. It was only after he'd gone that she realized he still had the menu.

Two events – an observation, a chance find – had coincided to define the day for her as somehow auspicious. The first came on the way from ZZ's, strolling caffwards in time for the lunch shift – three hours at double time, it being Christmas Eve and, technically, her day off. There'd been a frost, mostly thawed so that the street where Zeez lived was black and wet, except for rectangles of white where a hedge, a wall, a postbox had cast shadows. And, beautifully, a picket fence lay in facsimile on the pavement in a sequence of crystallized stripes. She'd stopped to look. The pattern was so flawless she wanted to believe the people who'd walked along here before her had kept to the kerb to avoid scuffing the frost with their footsteps. In time, she knew, the light would shift and the image would melt to zero, this being the way of things and not at all a reason to mourn, or you might as well watch a sunset and weep at its imminent extinguishing. During the looking, she made the discovery: there, near the base of the fence, a tooth. Human, complete with fanged root, ivory-coloured and free from blood or fragments of tissue. She picked it up, cradled in gloved palm for inspection, deciding it resembled – and she would have it made into – an earring. The tooth went into the pouch with the pendulum so she wouldn't lose it.

She'd shown Faye the tooth, over prep, revealed her plans for it – Faye being about as revolted as it was possible for a person to be without actually puking.

'*Why*, Clo?'

She'd shrugged. 'Serendipity.'

Working, imagining him alone upstairs in her bedsit – waiting for her, sitting or moving around above her head – she thought Ethan's turning up unannounced like this might be a third sign of today's auspiciousness. What it augured was anyone's guess, but she'd wanted to talk to him and now here he was, wanting to talk to her.

She took two large glasses of wine up.

'It's a party,' she said.

'What is?'

'The party is a party.' The music downstairs was audible, rever-berating. 'Free booze for me and Faye and Nigel, courtesy of the Rice-man. Festive spirit, and that.'

She said she was expected to make an appearance, sooner rather than later, and how about him joining her, them? *Are you a party animal?* He didn't need to answer, it was there in his expression and in everything she knew about him. He looked unwell, actually. But, whatever. She thought to herself that, maybe, they could talk a while up here and have a drink, using the bedsit as a social decompression chamber before going downstairs together. Ethan accepted a glass and stood with it, dead centre of the room. His boots, coat, gloves, scarf and woolly hat lay heaped in the corner, in imitation of a Guy Fawkes dummy minus the stuffing, minus the face. That smell again.

He sipped his wine, frowned, took another sip.

'What?' she said.

'This is sherry.'

She tasted hers. 'Fuck.'

Ethan went to the window, raising his glass to the light. The toy panther was there, on the ledge; he picked it up. She watched him. What the hell, it was alcoholic, swallowing some more of the sherry, and her lips were so syrupy that when she opened her mouth to speak they peeled apart like strips of dried apricot.

'I found a tooth today.'

She took it out, handed it to him, told him about the frost art on the pavement – its *perfect transitory beauty* – though not which street or how she'd come to be there.

'A guy in Flashville used to make sculptures out of leaves and twigs and bits of grass and that, then he'd set them afloat on the stream and watch them disintegrate.'

'Spoons?'

'No, another guy.'

She saw the menu now, on the draining board. Ethan remained at the window; it was the front one, overlooking the car park. Outside, a group of pubbed-up people were laughing and shouting and singing 'White Christmas'.

'You were parked out the back last week, when Gavin came,' she said, quietly. Simply. This was the first time they'd met, or spoken, since then. 'I saw the Toyota.'

Ethan turned to face her. 'You were in?'

'It was late and you were just . . . sitting there.'

Waiting, waiting, waiting for him to explain, because she'd spent the last week needing to hear him explain this. And then he cleared his throat. 'I came round to see you. But *he* was there, banging on your door.' After another pause, he said: 'I thought you were out.

I I I thought, even if you were in, if I knocked at the door after Gavin had gone you'd think I was him and wouldn't answer.'

He looked at the phone – on the floor, sitting on the nest of its own flex – as if it might ring at any moment, and the caller would be Gavin. Ethan asked if he was still hassling her and she shook her head and said that outburst seemed to have purged him of . . . of what? Of her, she guessed.

'You could've just phoned,' she said.

'I tried.'

And then she recalled pulling the jack so she and ZZ wouldn't be disturbed.

That night, after Gavin had gone and they'd heard the pick-up drive away, her and the Zeez had sat face to face on the bed in the dark, talking in whispers even though there was no need. Discussing Gavin, and Ethan, shifting to even more complicated notions. ZZ, a big shape in the black, said: 'Do you miss the life you left behind?'

She smiled. 'How d'you leave life behind? I take mine with me wherever I go.'

ZZ used his cigarette lighter to see by, arranging materials for a spliff between them on the surface of the sleeping bag. *Here, let me.* She took over, working in the inconsistent illumination, the lighter-fuel stink, the focus of the flame. And then it was done, he lit it for her, and she smoked and the room assumed another fragrance.

'You never think you might've messed up?' he said.

'If I do, I just salvage what I can and roll up a fresh one.'

'Coming here, smart arse.' The Zeez was laughing, fumbling for the spliff.

'Okay, so suppose you goof – what can you do? Go back and ungoof? Or just tick the Goofs I Have Made box and move on?' Back to her, the roach moist with his-and-hers spittle. She inhaled, held, exhaled through her nose. 'The cash is useful.' She shook her head. 'That's what jobs do, they fuck with your thinking.'

A smell of burning, of singed fibre. A live ash had landed on the bed; she licked her thumb and stubbed it out, conscious of an impression that the thumb, hand, arm, the action itself, belonged to somebody else and that she was no more than a spectator.

'Anyway, this thing with the cat is cool. I want to see it through.'

'Through to what?' ZZ said.

'To whatever.'

Ethan set the plastic cat back down on the ledge, took a slug of sherry. His shirt wasn't tucked in, the tails hung beneath his sweater; it was the red and white shirt, the one she'd said she liked. He hadn't shaved. In the light from the window, she could see that his stubble was snagged with bits of green lint from the scarf he'd been wearing.

'Don't take this the wrong way, Eeth, but what's that *smell*?'

'The lure,' he said. 'A distillation of cat-mint.'

'It's like . . .' She placed it now, remembering one of the women in the camp, with a baby – how old? ten months, or something – and the odour of nappies being boil-washed. 'I tell you what it's like, it's like ammonia.'

'Nettle family. Cats are very attracted to it – if it's growing in a garden, they'll rub up against it or roll around in it. They even feed on the leaves and stalks.'

Ethan explained how he'd come across some growing wild and had made up a batch, hiking out to points on the more likely of the cat's putative routes and spreading the mixture over walls, tree trunks, bushes and setting himself up near by in a hide – *to see if the lure lured*. Six nights in a row, he'd been out. But, zip.

'You cook it just like spinach,' he said.

She grinned. 'That's so cool.'

Ethan looked like he wasn't sure if she was taking the piss. 'You think so?'

'Yeah, most of the guys I meet these days stink of Woodbines.'

The phone rang. They stared at the phone. It would be Roy, she said, wanting to know if she'd deign to join them, though even as she spoke she was thinking ZZ and how she didn't want it to be

ZZ, now, in front of Ethan. She let it ring. They went on watching the phone till the ringing stopped and even then she could detect its echo for some seconds afterwards, passing like gossip from wall to wall in her bedsit.

'Why did you want to see me?' she said. 'Then, I mean. That night.'

Ethan answered right away. 'I wanted to ask you to work for me. Full time.'

'And that's why you're here now?'

'You wouldn't have to work downstairs any more.'

'I *like* working there. Kind of.'

He was shaking his head. 'This isn't your element.'

'Oh, right. Element.'

'How much does Rice pay you?'

'My earnings are frozen, pending a visit from the Minimum Wage Enforcement Inspectorate.' She smiled. 'Any year now.'

'I'd pay you double.'

'Money isn't . . .'

'The way we're working, it makes, in practical terms, it makes more sense,' he said. He was studying the floor, her feet. 'It makes so much more sense than than than the way things are now. It's going to . . . intensify, I think. The cat. The searching.'

And Ethan was off then, talking animatedly about Tumblejack Hill and the ewe carcass and how close, how fucking *close*, they'd come to witnessing that fucking kill, if it hadn't been for the sleet driving the sheep down off the exposed moortop and into the woods, for shelter. And how could she have been expected to anticipate that?

'Did you see what Inglis said?'

He meant the inquiry chairman's response to the leaked post-mortem (headline: ONLY A LEOPARD COULD HAVE DONE THIS!) *Mr Alam ought to need no reminding that a pathologist's role is to establish death by shooting, not to speculate as to who pulled the trigger.* She said, yeah, she'd seen it.

'You dowsed that kill, Chloe.'

'Maybe. Maybe not.' She shrugged. 'Maybe I dowsed something else.'

'No, you dowsed it. You dowsed it.'

She let it go, let him believe what he liked. 'Besides,' she said, 'if I give up my job I lose this place. The bedsit.' She saw, then, where this was leading. And before Ethan could spell it out, she stepped in with: 'Nap. Me living in the caravan is absolutely not going to happen.'

'You're not a town person. You suffocate here. What you, where you want . . . the caravan, living in the caravan would be the next best thing to living in a bender.'

She was almost annoyed enough to tell Ethan she had fucked, was fucking, had fucked last night and again first thing this morning, another guy. But she didn't. She didn't. She confused herself so much with the thought of these words that they died in her brain as synaptic impulses. But the compulsion for a sorting remained. She had to draft in her head, then for real, a swap of dialogue that would sort things, make things okay between them. Only, in this case, she had no idea what 'okay' constituted.

'Eeth, I *can't* live with you.'

He didn't reply, didn't react at all. He just stood there.

'I can work with you, yeah? But I'm not going to sleep with you.'

'Sleep. Sleep with, no, of course not. No.'

She sought signs in his face, his eyes, that a straightening had occurred. He was giving it the nods, now, lifting sherry to his mouth and lowering it, lifting and lowering, and she found herself saying, irritated herself for saying, she was sorry if she'd, if he'd got it into his head that . . . Anyway. And he lifted and lowered the sherry and said yes, yes, he understood now, and it was cool. She nearly smiled to hear him use the word.

'I was going to install a chemical toilet for you.'

She laughed. She laughed a lot at that.

'It's possible, with a chemical toilet,' Ethan told her, deadpan, doing that frown thing of his, 'to crap in such a way that the solution splashes your buttocks.'

'Oh, I'm there.' Laughing. Both of them laughing. 'I'm moving in tomorrow.'

When they'd done laughing, she pointed at the floor, asking if he'd had enough sherry to party with her and the others and how it might be fun – no hard feelings, and that. Some booze, some music, some chat. Roy demanding to know why farmers were worried about losing a few sheep when they were insured up to the hilt and anyhow, if there was a black panther on the loose, his arse was a kipper. Ethan shook his head. If it was all the same to her, he'd head off home now.

Sure, sure. Fair enough.

She went to shove her dreads back from her forehead and realized she was still wearing a paper hat.

On the doorstep, she said she'd see him soon, or they'd phone or something, yeah?, if anything happened; hugging him, in all his clumsy reciprocation, wishing him a merry Christmas for tomorrow. She aimed a kiss at his cheek, but his cheek wasn't there any more and nor was he. But the smell of cat-mint lingered; it was her smell too now.

40

ROD FAVERDALE (*sheep farmer*):

I took him up a bottle of scotch. It were the wife's idea – said she didn't like to think of the lad on his own in that caravan. Not on Christmas Day. I told her I didn't see how a bottle of my scotch would be much company for him, but she'd wrapped it by then and was shoving me out the door.

He was fixing the fence. Some pickets had broke or worked loose – what with the sheep using them as scratching posts – and he was packing the holes with hardcore and shoving them back in. I didn't say owt, 'cos I knew I'd get roped in to doing it for him. Said he was going to repaint it after. Oh, and did I have a mop he could have a borrow of, so's he could clean the outside of the caravan? There was a bucket on the steps and I could see he'd been having a go at the windows.

The bitch was there. The retriever. Skinny. Leaner than a working dog, 'cept it didn't look like she was being fed proper.

I goes: 'Bit early for spring cleaning, int it?'

'I'm getting a toilet installed.'

Then he started on about a shower – would he need a generator, or a pump, or could he put up a tank so it worked on gravity? And how would he heat the water? I'm standing there like a lemon with a bottle of scotch in frilly wrapping, and I'm thinking it's taken him the best part of twelve month to decide he don't like shitting on my land.

'What's brought all this on?'

'My lover's moving in with me.'

Just like that, he said it. His lover. All I could think of was that beanpole lass with the shaggy hair – the Scarecrow, the wife called her. And I'm thinking we'll have a fucking peace camp pitched up here if this carries on.

Lover.

Anyhow, I gave him the scotch and he said what was that for? – like he didn't realise what day it was – and I told him it were a Christmas present. No thank you or owt. He just went back to fixing the fence like I wasn't even there. And I'm thinking: whoever she is, pal, she's welcome to you.

41

Her footsteps on the stairs seemed, to her, to produce the asymmetrical percussion of someone with one shoe on, one shoe off. Only, she wasn't wearing shoes so there was no explaining the lopsided racket of her descent. She opened the door and there was Ethan, distracted, as if he'd been trying to puzzle this out as well. *Hiya!* Her boots stood against the hallway skirting, which was good, seeing as she'd been unable to find them anywhere upstairs. She sat down and drew them on, tugging the mud-stiff laces.

'Yesterday – the whole, entire day – is a blank,' she said. 'A total blank.'

'It was my first anniversary.'

'Was it?' She raised her head, her dreads, from what she was doing. 'Yeah, it was, wasn't it? First of Jan. I should've remembered.'

She'd wasted the day: hungover, stunned by dehydration and tiredness, fragile, nauseous, coiled alone on her bed in a state of lethargic self-pity, redolent of a sleepy-warm smell, and of booze and stale spliff and sex.

'You left the phone off the hook,' Ethan said.

'I tell you, one ring and all the capillaries in my brain would've imploded.' She imitated the noise of an implosion. 'You missed a brilliant night.'

'Is that new?'

'This? Yeah. Yeah, it is actually.'

Her daypack, looped over one shoulder, had slipped to the crook of her elbow. The pack – black, natch – still had a triangular label strung to the strap, bearing the imprint of a boot tread and the legend: TAKE A HIKE. She put it on properly.

She fixed on his face, a hard critical look. 'Eeth, are you eating?'

'Eating? Of course I'm eating.'

'And this stuff you eat contains calories, does it?'

'My face always looks thin in winter.'

He tried to explain this, the cold contraction of skin over bone, but didn't make much sense. She told him she'd packed food to last them till morning, as well as a flask of strong coffee with a nip, for *the long dark hours of vigilance*. It would be kind of surreal, she said, spending a night there again. She feigned jokiness, but she was edgy and sensed in him an apprehension as acute as her own. Ethan was stroking his face, testing the flesh like he was going over in his head what she'd said about calories.

'Yesterday lunch,' he said. 'Soup. I spilled some and had to retype two pages.'

'You haven't eaten since then?'

'Why surreal?' Ethan said.

'Why d'you think?'

She stood, stamped her feet, stubbed the toecaps against the jamb and was into the yard before him, off up the street. It was bitter. Inside the pick-up, their breathing, their body heat, filmed the windscreen and when Ethan snapped the heater-vents to max particles of debris – dead insects, dust, pieces of leaf – blew into the cabin.

Yesterday she'd managed, at least, to drag the phone to the bed and call Mom to say happy New Year, to chat. She wished she hadn't. Carrying around with her ever since the advice, the admonishment, the warning, the *taste* of her mother's disapproval.

'What you do, if you misuse the pendulum, is misuse yourself, because the tool is only an extension – an indicator – of the intuitive powers of the internal dowser.'

'I know that.'

'Then act like you know that.'

'Mom, this is not misuse. I dowse myself all the time about stuff.'

Her mom told her, after they'd jawed a while about Ethan and ZZ and the cat, but mostly Ethan, that she believed her daughter was going with whatever this phase of her life swung her way, like it was some kind of existentialist experiment. Like it was a game. She was doing future with the lives of more people than just herself, and seeing only beauty in the patternlessness of potentiality.

'Don't go there, hon.'

'Where?'

'You know what I'm saying.'

She did. She knew Mom wasn't talking about a place, but about deviation from the four stages of the dowse: Balance, Equilibrium, Vision, Oscillation. Skipping to the fourth without due attention to the other three was a trademark of the novice. For her, with her training and skill and experience, it was just plain reckless. Yeah, yeah.

Twice she'd dowsed the map and twice the pendulum said 'yes' as the pointer touched the same square. Both times, she distrusted the response. How to tell if she'd dowsed the site, the cat, or herself? The emotional and physical associations were too potent, too personal for her to believe she wasn't misdirecting herself along a false trail of her own unconscious. Swinging the bob, but invoking the idiot.

Nap. She'd phoned Ethan and told him they should leave well alone.

And they would've done, only he caught a radio interview with a woman who claimed to have heard the call of the beast. She lived alone in a former gamekeeper's cottage, two K from the nearest metalled road. On New Year's Eve, past midnight, she switched off the television and, as usual before retiring, let her dog out. Waiting on the back steps, she heard a distinctive cry from the woods beyond her garden. The woman, a former music teacher, said: *It started on the fourth note above middle C, which is to say F, and rose up the scale a further five intervals, ending on the next C. This was repeated three times, with a short break between calls. Finally, there was a loud grunt or exhalation.* Only a large, deep-chested animal could have produced such resonance and strength. A country woman, born and raised, she recognized its sounds: the blood-curdling cry of a fox, the appalling shrieks of a captured rabbit, the territorial threat-call of a feral tomcat. *It was none of these. It was absolutely bestial.* Her dog, a Jack Russell called Caitlin, had leaped into her arms and cowered there, whimpering.

Ethan located the cottage on his map, and the woods behind it. Woods he'd never visited. Woods that lay just outside the hypothetical territory he'd plotted for the cat. Woods that would have been felled for a bypass that was no longer to be built. Woods she'd map-dowsed, twice, with deep distrust. Woods she'd lived in.

This was Flashville.

'We called this one the Big Lick,' she said.

'You had names for the trees?'

'Just the unusual ones.'

This time of year there was a sense of space and light, but the bare canopy told of the dome of gentle seabed-green that formed here in summer and which, for some reason, was how this place played in her memory. Today, it was too white. Too hard. Too naked. The ground was crisp with partially frozen mud and leaf mulch the colour of molasses, the defoliated trees making black river systems against a featureless sky. Words and footsteps snapped in the brittle air, and from elsewhere in the woods came the clamour of rooks returning to their nests as the afternoon aged. She performed a slow solo circuit of the oak – ancient and ugly, maybe three centuries old. Awesome.

'Why Big Lick?' Ethan said.

'Short for Big Liquorice.' She indicated the greeny, grey-brown trunk that took six folk hand-in-hand to encircle. It looked as if several thinner oaks had been grafted on to one another . . . *like giant sticks of liquorice fused and given a half-twist*. 'It's a mutant,' she said. 'A tree tree, genetically modified to sprout clones of itself.'

'Liquorice is black.'

'Proper liquorice isn't.'

Being here at all was weird, being here with Ethan . . .

He was gazing up into the branches, and she guessed he'd be

trying to estimate the height; he pointed, she raised her eyes too –
spotting a length of bright blue nylon rope, frayed at the end,
suspended from one of the limbs like a fluorescent vine.

'We had a platform up there. One of the bailiff's gang tried to
dismantle it and fell and dismantled his collar bone instead.'

The cheers, the whoops, the applause, re-created themselves in
her imagination.

It wasn't just him – Ethan – it was the hollowness. The utter
stillness. How did somewhere that had been so teeming with life,
so *full*, get to be so empty? So post-nuclear holocaust empty. Since
having the tooth-earring made, and looped in her left lobe, she'd
found herself habitually fretting at it. She was doing this now.

She'd anticipated – what? – not Flashville, sure, but evidence of
habitation or, at least, disturbance: lozenges of compacted soil
where benders had stood or boardwalk pallets had been laid, unused
kindling, ashes, litter. But, months after disbandment, the rope was
the only immediately obvious clue that the camp had ever existed.

Ethan must've been thinking this too, because he said: 'You
wouldn't know there'd been a protest.'

'You would. If there hadn't, we'd be standing in the middle of a
fucking four-lane highway.'

She conducted him, sketching with her hands the absent elements
of the camp's configuration, pacing out approximate distances,
narrating, describing; merging images in his mind, for him, with
the ones he must've preconceived. Aware all the while that it wasn't
only him for whom she was trying to revive the place. Ethan toured
the woods with an air of archaeological conjecture, reconstructing
– by his questions – something closer to Iron Age settlement than
to eco squat; its departed inhabitants, he said, were no more alive
to him than jigsaw skeletons of unearthed bones.

The Chloe I envisage dwelling here is the Chloe of a previous incarnation.

She had no idea what he meant by that. Then she thought of
Richie, of Spoons, and decided that maybe she did.

'Incarnation,' she said, smiling. 'I swear your vocabulary is starting to expand to accommodate mine.'

She wanted him to shake his head and say *nap* and smile, but he
didn't do any of this, he simply stood looking around like he was
lonely and sad and confused and a long way away from her even
though they were just a few steps apart.

'This was our bender.' She pirouetted, hair flailing. 'It looked for
all the world like a buffalo in a tarpaulin poncho. Four of us had to
share.' Counting them off: *Plum, Giraffe, The Blessed (Virginia),
Blinky.* 'The four hoarse women of the apocalypse.'

'You shared.' A statement, flat and sullen.

'We had to. We just got on with it.'

She was aware of his scrutiny, as she stood where the bender
had stood, and it was as though he was mentally enclosing the
space around her – sketching in her home, visualizing her inside.
She guided him to a natural depression near by and scuffed at the
detritus to expose a rough circle of charred earth.

'This was where we cooked.'

'Where were the tunnels?'

She offered him a smile. 'Underground, mostly.'

'I'd prefer . . .' Ethan frowned. 'I'd prefer to live in a tunnel than
a tree-house.'

'Claustrophiliacs.'

'What?'

'That's what we called people like you.' She paused. 'People like
us.'

She took him to the tunnels. They were detached from the
grouping of benders, set into a shallow embankment where the
ground eased down among young birch to a beck, beer-coloured,
swollen with recent rains. The opposite bank had been coppiced,
creating a false clearing and, fleetingly, an illusion that the afternoon
was brightening not darkening, that a last splash of light would defy
the day's closure.

'I thought they'd have collapsed them,' she said. 'You know? Or
blocked them off or something. Stop kids going in.'

Ethan halted with her beside the stream as she looked up towards
the two black incisions – an *n*, and an inverted *v* – set diagonal to

one another, some thirty metres apart in the incline. The nose and eye, she always thought, of an unfinished Hallowe'en pumpkin. She recalled the mud, like melted caramel on Spoons's denim overalls when he'd done his stints at the digging, the propping, the sinking of air vents. She was glad the tunnels hadn't been demolished.

'I spent six days in there.' Pointing to the one on the left. 'You had to crawl in, then it opened out into a kind of chamber. The Home Dome. Two hours' Torch Time a day and just about enough room to sit up.'

'By yourself?'

'Nap. Two of us.'

Ethan shut his eyes, pressed them so firmly with thumb and middle finger she couldn't believe it didn't hurt. He dropped his hand, opened his eyes again. Blinking. She studied him in profile: his cheek, the tip of his nose, rouged with cold, lips slightly pursed, gaze fixed on the tunnel. Individual hairs in his eyebrow were distinguishable. He released a breath-cloud, coughed, raised a gloved fist to his mouth, coughed again and, without looking at her or even, so it seemed, addressing her, he said: 'Two of you.'

'Being on your own in there for so long . . .' she said. 'Can you imagine it?'

'You'd come out knowing yourself better than when you went in.'

'I don't know. With me, I think I'd dig around inside myself so much I'd just end up more of a mess. I'd scare myself, actually.'

'You dowse yourself . . . your *self*. What's the difference?'

'It's the difference between transcendental meditation and tripping on acid.'

She was drifting off, away from him and the conversation, moving up the slope towards the entrance to the Home Dome. Darkness was imminent, and Ethan would be anxious to scout for places to pitch a hide, or even to search – or dowse – for signs that the cat had been, or would be, here. But there was something they had to do first, 'cos – curiosity, or intuition, or an altogether different attraction, or whatever – she was being drawn in and needed to know why. *Hey, Eeth.* Her cry put up a pair of pheasants, the metallic alarm calls running like a commentary beneath the clatter of their flight. The woods hushed again. And she was there, at the tunnel's mouth, beckoning him.

She went first, on all fours, a torch held Flashville-style above one ear by an elasticated headband. Ethan crawled in after her, laser strands of light from his own torch zapping beyond her, the scuffle of his progress in synch with the left-right left-right drag of her elbows, knees, feet. Damp filmed the walls and ceiling with a pale sheen, as though the earth was sweating. She sweated too. Each exhalation was warm and wet, spit pooling in the hang of her lower lip. And when she inhaled, the air was stale and cold and stank of rotting mushrooms and of something unidentifiable. No talking. The only noise was their breathing, and the chafe chafe of their propulsion – a mechanical, metrical action that was as much to do with the familiarity of being here as any of the sights or smells or sounds or textures. She felt no sense of panic, of confinement or suffocation, or of the fatal weight of earth shored up above and all about them, and wondered if Ethan did. Or was he utterly focused on the torch beam, as she'd instructed him? As Spoons had once instructed her. Condensing the tunnel to the disappearance and reappearance of the other person's bootsoles in the spill of light ahead of you. Only that.

'I can see the dome.'

Her voice retreated from her along the passage, dead and mono-syllabic. What she could see was the tell-tale alteration in the nature of the shadows beyond the range of the torch. She quickened. The light reached the dome now, expanding around its curved walls as if the beam was a bore of water sluicing along a sewer. A minor tilt of the head, the chin, adjusted the angle of illumination. She saw it then. On the floor of the Home Dome, maybe five metres away. And the seeing of it braked her so abruptly that Ethan barged into her from behind. A word escaped from her with the sound of a kiss. Even though the word was hers, she didn't know what it was, or if it was a word at all or an exclamation, a simple and sudden expulsion of air. The sound came again and she knew then that she was gagging.

'What is it?' Ethan: urgent, tense, anxious.

She didn't reply. What she did was edge forward so he could manoeuvre into the chamber with her. What she did was lean against the arc of the wall, half squatting, half sitting, head tipped right back, one hand over the lower half of her face, eyes shut, making herself as small as she could. Crying? Yes, she was crying. She was crying. The stench achieved its impact now. Ethan would be looking where she had looked. Where she no longer needed to look, because the image was beyond erasure in her head: the carcass of a young deer, partially eaten, its eyes open and so intelligent with torchlight that her instant and shocking thought had been that the creature was still alive.

42

SUSAN REANEY (*housing officer*):

The day we broke up was awful. It was a Sunday, we'd just got back to his place after taking Erica for a walk. While we were out I'd been trying to find a way to tell him, but it wasn't until we were home that I managed it. He just sat there and heard what I had to say without interrupting. Didn't say a word. You couldn't even tell what he was thinking from his expression. Once I'd said my piece he went on sitting there, staring at me in silence for what seemed like ages. Then he asked me to marry him. Just like that.

'Susan, I think we should get married.'

I almost burst out laughing. But I could see he was deadly serious; he looked so earnest – so desperate, to be honest – that I felt quite sorry for him. He was nodding away to himself, not even looking at me now. Yes, we should get engaged and then get married and then I could move in with him. It went on like this for a few minutes. I just couldn't make him understand that not only did I not want to marry him, I didn't even want to go on seeing him. In the end I lost patience, and I suppose I was nastier than I'd meant to be. Ethan went very quiet again. Then he got up, calm as anything, put his coat back on and let himself out without a word. There was no anger, no slamming of doors, he just walked out of the flat and left me there with his dog. It was as though we were at my place rather than his and he felt he should be the one to go.

I wasn't sure what to do. After a few minutes I decided just to go home. But the front door was locked – Ethan must've locked it on his way out – and it couldn't be opened from the inside. I looked for a spare key but there was no obvious place where one might be. The back door was locked too. I wasn't panicky or even irritated at that stage – it was just so farcical. So I sat down and waited for him to come back. After a while – half an hour or so – I began to get annoyed with him. It was ludicrous, pathetic. I went to see if any of the windows were open, but it was a cold day and they were all shut – double-glazed, with security locks, and no keys anywhere, that I could find. I must have searched every drawer and ledge in that flat, Erica traipsing round after me like it was a game. I was literally imprisoned in his flat. I couldn't even call for help, as Ethan didn't have a phone. Then I thought: what if a fire broke out? I'd be trapped, I wouldn't have a chance. And once panic set in it wasn't long before I was imagining him at the front door, pushing a lighted rag through the letterbox. Was he capable of that? How do you know what any man is capable of? All I knew was, I had to get out of there. Right away. I had to smash a window and climb out. I started searching again, for something, anything, to break the glass. I more or less ransacked the flat before I found a toolbox under the kitchen sink. I opened it, hoping to find a hammer, and there – in the top compartment – was a set of keys tied together with string. Window keys, door keys. I tried one on the front door, and it worked, although I remember my hand was shaking so much I took several goes before the door opened.

Afterwards, I wondered if Ethan had planned it, somehow, or at least prepared for such a situation. Knowing I'd have to smash my way out, knowing I'd look for something to do it with – hiding the keys with the tools, where he knew I'd find them. You start to think like that. It's paranoid, but you can't help yourself. He didn't show up at work for a few days. When I confronted him, he blanked me. Wouldn't even talk about it. I heard later that he'd handed in his notice and, within a month, he was gone. I never saw him again. And in the papers, now, they refer to me as his *ex-fiancée*.

43

With the hide assembled, they sat inside and waited, seeking movement, a shadow, a slink of black on not-so-black on the opposite
slope as the predator, the killer, returned to finish feeding. But all
she could see was the fawn – ruptured, broken, 24-hours dead, Ethan
reckoned. In his files, the carcass photos were fakes, contrasted to
the real thing. Murder scene mock-ups on the covers of whodunits.
Pure porn. What it was about the fawn, more than the sheer sensual
gore, was its utter absence of composition.

'You get used to seeing death . . . I dunno, *choreographed*,' she
said. 'In films and on TV and that.'

'Hn.'

'The position of the limbs, the head, even the blood – they're all
arranged just right. A painting, guiding the eye of the viewer.'
Art-school speak. She shuddered with cold. Talking in whispers,
unable even to see each other's faces. 'Sorry, I'm freaked.'

From his silhouette, she could tell that Ethan was staring straight
ahead at the tunnel; he'd been talking about how – with materials,
time, expertise – they could've rigged up some kind of trap: a gate,
like in a zoo, primed to drop shut once the animal went in. She saw
bars. She saw Ethan and her rolling a boulder across the entrance.

'I could smell it,' he said.

She nodded. For her, it wasn't an odour but a response. A
trembling. Some dowsers – her mom – were 'tremblers', using
themselves, their hands, their body, as a tool; not her, till now, but
in there she'd dowsed the cat without the pendulum, without even
dowsing. It was as though the cat had dowsed her, murmuring to
her six senses:

I was here, I was here, I was here.

She wasn't handling this. The shock. Being in a confined space with . . . that. And what if, jesus, what if the cat had come back while they were in there, trapped inside? Ethan said it would've scented them and kept away. Even so they crawled out a fuck sight sharper than they'd crawled in.

'Me and Richie used to tell each other ghost stories in the Dome. Spook Time.'

'You don't call him Spoons now?'

'Nap. Not any more. Not since Flashville.'

'Spoons is dead,' Ethan said.

His words were little more than breath impregnated with a sound that, for her, contained his meaning. Sub-audible, almost. Was that possible? Like lip-reading – only telepathic, so you'd communicate in the dark by the quality of each other's exhalations. With Richie – Spoons – she'd come close to this in the six days before the surfacing.

'When I saw the deer, the fawn,' she said. 'Before I realized what it was –'

'You thought it was alive.'

'I thought it was Richie. Just for a second, not even a second, I saw the shape – the ribcage, actually – and I thought, somehow, I'd abandoned him down there and come back months later to find his corpse. Like, I'd left him to die. To rot.'

Dowsing is not a metaphor for life. Mom (c. 1989, '90, '91, '92 . . .). In dowsing, you sometimes retraced your steps and dowsed again – to suss helpful responses from the unhelpful, to weed out the idiot, to be sure of yourself. You might have to go back to situations you thought you'd already dealt with.

In life, hon, leave your past alone. Learn and move on.

So what in the name of whoever was she doing here in this place that was, and was not, Flashville? Thinking about a guy who was, and was not, Spoons. Sitting here, in concealment, with an optically enhanced monochrome field of vision – drawing every last grainy nuance of definition from the, to the naked eye, unavailability of light. She had the notion she was spying on her previous self. She was a CCTV camera aimed at the tunnel, waiting for Plum and Spoons to emerge.

But Spoons was dead. Spoons became Richie became nothing. Plum had died too. She'd become Chloe Fortune: waitress, dowser, bedsit dweller, retired environmental activist, casually sexual with a mountaineer, carefully asexual with a pursuer of cats.

It would do, for now.

In the caff, on the morning of the eve of a new year, Roy asked where she saw herself in twelve months' time and she said she never saw herself in that way, futured.

'These woods mean zip to me now,' she told Ethan. 'I mean, I'm glad they're here – as woods, yeah? – but I suppose what I'm saying is this isn't Flashville any more. Flashville ended when the mob demobbed. Its existence is conceptual now, you know?'

Ethan didn't say anything.

Midnight, by his illuminated watch. Her buttocks were numb, legs heavy with stalled circulation, her feet pulsed; she shifted position, but there were only so many posture variants on offer and she'd done them all. How could he remain so motionless for so long? Hours of vigilance reeled exaggeratedly ahead of her. She pictured 'discomfort', dismantling the letters, rewriting them in a senseless anagram, repeating this to herself as a mantra of endurance. She freshened their beakers. In earlier vigils they'd slept in shifts, but this time they both wanted to stay awake for the duration, jolts of caffeine holding them close to alertness. She'd be drunk soon, what with all the whisky in that flask. Each swallow of coffee dropped a plumb line of heat inside her.

'Are you pissed?' she said.

'*Shh.*'

She heard it herself then, set the drink down and raised the infra-bins. Starting at the tunnel mouth and scanning outwards until she saw what she knew Ethan must've seen through the zoom: the dark flank of an animal loping among scrub away to the right. Tracking it. Tracking it. And there it was, out in the open on the slope above the beck, feet peck-peck-pecking through the leaf litter, shoulders down, head up, snout up, tail fanned behind it. A fox. The dissipation of adrenalin left a sour taste. She felt it in Ethan too – an easing of muscles, a subtle release of air held too long in the lungs. The fox hesitated, suspicious, nosing the air – first in their direction, then nodding at the gaping hole. It went in. It came out a few minutes later with the complete leg of a young deer in its mouth, like a dog with a cumbersome stick. The white, weighty, meaty ball of the hip joint was dragging along the ground.

She lowered the bins. 'I have to dive out for a pee.'

Sometime around two a.m. on New Year's Day, she and ZZ had shagged on Tab Ten – this being alcoved from view of the caff's picture window, though she was so hanging by then she'd have done it on One with the lights on. She smiled now to think of it.

The Zeez. He wasn't Richie or Gavin. He wasn't Ethan. That was the deal.

And here she was, forty-eight hours on, spending the night with a guy who *was* Ethan, camouflaged in woods in the cold, so dark she found herself imagining his face – its binary strokes and circles – as coloured shapes arranged, childlike, on an oval of felt.

'Smile,' she said.

'What?'

'I want to see if it feels different in here when you're smiling.' She heard the shift of clothing and guessed he'd turned his head towards her. Frowning, she thought, making his eyebrows meet. 'You're not smiling, are you?'

He paused, then said: 'No.'

'Fair enough.'

She unwrapped another of the sandwiches. Ethan had eaten none, and declined again. The hide smelled of egg mayonnaise and pepper, whisky and coffee. It creaked if either of them moved and, when a breeze got up, holly leaves fretted like fingernails at the canvas. Like mice. Like uncooked rice on glass.

'Go on, Eeth, have one.'

'I'm not hungry.'

'Eventually, you start to digest your own stomach.'

They shared the last of the coffee. She had no idea what time it was. The cold was no longer outside of her, but generated from within – from the deep hollows of her bones – and radiating outwards through her veins to every part of her flesh. The booze did not warm her now, even as an illusion, but there was enough of it in her system for her not to care. She shut her eyes, fantasizing herself snug in bed inside a sleeping bag.

When she woke it might've been five minutes later, it might've been an hour.

It took a moment to comprehend where she was, and why, and who with. Her neck ached. Her head was tilted right over to one side, Ethan's side, resting on his shoulder; her ear felt damp, reddened and slightly painful. Half her body was warm, the other cold. She jerked upright but the sensation in her cheek was unchanged, as though the contact with his collar bone continued despite the abrupt disconnection. This was like coming round after slumping asleep in a train seat: stiff, disorientated, flushed with an unspecified embarrassment. Her mouth tasted of everything she'd ever eaten.

'Sorry,' she said.

The glow from Ethan's watchface made a point of focus in the black between them. 'Four thirty-two.' The light snapped off. 'You've missed nothing.'

Waking, she'd had a residual impression of talking aloud in the final moments of sleep. But, on hearing Ethan's voice, she realized he was the one who'd spoken and it was this – his mumblings – that had nudged her awake. She rewound for the sense of what he'd been saying, but found nothing.

'Were you using the microcassette just then?'

'No.'

'I thought I heard you talking to yourself.'

'No.'

'Ethan, I heard you.'

After an age, he said softly softly softly: 'I was talking to you.'

'Me?' Leaning against him, head to shoulder, and all along he'd believed her to be awake, conscious, voluntarily intimate. 'Tell me you knew I was asleep.'

'Yeah, I knew that. Yes.'

'So, what were you saying?'

'I told you I loved you.'

The two of them, enclosed in a void that could've been anyplace, could've been a dream or drunken hallucination, but suddenly sober she listened to him say the love triptych again – the *I* the *Love* the *You* – hearing him repeat the unanswered litany he'd muttered to her as she slept: the caravan was ready for her, he'd installed the toilet, a makeshift shower, and the place was done up, warm(ish) and clean and tidy, it was just a case of handing her notice in, and agreeing a date and time for him to collect her.

'I can't do that, Ethan.'

'Why not?' His perplexed tone belonged to a man adding a column of figures for a second time only to arrive at a different total. 'I don't understand why not?'

'Because . . . basically, because I don't want to. I don't want what you want. I don't feel what you feel. Sorry, but that's the way it is.'

'You you you do feel it.'

'No, I don't.'

'You slept in my bed.'

'I know.' She exhaled. 'I know.'

'And just now . . .'

'Ethan, please. Don't do this to yourself.'

This had the quality of, and the potential to become, an ending – an unravelling – similar to, but not quite the same as, all the others in her experience. She let the flat smack of her words resound and fade to quiet, uncertain what to fill this quietness with but sure that she would have to be the one to fill it, because Ethan's was suddenly the silence of someone who'd never speak again to anyone about anything.

44

She was due at work by six. The long haul to the Toyota, the drive back to town; she could use a shower before her shift. They should set off, now. Not just because of the caff but because she didn't want to be here, with him. Like this. After the – what? – the *separation* that had occurred. Two separations: one between them, one between them and the vigil. The vigil was no longer about the cat, but about the two people in the hide. Only, she couldn't be doing with such intensity, such oppressiveness. Cold, stiff and dirty; she'd had enough.

'Come on, let's quit.'

'I'm not leaving till after daybreak,' he said.

'I have to –'

'I'm not leaving.'

She stared at the place where his face might be. 'And I get back how, exactly?'

'I don't know.' She felt him rock forward, then back again. Heard the agitation in his voice. 'How . . . how do I know? How do I know how you get back?'

He seemed to occupy more of what room there was in the hide, spreading into its spaces, enlarging himself, jolting her, pressing against her. How far to town from here? Eight, nine K? Couple of hours, on foot. Longer, given the dark, the woods, the hills and how tired, how fucking tired and semi-boozed she was. Even if she left now, by herself, she'd be at work later than if she waited with him until after the dawn. To be stranded out here with him, *dependent* on him, was too exasperating to think about. And him acting as though somehow this was all her responsibility.

'Roy'll be well chuffed.' Like this was the issue. All the while, the rocking back and forth beside her. Why was he doing that?

What she wanted, above everything else, was for him to stop doing that. 'Look, I want to go home. Just take me home, okay?'

'This is a vigil.'

'*Ethan.*'

'Nobody leaves until I say so.'

Being just about the most ridiculous remark she'd heard in ages. But Ethan said she wasn't to laugh at him because he was serious: he was staying, and she was staying with him. As he spoke she was weighing the choice of acceding to this, or two hours of solo foot-slog . . . and deciding there wasn't even a contest.

'I don't usually do melodrama, Eeth, but I really can't pass this one up.' Easing herself from sit to squat to stoop, fumbling to loosen the flap of canvas that would free her from him, from the hide, and into the woods. 'That's me, then.'

Moving clumsily, noisily among the trees, the play of the beam erratic and disembodied and seemingly unrelated to her. It was as if the torchlight and the sound of her progress belonged to two people, one pursuing the other but unable to close the distance. Using the pale elongated cone of yellow as a tracer through the enshrouding black. She knew these woods and she did not know them at all. In places where there was no trail, she forced her way through, one hand protective of her face. A minute, maybe two, since leaving the hide and already she might've been lost in the depths of an immense forest. She knew this was the night talking, the solitude, the rude and startling commotion she made in the silence. If she was afraid, she was afraid of herself. All she had to do was walk for as long as it took to reach the nearest road, and the woods would be gone.

The cat.

She was alone in the woods in the dark with the cat, being stalked, and in the instant this thought struck her she heard a noise that was not her. Away to the left – the left? – no, the right, the right and behind her. A noise that was not the rush of the wind in the trees, or the echo of herself, or any of the night-time creaks and sighs and shuffles of woodland. This was deliberate, animalistic. Violent. This was the noise of something large moving urgently among the inadequate resistance of static things – undergrowth, bushes, branches – as though towing them in its wake.

To the right and not so far away now. Closing in.

Small yips escaped from her mouth as she picked up the pace: jogging, running, turning her head, the torch, to try to see what or where it was and how near but seeing nothing and only having the noise to tell her of its momentum. And even the noise now could not be placed. The noise was all around her. It was everywhere. Branches caught her face, her clothes, she tripped on tree roots, slipped, fell to her knees, raised herself again and almost immediately stumbled down an unexpected slope, scrambling up the other side and out on to a broad logging trail. And there it was, halted ahead of her on the track at the limit of her torch's range – a glimpse, in a faint reflective gleam, of the white of an eyeball, teeth, a cheek.

Ethan.

She stopped, hands on hips, wide-mouthed, breathing so fast and furiously that not just her lungs but the entire upper half of her body was working to collect enough air. Blood fizzing in her ears. The pair of them watching one another in the crossed swords of their torch beams.

'Jesus, it's you.'

He approached, a hand raised against the dazzle as she kept his head centred in the shaft of light. His breathing was as laboured as hers. 'It's me,' he said.

'Why the . . . why the *fuck* didn't you call out or something?' The glare left his face as she used her torch to gesticulate, drawing an arc across a silvered stand of trees to the side of the trail. 'I thought . . . Ethan, you've just frightened the shit out of me.'

'You thought what?'

'Why didn't you just call out?'

'I had to catch you.'

'Coming after me like that. I mean, fuck.' She inhaled deeply through her nose and out through her mouth. 'All I could hear was this . . . *crashing*.'

He eased closer still. She bent forward at the waist, lowering her head, then lifting it, frisking her dreads. In the torchlight, Ethan's face glistened with perspiration. It looked unnaturally white. The shock, the fear, the relief had become anger now, and she was forming something to say to him – something raw and spiteful – but he reached out and carefully, tentatively placed a hand on her head. This action surprised her into silence. His fingers were searching among the thick ropes of hair for the contact of her scalp. The touch of her skull, its veneer of warm, damp skin that she became conscious of only as a consequence of the gentle pressure of his fingers. The thought occurred to her that this was the first time Ethan had touched her hair. She didn't flinch or beat his hand away. Like a spider in her palm, the sensation was neither pleasant nor unpleasant – simply unusual enough, fascinating enough, for her to allow herself to experience it. He was a phrenologist, she decided. Reading her. Waiting for her to show him what to do next. What she did was lean back a little so that his arm was fully extended, only the tips of his fingers remaining in contact with her skin. She spoke quietly, insistently.

'Take me home.'

He took a half-step towards her, increasing the weight of his touch, which was no longer a touch but a grip, fingers and dreads interlocking. *Don't, Ethan.* Now, too late, she went to withdraw his hand, herself from his hand, but he had her hair and he wasn't letting go, he was tightening, tugging, tearing the roots as she resisted the draw of her head, her face, her mouth towards his. *I said don't!* He tried to kiss her and their teeth clicked hard together and she felt the sharpness of her own teeth against her lip and the taste of her own blood. She was not, she was not, she was *not* letting him kiss her. Pulling, pushing, the panting wordless tussle, the description of dizzy circles as they revolved on the axis of each other's total determination. And she sussed in that appalling instant that Ethan was physically stronger than her, and that willpower –

the power of her will against his – was not where this fight would be won and lost.

She made a sound like a scream. She aimed a kick, a punch, but there was no purchase, no room, and all she did was lose her torch. He'd brought her to her knees, pulling her down down. She swore, yelled, shrieked at him to stop just to stop just to *oh please* let her go, but he went on without a word – his only language, the grunting of the effort of what he was doing. He was dragging her along the ground by her hair, by her *jesus* by her fucking hair only he couldn't he couldn't. He let go. She was lying face down on the muddy track and she didn't know where Ethan was. He was gone: he'd let her go, he was gone. That was him, moving away through the woods. Then, as she rose up on to all fours, something exploded against the side of her head.

She couldn't move. She was lying on her back and she couldn't move.

Why couldn't she move?

Her arms, her legs, were heavy. Not heavy, paralysed. There was no way to lift them or to move them at all and her clothes – her jacket, jeans – were too tight for her, sucking at the flesh like shrinkwrap, like a Chinese burn.

Her head hurt. Her scalp hurt. Her ear hurt. Her legs were cold.

She raised her head and there was enough light in the sky and in the woods for her to see herself starfished on the ground on the slope where the hide had been. Those things – grey, what were they? – those things were the pegs, the tent pegs he'd used to stake out the hide. Only, they weren't staking out the hide any more, they were staking out her. One for each ankle, one for each elbow – driven hard through the fabric of her gear and into the earth.

Her jeans, her knickers, were yanked down beneath the knees.

She looked at herself for a long time, then let her head tip back and closed her eyes and registered the bruising and the ooze of the gunk that seeped from her.

45

GREG "ZZ" HOLLAND (*shop manager/climber*):
You could go your whole life and never meet a woman anything like her. She was a mountain: you had to comprehend her, and yourself in relation to her, before deciding the nature of your involvement, or whether you even wanted to go anywhere near. I don't mean to sound arrogant, but I've been around a lot more than Ethan and I think I read her better than he did. And, certainly when it came to Chloe, I think I read myself better than he read himself.

Does that excuse what he did? No. Absolutely fucking not. What he did was unforgivable. I'm just trying to make the point that . . .

. . . look, Chloe made little allowance for her impact on those around her. I'm not saying she was callous or manipulative or a control-freak. Not at all. She wasn't. She just strutted her stuff and, basically, it was up to you to find a safe route into her life – if that's what you, or she, really wanted – and out again. I liked her a lot, as it happens. But I appreciated, from the start, the limit of our connection and the dangers of being distracted from that limitation. And I understood, as she did, that the true solution to being controlled – by a person, or a situation, or an environment – is not to seek control, it is to seek self-control.

In the dazzle of a woman like Chloe you could blind yourself to that.

46

Riding in a transit van with a guy who claimed to be a punter. One of Roy's irregulars. Recognized her by her hair, he said, only she didn't recognize or hardly look at him, though he swore she'd served him up a Full English just a week since. He told her his name, like she gave a shit about his name or anything about him. She stared out of the window – not even out, but at, the window – not talking or replying, not explaining her roadside presence at whatever time it was in the middle of nowhere, or the state of her. Observing none of the conversational courtesies from hitch-hiker to driver. Finally, the guy absorbed her silence into a sullenness of his own. Dropping her a few streets from the caff, and she was away before the *don't-fucking-bother-to-thank-me-then* routine.

'It's the journey,' Roy said. 'All those stairs from first floor to ground, all that traffic.' He shook his head. 'If you want my opinion, it's a miracle you made it to work at all.'

'*Roy.*'

This was Faye.

Roy looked at her properly now. And then they were sitting her down, pouring her tea with multiple sugars, and she was trying to stand up, telling them it was okay it was cool she was fine, and if they'd just stop fussing over her and let her get on with her job – 'cos time was dosh, here – and she was late enough already.

'Take her upstairs.' Roy, talking to Faye – like she wasn't there, or like she was a child. 'We've only four in, and two of them are asleep.'

Sleep. She so badly wanted to sleep.

'I'll be all right,' she said. 'Just let me get cleaned up.'

Roy gave her the day off on full pay. He told her she looked like she'd spent the night in a freshly dug grave, like she'd risen from the dead. She pulled a face at the sweetness of the tea, but it was hot and good and she closed her hands around the mug for the penetrative warmth. One of her fingernails had levered up from its bed, hurting out of proportion to the other sorenesses. When she went to toy with the earring made from a human tooth she found that it wasn't there, and that part of her earlobe wasn't there either. Her shoulders began to shake, discomposing the surface of her drink.

'Come on,' Faye said.

Faye went to relieve her of the mug but she carried it herself, careful not to lose any as she allowed herself to be escorted from caff to bedsit.

'D'you want to talk about it?'

'Nap.'

'Want me to call anyone?'

'Could you put a CD on?' She named one and Faye sorted it. 'Thanks.'

Eighteen hours since she'd left, but it felt like weeks; the music helped, almost restoring the place to her, in its unviolated and private familiarity. Faye assisted with the removal of jacket and boots, which meant setting the tea down and she absolutely didn't want to do that. She was made to see it was okay – the tea taken from her, then handed back intact. Faye noticed, she must've done, the holes, the rips in her clothing. But she said and asked nothing. The role of helper seemed to have sobered Faye. Aged her. Suddenly Faye had to be the older, wiser, least childlike of the two women.

'I need a shower. No, a bath. I have to have a bath.'

'Sure, I'll run one.'

She listened to the turmoil of the water, watched steam gasp through the half-open bathroom door and disperse to nothing. Odd details, unnoticed until now, became sudden points of fascination: a discoloured rectangle of wall where a picture had hung; a rubber doorstop set into the floor to protect the skirting. How was it possible to have lived here all these months without registering them? She tried to press the injured nail back, but it was mostly detached; in the bath, in the hot and softening and anaesthetic water, she would remove it altogether. She visualized herself doing this.

The bedsit still smelled of the sandwiches she'd made for the vigil.

She crossed her legs, leaned forward and clasped her arms around her knees. She stood up, went over to the phone and pulled the jack. At the front window, she searched the pay-and-display for red, for a pick-up . . . there was something similar, but blue, a Mitsubishi. She shut the curtain. She checked the back window too – the yard, the service road – and closed that curtain. The room was gloomy: greys, greens, blues, blacks. She snapped on the light; in the same instant the pipes screeched with the turning off of the taps, so that it seemed, phenomenally, as if the flick of the switch had also effected this.

Concussion. She'd been knocked unconscious by something, by him, and she knew if you'd suffered concussion you ought to go to hospital, you had to be X-rayed, *detained overnight for observation* because . . . because of brain damage, was it?, or a fractured skull or haemorrhaging or whatever. How was her vision? Blurred? No, it was fine. Her head ached but she was okay, she wasn't dizzy and her vision was fine. If she went to the hospital they'd want to know about more than just the concussion, and she wasn't ready for that yet or even sure whether she'd be ready for it at all.

Sleep. Bath, then sleep.

She went to the sink and puked. It tasted of coffee and whisky and egg mayo.

Naked and goosebumped and alone, Fayeless, in her bedsit, beside the bath.

The police. What she should do was call them. Tell them. Or go to hospital and tell them so that they'd tell the police and she could be questioned. Only, she wouldn't be questioned, she'd be interrogated.

She'd be examined.

The police were the police the police were . . . filth. They were The Filth.

She looked down blankly into the bath, its heat condensing on her skin. If she was going to call them, she should do it sooner rather than later. Now. She should do it now, before this: the cleansing.

No. No.

She stepped in and submerged herself.

She soaked until the water was tepid, drained it, replenished it. She had three baths. If the tank hadn't emptied she'd have had a fourth, a fifth. She dried off, put on a baggy T-shirt and tracksuit bottoms and went to bed. But the moment she lay down she knew if she stayed there she'd never manage to raise herself, her rigid and pinioned limbs. So she piled the sleeping bag and pillow in a corner of the room and slept there, half sitting – door locked, phone disconnected, curtains drawn, light blazing.

She dreamed she was a starfish, inert on the seabed, gradually being obliterated by the shifting floating glimmering particles of sand.

Waking in the late and already dark afternoon, she plugged the phone in and dialled her mom. No answer, no machine. She hung up and thought about ringing ZZ, but didn't.

She toasted bread and binned it, partially eaten.

At the end of her shift Faye came, asking if she'd like company for the evening, the night, and she told her no. Thanks, but no, she'd be okay now. Then, as Faye left, she called after her down the stairwell and they ended up crashing at Faye's: eating, a little; boozing, a lot; jawing until the small hours.

She was puny and fragile and defenceless, just so many brittle lengths of stick to be snapped. She was sticks and filth. What she was, what she was . . . what she was, was so weak and pathetic she transferred whatever capacity for strength she had to the people who would harm her. She made it feasible, legitimate, for them.

For him.

I am a cunt. She told her mother this. *Mom, I am nothing but a cunt.* Only, the phone was ringing ringing ringing and nobody was picking up and she was telling it to the tone. She told it to Faye. Faye held her tight and rocked her, only she didn't want to be rocked so Faye simply held her and murmured things that contained no meaning.

The next day she worked a full shift at the Place and was, according to Roy, *of no practical use to anyone whatsoever.*

But she did it. She did the shift.

Working the tables. Taking all the chat from the punters who wanted to know who'd died, who said *cheer up, love, it might not happen* . . . until the boss pulled her off front-of-house and assigned her to pots and prep.

The snow surprised her. After a second night at Faye's, she awoke early and parted the curtains on the street's transformation to pure and cushioned sodium-lit lemony white. Nothing was falling now and it was as though the snow had been laid whole, in one go, rather than compiling itself in subtle accumulation. It sat deep on the ledge. Hoisting the sash window, she feathered her fingers across the frozen crust and withdrew them, damp and icy, and pressed them to her cheeks. She scooped up a double handful and sluiced her face, her neck, sucking in her breath at the shock of it. Fragments of slush collected in her eyebrows and in the folds of her ears and slopped on to her bare feet.

She went into the other room to wake Faye. *Come and see!*

Five eighteen by the red numerals of the video. The two women stood, looking out. Across the road, a great slab of snow dislodged from the roof of a house and slid off in slow-motion, exploding almost silently on the angle of the bay window below. A chain reaction set in along the terrace, one rooftop after another shedding its load in a sequence of perfect, perfectly wonderful avalanches.

The Zeez once told her it was all to do with the degree of incline, the nature of the snow, ice, rocks or whatever, and other contributory factors she couldn't recall. If ever she was caught up in one she was to flap her arms and legs, like this, and 'swim' with it. Unless it was rocks, in which case you were fucked anyway. She remembered that much. Also, this: the people killed in an avalanche were most commonly the ones who'd caused it. *Sometimes a word is all it takes. A cough. A sneeze, and . . . wumph.*

On the third morning post-Flashville, she called in at the shop.

'Can we talk?'

ZZ glanced at his assistant, who shrugged – what was it to her? – and he said *yeah, come on through.* Through. In the back, among the stacks of stock where they'd done it one lunchtime, braced against a carton of Karrimor 80-litre rucksacks, various colours. He went to shut the door but she told him to leave it.

'I thought you might want some privacy.'

'I want the door *open.*'

'All right, all right. There.' He wedged the door wide and switched on a two-bar electric heater. 'Can I get you anything? A coffee? A more affable disposition?'

She didn't smile, or even answer. There was an oddness to the room – the cast of light, the timbre of their voices – and it took a moment to suss out: a layer of snow on the corrugated perspex roof, subsuming everything. She smelled burning dust.

'I called you a couple of times,' the Zeez said.

'I've been staying with someone.'

'Ethan?'

'No.'

He pointed to the side of her face. 'Did he do that?'

She wasn't sure whether he meant the bruising or the ripped earlobe. She let it go. Sitting on a box, standing again, craving somewhere to walk, to drift, that wasn't hemmed in by stock or by him. ZZ's hands were pocketed and he was propped against the whitewashed wall, sweater sleeves hoiked to mid-point on his forearms. The dense hairs on his wrists were raised by cold and by the taut fold of the cuffs.

'You look terrible,' he said.

'Yeah, like, my appearance is extremely important to me.'

'I'm not talking about your appearance, I'm talking about you.'

'Uh-huh.'

ZZ couldn't tell her anything about herself. She knew better than anyone that – for now, for a long time to come, possibly for ever – she was much smaller than the sum of the damage done to her.

'You got any dope?' she said.

'Not here, no.'

She scrubbed the air with her hand. Anyway, a spliff wasn't what she wanted. She wasn't sure what she did want. Or why she was here. Or what she wanted to say or do, or for him to say or do? What *could* he say? He couldn't say anything. She'd simply sensed the need to see him. There was a strength within ZZ that she'd imagined she might draw on, somehow, given that her own had been reduced almost to zip. But, now, seeing him – with his imposing physicality – all the strength he possessed seemed to have concentrated at the surface of his body.

I have to go. She could say that. Just walk right out.

The boxes were really bugging her, she tried to shift one, pushing it, pulling it, but it was too heavy and she had to walk it corner by corner across the cement floor. She occupied the space she'd created for herself. ZZ was stepping towards her, arms spread – *hey, hey Chloe* – because crying did that; it made people want to touch you, to hold, to clasp, to stroke, to enfold you, to make you shush. It softened them. They became soft and they said *shushshushshush*.

'No!'

She raised both hands, palms out; the Zeez looked at her hands, then at her eyes and he stopped. He stopped right where he was and didn't come any closer. She wiped her face on the sleeve of her jumper and filled herself with breath. With oxygen.

And she told him about the rape.

47

MR BARKER INGLIS CBE (*chairman, MAFF inquiry*):
At the outset of my inquiry it was suggested in some quarters that
I would be inclined, personally and politically, towards implacable
incredulity – that, almost irrespective of the evidence, I would be
beyond persuasion in the matter of the so-called Black Beast. That
I would be that 'man of science' who, according to Dr Mortimer in
The Hound of the Baskervilles, 'shrinks from placing himself in the
public position of seeming to endorse a popular superstition'. This
charge was, always has been, and remains a glib misconstruction
of both my brief and my motives. On the contrary, I have endeav-
oured to be rigorously open-minded, as I hope and trust has been
demonstrated in the pages of my final report contained herein.

Moreover, my approach has been one of positive scepticism,
which is to say an intention to seek to extract <u>explicit proof</u> from
the accumulation of <u>implicit evidence.</u> In this sense, I set out to
prove that there *was* a 'beast' rather than to prove that there was
not, for to prove a negative would have been an onerous task
indeed. Even if there was an absence of evidence of the 'beast' this
would not – logically, or empirically – constitute evidence of its
absence. This will doubtless be seized upon as an admission (or, at
least, leave the door ajar for those predisposed towards belief over
disbelief). However, the plain fact of the matter is that it would
have been no more possible for me to prove the creature does *not*
exist than to prove there are no fairies at the bottom of the garden.

48

The call came that afternoon. She was at the bedsit, preferring to be alone there rather than at Faye's, who was on shift; reassured too by the familiar sounds and smells of the caff right beneath her. The phone's sudden shrillness shocked her. The easiest thing would have been to ignore it, or to pull the jack. But she didn't. When the ringing persisted, she raised the handset to her ear, wordlessly, letting the caller speak first.

ZZ.

On the mobile, the reception frosted with break-up. But she gathered enough of his words to understand that he was on his way to town from Ethan's place . . . *you've been* . . . *Zeez, what the fuck* . . . ? ZZ was picking her up, ETA ten minutes, to take her back out there with him. She tried to cut in again but he said it was okay, it was cool, it was safe, but it was important, it was absolutely important, for her to come and if she'd please just let him finish he would tell her why that was so.

The Cherokee surfed the packed snow on the track that traversed the undulant cake-icing fields of Faverdale's land. In town it had begun to turn to slush, but not up here. A plough had been through, piling cliffs of white to either side of them where the drifts were deepest. It was like driving in a bobsleigh run. Only as they passed the farmhouse did she see the smoke. Filaments of grey against the blank sky, scrolling upwards over the sycamores that hid the caravan. The smoke was the diluted smoke of a cigarette that continues to smoulder after it's been stubbed out. As they neared, charred scraps of debris wheeled above and about them on the breeze like so many birds.

The caravan wasn't a caravan any more. It was a pair of wheels without tyres, an axle, a chassis, the crippled metal skeleton of its superstructure, a stoop, and smoky damped-down charcoal gloops and slabs that might've been anything, but included, recognizably, a typewriter. Hosewater sludge surrounded the wreckage, and the snow beyond was sneezed with smuts. Her first image was of Pompeii: the grimacing, burned-alive fossils of a man and a dog. She asked, she had to, to be sure, to be absolutely sure in the shock of it all. The policeman, standing by the picket with Mr F., wanted to establish who she was – her *connection to the occupant* – before answering.

'No bodies,' he said, at last.

'He's done this hisself.' This was the farmer. 'I thought it were kids again, but the wife reckoned the Toyota came down by our place not two minutes before she saw the smoke.'

Their gaze – hers, ZZ's, Mr F.'s, the policeman's – was drawn to the ruins in the way that people in a room will gawp at the TV even when it's turned off. An oddly sweet stink of plastic, and of school science labs, filled her nostrils. The smell, for all she knew, of a chemical toilet destroyed by fire. She wondered if the solution had exploded. Would it explode? Then she recalled the cactus she'd given him, and tried to picture how that would've burned. If she was meant to feel something, she didn't know what it should be. She felt nothing. She was present at the aftermath of a dramatic event which had nothing at all to do with her. This used to be a caravan, and now it wasn't.

She caught herself on the point of holding ZZ's hand and pulled back.

'Any idea where he might be?' the policeman said. His eyes, brimming with wet from the wind, resembled those of a fish. The wind, the cold, appeared to bother him. The cold appeared to be a big part of him not wanting to be here, doing this. 'Eh?'

She shrugged.

'You haven't seen him today? Or spoken to him?'

'Nap.'

He watched her, like he disbelieved her, or like he didn't much appreciate how she looked and, in particular, how she looked at him. She fretted at her fleece hat, not sure how much it concealed; thinking her consciousness of the damage might somehow transmit itself to the policeman. It was starting to snow again.

'If he contacts you, Miss Fortune, or if you think where he might've gone . . .'

'Yeah, yeah. Sure.'

He wrote on a pad, tore out the page and handed it to her. A phone number, a name: *PC Monks*. 'D'you know of any reason why he might've done this?'

She could've been glib. *Maybe he wanted to keep warm, yeah?* Or she could've revealed a reason – the background to a possible, putative reason; but, for all that she'd learned of Ethan's reasoning, she didn't know the reason for *this*. So she simply shook her head, peripherally aware all the while that ZZ was giving her the hard stare.

She imagined a skein of ice crystals on the cushion, cracking minutely as Ethan awoke. He would've perspired, the damp fabric freezing in the places where his head no longer rested. She imagined him nudging the curtain, to find the window laminated with frost; she imagined him thirsty, stiff, not quite knowing where he was or what time or even what day it was. It was late. He'd worked into the early hours and crashed the morning away. Easing out of bed – Erica watchful from her basket, her breath, like his, spinning pale streamers of fog; she imagined him stooping his way to the door, his own stale odour lifting into his face on a convective wave of warmth. She imagined him opening the door to let Erica out, and his surprise at the snow that had fallen while he slept and which lay captured in the natural trap of the U-shaped pitch, the larger drifts banked against the side of the caravan itself. And the snow, in all its pure brilliance, would be significant to him. It would be portentous. Being the way his mind worked, now.

All of this, she imagined.

There would be no water. The pipes, the butt, frozen – the

repeated depression of the treadle producing no more than a gasp from the tap. No food, either. Or, maybe, just a few crackers softened with age and a tin of – peaches? – no, pears. She imagined him devouring the pears with his fingers, then feeding the crackers to Erica, posting them into her mouth one after another like letters. Saying: *That's it, Reeks. That's the last of everything.* And Erica would flap her tail at the sound of Ethan's voice, because there was nothing he had done, or could do, that would extinguish a dog's devotion.

The date. He would make a mental, or even literal, note of the date. The snow . . . what if the falling of the snow was an affirmation of an earlier sign? Ethan having been awoken sporadically in the night by the cold and by his own agitation, dislocated, flitting between sleep, half-sleep and wakefulness, reaching a conclusion. She imagined him reaching an unconscious conclusion, then waking to snow and an assimilation into the conscious mind of the certainty, the absolute resolution of what he would do today.

Finally, she imagined this:

The stripping from the walls of everything pinned there, and the littering of the floor; the emptying of the files – documents, photos, maps, notebooks, sketches, tapes, scattered about along with their storage boxes. Within minutes, the caravan would be strewn with the work of more than a year. Just so much refuse. The heaping of the seat cushions, bedding, curtains, clothes on top of all this. Ethan would be warm and a little light-headed, weak with hunger and nervous tension and days, weeks, of depletion and the momentous fact of these actions. Done. Surveying the result – the pyre – from the doorway and finding that he was neither sad nor regretful but curiously exhilarated.

A single match, she imagined, started the fire. Using a report of the vigil in the woods at what was once Flashville – rolling it tightly, giving it a twist, igniting one end and placing these pages among the others. On the stoop, watching the first tentative flames gain in confidence, consolidate – encouraged by the air from the open doorway. There would be a pattern, a logical progression to the flames' spread into the interior, although it would seem

opportunistic and arbitrary; a casual, fluid lapping enlivened by
sudden flares and combustions. Ethan had started one fire, but now
there were several, apparently independent of each other. The
cushions did not look to be alight, yet their fumes hung a dense
black smog beneath the ceiling. It was no longer safe to remain.

She imagined him turning away. Retracing his steps in the snow
to the Toyota. Climbing in alongside Erica and driving off down
the track, a vibrant and final image of his home framed in triplicate
in the vehicle's mirrors.

'Portentous of what?' ZZ said.

'Who knows?'

They were in the Cherokee, parked at the mouth of the U, the
engine idling, the heater on full blast. The snow was thickening,
eddying, splatted against the windscreen by the wind. PC Monks
had driven off, Mr F. had trekked back down to the house. It was a
fumble for the sense of all this, the imagining, because something
was happening and, for the life of her, she couldn't suss what it
was.

She turned to look at the Zeez. 'Why did you come up here?
Before, I mean.'

'I wanted to confront him.'

'Confront. As in, beat him up. Give him a good kicking, yeah?
Like, being a girl, I really need a big strong guy to sort things for
me.'

'Chloe –'

'Or did you want to nail him down and fuck him, so he'd know
how it felt?'

ZZ didn't answer.

She feigned a sigh, a swoon: 'My hero.'

'I had to confront him with what he'd done to you.' He expelled
all his breath at once. 'Look, there wasn't any plan. I just came up
here. I was so angry. Outraged. I drove out to see him without any
idea what I was going to do or say.' He gestured at the pitch. 'And
then, when I get here . . . this.'

Silence. The mesmeric observance of the snow. She splayed her fingers above a heater vent and invited the ache of revived circulation.

'I think you're wrong not to tell the police,' ZZ said.

Being more or less verbatim what she'd already had from Mom, eventually, and from Faye, and from herself – in those moments when she made believe that counsel for the defence would not ask her: *What you are saying, then, is that you were raped, but that at no point during this alleged rape were you conscious?* So it would be reduced to – what? – assault. Aggravated assault or ABH or whatever. Oh, and criminal damage to one jacket, one pair of jeans. And for this she was supposed to let a PC Monks-type or his professionally gender-sympathetic WPC equivalent mess with her head. And she was to submit, belatedly, to forensic investigation of her vagina.

Like, yeah.

'You got an O.S. map?' she said.

The Zeez leaned across to pop the glove compartment. She withdrew the map and arranged it on her lap, tracing the surface with her fingertips, smoothing, studying the features by touch alone with the deft shuttle of someone reading braille, or playing the piano with their eyes shut, or making lace. She conceived of a map made of lace, points of interest plotted by the threads of their paths of interconnection.

'Are you dowsing him?'

'That's why you brought me here, isn't it?'

'You are dowsing him.'

'When someone goes missing it raises . . . it embodies the possibility of finding them. Ethan's missing, and you want to find him – you want *me* to find him – 'cos he's there to be found.' She smiled. 'You're a climber, you should be able to relate to that.'

'Any minute now, I'm going to know what you're on about.'

'Why d'you climb a mountain?' She made a pyramid with her hands, made her voice deep with manly, climberly cliché. 'Because it's there.' Hands still set, she said: 'A mountain creates the conditions for it to be climbed.'

ZZ laughed. 'Most of the ones I've climbed have created the conditions for you to die up there, or fall off, or give it up as a bad job.'

What it was, also, was Ethan. The probability of Ethan's wish to be found. Not soon, because how could he have known of her connection to the Zeez, or anticipated him turning up when he did? But she suspected that – eventually, ultimately – Ethan intended to be found. *Torching the caravan, right* . . . The torching of the caravan, she said, was a beacon. And a sincere vanishing act didn't begin with the lighting of a beacon but with an inaudible, invisible, intangible slinking away.

'I don't have a good feeling about whatever he's doing,' she said.

ZZ, nodding beside her. 'Nor me.'

She considered this. What he'd done to her and what he might be in the process of doing to himself, and whether there was anything left within her – a residue – of the Ethan, pre-Flashville vigil, for her to care enough to want to save him. And what there was in her head was a mosaic of hatred, but also pieces that were something other than hatred, whose colours were close to hatred's and yet were not quite the same.

'Your call, Clo.'

'I know.'

'You take us there, I can be the one to bring him back,' ZZ said.

'Part of me doesn't even want to look for him, or think about him at all. Then there's a part wants to find him so badly I scare myself.' She shook her head. 'We're talking prime "idiot" territory.'

One delusion in dowsing being the belief that if you wanted to find something badly enough you would find it. *You want it badly, you'll seek it badly* – Mom. Stood to reason that to look for an object you had to be objective, not subjective; you didn't *look*, you made yourself conducive – amenable, receptive – to *seeing*, to a coincidence in time and place of the seeker and the sought, the seeking and the being sought.

The map. Dowsing once more with the tips of her fingers. Letting the response – the sensation, or its absence – reveal to her the truth of her desire to find him.

There. *There.*

She showed ZZ on the map where she thought Ethan would be if he wanted her to find him. A place of significance to him, in relation to them, being the site of the first personal demo of her facility to dowse 2-D: the secluded woodland camp where, all those months ago, she'd recovered an empty can, a spoon, two matches and a tent peg.

49

A descent into town to raid the Zeez's shop – snow goggles, crampons, thermals – then loading up the Cherokee and heading back out on the moors. In town, the falling snow was benign, picturesque, but here on the high roads it raged at them. She navigated as far as the track she'd once hiked up, and where Ethan had parked for that slog to the campsite. Even before they reached the stop-off point, the twin tyreprints – partially confused by fresh snow – reeled ahead of them, drawing them on like a tow-rope or like a thread through a labyrinth. And even though she'd dowsed this she was surprised when a final bend fetched the pick-up into view, because it had seemed to her as if they could follow the tracks for ever without catching up with Ethan. Or as if they'd imagined the marks somehow belonged to their own vehicle and, all along, they'd been pursuing themselves. ZZ slowed, braked to a halt behind the Toyota and stilled the engine. They stared silently through the windscreen. A burn-out: the red paintwork blackened and blistered or seared off altogether, the windows corrupted to sheets of smoked glass. It was a dead thing. It was the cockpit of a crashed and decapitated light-aircraft.

'This is for real now,' ZZ said.

He said that and then just sat there. Which was fine. She was cool with that. If he'd tried to hurry her, if he'd been decisive, sorting her, compelling her to urgency, to jump down from the cab and set off after Ethan on foot – *come on, come on* – into the woods . . . if the Zeez had done any of these things, she would've made him drive her clear away from here. But he didn't. What he did was sit, as she sat, stalled, as she was, by the sight of the pick-up. Being confronted by evidence of how close they were, and by the latest act in a sequence of self-destruction, did not tilt her towards certainty but towards doubt. Did she want to be here? Did she want to go on with this? *This is for real now.* And it was only ZZ's hesitancy, his recognition – conscious, inadvertent, intuitive or whatever – of *her* need to hesitate, that let her ease back from quitting. In the end, she was the first one out of the vehicle.

And that was when she noticed the bloodstained snow at the edge of the track, where a trail entered the trees. The colour was wrong. It was the browns and oranges and dull deep reds of old blood; not spilled blood but a wipe, a graze, a smear of rust. It was the blood soaked into a chopping board from the prep of raw meat. A rook took off from this patch of discoloration, carrying something – a shred of red – in its beak. She recalled a story told to her by Ethan: last spring, he was out stalking when he saw crows picking at what looked to be fresh carrion. Thinking, hoping, hardly daring to believe he might've stumbled on a kill, he drew nearer . . . only to find that a ewe had delivered her young, and that the birds were feasting on the steaming afterbirth.

ZZ squatted to inspect the stain, but if he had a theory about it he didn't let on.

There was no script being written in her head of what was to come. No rehearsal of the speech or deed or attitude to be played out. This, in any case, coming under the category of future, which she didn't do. All she had was a nebulous, unfathomable sense of acting for herself, not for Ethan, without any idea of what the act might be.

'I don't know what I'm doing,' she told the Zeez, as they geared up.

'Perhaps you don't need to know that until we find him?'

His remark being the sort of thing she'd have come out with – to someone else, or to herself – before Ethan made her afraid to live and think and *be* like that. But she wasn't afraid now, being here; not simply because ZZ was with her, but because of Ethan. This time, he seemed to have marked himself out as the victim of any harm to be inflicted. He was the one in danger now, not her.

An image: Ethan waving to her from the top of a tall tree in the instant before he jumped.

ZZ reckoned Ethan had been the one to misread her, to misconstrue the signals; being only half true, because signals had been transmitted – briefly, bafflingly – and then revoked; and it was Ethan's failure to handle the revoking that was the problem. She'd halted. She'd halted herself, she'd halted them. And that should've halted him. But he went on, fabricating a huge and unstable edifice of expectation that was less and less to do with her and more and more to do with him. She had to absorb Ethan's misreading, but she also had to absorb her own. She was the dowser who'd failed to dowse him. The seer who'd failed to see him, or where he was leading her. Mom had been right: he was the unaccounted variable in all this. In failing to read him, or to read herself because of him, she'd invoked – she'd become – the idiot.

We are two people at the margins.

Her partial explanation of the attraction – to Mom, back near the beginning of Ethan. Only, it had taken longer than it should've done to suss that they were also two people irredeemably and disastrously at the margins of one another.

The woods looked unlike her memory of them: in leaf, in early-autumn sunlight. But she knew woodland too well to be fazed by this or misled by the superficial uniformity. And once she'd located the beck where Ethan, in her imagination, had strip-washed upstream from here on a warmer, gladder day than this – there was no getting lost.

'This takes us right to him,' she said. 'Another couple of K.'

'Okay.' ZZ was wearing his goggles, hers were pushed up on to her forehead. Snowflakes accumulated in his beard and in the fabric of his hat faster than they could dissolve. 'The dog ought to hear us before he does.'

'Uh-huh.'

Since the blood, she'd kept herself from thinking about Erica. There'd been no other stains, nor bootprints or paw prints, though she guessed Ethan would know of a more direct route than theirs. They pressed on, the trees in this older, denser section of the woods sieving the blizzard, lessening its potency, protecting them from the worst of the wind. But they were on high ground now, and still climbing; the cold was fierce, despite the shelter, and the going was rougher. Soft mud under soft snow, slush, ice at the beck's edges that splintered beneath their tread like thin sheets of perspex. Her legs and lungs smarted; in trying to keep pace with ZZ, she'd snagged her calf on the sharp metal tooth of a crampon.

An hour from the Toyota, they reached the place.

The tent.

She sensed a presence inside, and that it wasn't Ethan. Erica. Erica was in the tent. But there'd been no barking and she hoped she was mistaken; she hoped the tent was empty. The caravan . . . the pick-up . . . the dog. She shook her head, as though this might somehow dislodge Ethan's logic from her thinking. As ZZ went to unzip the flap, she made him step aside. *I'm doing this.* Crawling in was so redolent of entering the Home Dome that she closed her eyes against the memory of the mutilated fawn. When she reopened them, the form of a dog materialized in the dimness: on her side, motionless, her flank maybe, maybe not, swelling and sinking – she couldn't tell – but if she placed a palm there she'd know if Erica was dead. At the pressure of contact, Erica raised her head to look at her and released a single, plaintive, pathetic whimper.

ZZ was scouting this side of the beck; she heard him tramping about, calling Ethan's name. It sounded like a sneeze. She was in the tent, feeding chunks of glucose to Erica as she lay there, enfeebled by exhaustion and malnutrition. *If he shows up, shout.* That was her role, now, to wait for Ethan to come, or for him to be fetched from wherever he'd gone. Being just about anywhere, Zeez reckoned; and, with Ethan having at least a two-hour start in steady snowfall, what odds on deciphering a trail? As he'd prepared to leave her, ZZ had surveyed the woodland as if it was ranged against him – as if the trees, the weather, were in conspiracy. As if

Ethan wasn't hiding, but being hidden. She thought about this, and decided that maybe there wasn't so much of a difference.

'If he's out in this for too long . . .' The Zeez had left the sentence there.

'What?'

The survivalist spiel: with body temp at thirty-seven and an actual temp of, ZZ guessed, minus one or two – lower, if Ethan had moved up on to higher ground; lower still if he'd left woods, where you were talking serious chill factor . . . say, eight or ten below zed. *That's a forty-seven degree differential to make up.* Meaning a diversion of energy into combating the cold, at the expense of other vital bodily functions: muscle activity, heart rate . . . a slowing of the pulse, cardiac arrhythmia, lethargy, immobility, confusion, amnesia, loss of consciousness. ZZ had stopped at loss of consciousness.

From the direction of his cries he must've crossed the beck now. *Ethan! Hello! Hellooo! Eeethaaan!* Becoming distant again, as ZZ widened the sweep of the search. He'd told her he wouldn't return until he found Ethan, or until the onset of dusk forced them back to the Cherokee. She was to wait. She was to look after Erica. She was to call if she needed him and he would be there for her and she would come to no harm.

ZZ. The grizzly. The bear in the woods who could pick Ethan up like a branch and break him. If she'd possessed ZZ's strength she would never have been raped.

But the only strength she had was her own.

He'd asked if she could dowse for Ethan – here, not on a map but for real – and she'd taken the pendulum out, but . . . a shake of the head. *Nap. Nothing.* Sometimes it worked, sometimes it didn't. And she'd let him believe that, because if he believed that he would go off by himself to search, and she'd stay in the tent while he drifted further and further away. It had taken the dowsing to make her realize she wanted this: for him to go, for her to be alone for the – for the what? – for the enactment. The completion. Whatever this was, it was hers to complete.

The finding of Ethan. The moment of revelation. These belonged to her.

So she was alone, now, Zeezless. She was retrieving the pouch from her pocket and, for a second time, freeing the pendulum, enclosing the bob in her hand for the harmonization of temperatures.

Focus. Composure. The emptying of her head of everything that was not this.

When she was ready, she paid out the weight and allowed it to calm at the end of the cord. Inside the tent – no wind or snow or cold or any disturbance at all – she dowsed. Compass point by compass point, visualizing Ethan, naming him, seeking the direction he'd taken, posing the internal question: *here? here? here?* Attending to the response that was the true one and not the idiot, or the distraction of him, or of herself. The swinging of the bob.

Here. This way.

She fed the last of the glucose to Erica, stroked her, spoke to her, then left the tent and zipped it shut. Looking and listening for ZZ. He was out of sight, his voice so faint that he was as far away as it was possible to be without straying out of range.

An emergence. The leaving behind of the trees. After an uphill hike among snow-laden low-slung branches, she found herself at the foot of a snowfield that ascended to what might've been a horizon but for the whiteout. She knew this place. She'd never been here, but Ethan had told her about it: the lookout point. Each morning of the stalk he had come up here to fix his binoculars on the caravan, away across the moorside – like a creature in a burrow, he'd said, fearful of intruders, digging a second burrow in order to spy from its entrance on the first. The blizzard was relenting, easing to a shower of fine flakes slashed sideways by the wind. As she climbed, the grey-on-grey pencil line of a summit became discernible, its surface skimmed into such a wild white spume she couldn't tell if the figure she glimpsed in silhouette up there was a figure at all, or just a pattern, a pixilation, in the snow spray itself. But she saw it again, solid and inert, and knew that it was real: maybe a trig point, or a cairn; but what it most closely resembled was a statue of the Buddha, seated in the lotus position.

Ethan was naked. Cross-legged, facing out into the obliterated landscape, snow banked around his legs like a plinth, his clothes in a neat snow-caked pile beside him. The skin was so discoloured he might've been sculpted in amethyst. She wasn't sure how frostbite looked, but there was something grossly wrong with his fingers, his nose, his ears. And there in the lumpy drifts in front of him was exposed flesh and bone and blood; she thought at first it was his feet, that he'd done something to his feet. But it didn't look right and, clearing the snow, she uncovered the remains of a carcass.

The fawn.

Rotten, degraded, decomposing. She saw that a hind leg was missing. She saw too that each of the other legs was staked to the ground by an aluminium tent peg.

Ethan's eyes were open, frosted with false white lashes. The pupils were tiny points of black, the gaze dull and vacant and unfocused, but not yet, not quite, the gaze of a dead man. His lips were purple, the lower one misshapen and encrusted. Placing an ear against them, she felt the merest damp brush of his breath.

'Ethan.' She exhaled into his face and detected a flicker of reaction. 'Ethan, it's me. It's me.'

His eyes moved fractionally to fix on hers. There was a moment of recognition, of engagement, then his gaze dulled once more. But in that instant she knew he'd seen her and whatever remained vibrant inside, in his brain, was processing the information that this was her – Chloe Fortune – and that she'd come for him. He couldn't have planned for her to be here so soon, to reach him while he was still alive; so he must've been prepared – he must've *wanted* – to die. To kill himself. But there had been a brief, unmistakable flare of hope in his eyes just then. He was close to death but he had not died yet, and he understood that she was here and she could save him. And she saw enough in his fleeting response to realize that –

having led himself to the place where his death was, and having seen *her* – he desperately wanted to be saved.

There was still time. She could wrap him in her jacket and somehow help him down from here to a lower, more sheltered place, to the woods, to the tent, where she could call out to ZZ, who would know what to do to make Ethan warm and safe, and to enable him to survive this. To live. With her help, he could be saved.

She looked at the carcass. The pegs.

Ethan was almost comatose, now. This had to be done quickly before she lost him. She positioned her face in front of his as she had done before, reviving him again with her breath, locking on his gaze so that he had to look at her, see her, register her once more. And what she sought in his eyes was the awareness, the absolute certainty that everything was sorted.

There.

She stood up, bashed the snow from her knees and left him, heading back down the slope that would bring her, eventually, to the tent. Where she would wait for ZZ to return with the news that Ethan wasn't anywhere to be found.

50

MEREDITH BECK (*moorland tour guide/paranormal investigator*):

The 'official' version is that he was stranded in a blizzard while trying to lure the Black Beast with the carcass of a young deer.

Cause of death: hypothermia. Verdict: misadventure.

He was a madman. A man who had driven himself mad with his obsession. He had it coming to him.

The damage to his body was as a result of frostbite and scavenging.

And, naturally, there is not – and never has been, nor ever will be – a Black Beast.

These are the conclusions that officialdom is content for us to draw.

An alternative conclusion, coming so soon after Barker Inglis's inquiry report, would have been deeply embarrassing for the Ministry. And such a conclusion could not be allowed to take hold in the popular perception. Thus, the smokescreen of the coroner's verdict.

The pathologist, of course, is a party to the cover-up. I pity him. Each time he sleeps, that man must relive in his nightmares the moment when he drew back the sheet and saw, etched upon that body, the marks of the true killer.

Acknowledgements

Of the numerous publications I consulted in researching this novel, the following were especially useful: *The Elements of Pendulum Dowsing*, by Tom Graves (Element Books, 1989); *Dowsing for Beginners*, by Richard Webster (Llewellyn Publications, 1996); *The Beast of Exmoor – Fact or Legend?*, by Trevor Beer (Countryside Productions). Two television programmes were also very helpful: *Strange But True?* (ITV, 3/10/97), and *The X-Creatures: Big Cats in a Little Country* (BBC1, 23/9/98).

My interest in dowsing was first aroused when I interviewed a professional dowser, Mark Butler, for a feature in the *Oxford Times* (17/4/92). And I am grateful to Nigel Mortimer, ufologist and dowser, for his inspirational guided tour of Ilkley Moor. (The character of Meredith Beck is a figment of my imagination and in no way modelled on Mr Mortimer.) Thanks too to my good mate Andy Jones for supplying me with a sheaf of cuttings on the beasts of Bodmin and elsewhere. Information on the Brocken Spectre came from the climbers, Bryan and Mark Hockey. For the idea of the *soror mystica* I am indebted to Lindsay Clarke's novel *The Chymical Wedding* (Jonathan Cape, 1989) and to a conversation with him about alchemy.

The critical input of my agent Jonny Geller, at Curtis Brown, my editor Tony Lacey, and his assistant Jeremy Ettinghausen, at Penguin, has been much appreciated. And a stunning critique of an earlier draft by a friend and fellow writer, Phil Whitaker, helped salvage this book from the mess I was making of it. Finally, my heartfelt thanks to my wife Damaris for her love, support and criticism – and for making it possible for me to write this novel at all.